Agatha Christie®

Poirot's Early Cases

HARPER

HARPER

An imprint of HarperCollins*Publishers*
1 London Bridge Street
London SE1 9GF
www.harpercollins.co.uk

This paperback edition 2016

First published in Great Britain by
Collins 1974

Agatha Christie® Poirot® Poirot's Early Cases™
Copyright © 1974 Agatha Christie Limited. All rights reserved.
www.agathachristie.com

A catalogue record for this book is
available from the British Library

ISBN 978-0-00-816484-3

Set in Sabon by Born Group using Atomik ePublisher from Easypress

Printed and bound in Great Britain by
Clays Ltd, St Ives plc

MIX
Paper from
responsible sources
FSC www.fsc.org **FSC™ C007454**

FSC is a non-profit international organisation established to promote
the responsible management of the world's forests. Products carrying the
FSC label are independently certified to assure consumers that they come
from forests that are managed to meet the social, economic and
ecological needs of present and future generations,
and other controlled sources.

Find out more about HarperCollins and the environment at
www.harpercollins.co.uk/green

CONTENTS

The Affair at the Victory Ball

Pure chance led my friend Hercule Poirot, formerly chief of the Belgian force, to be connected with the Styles Case. His success brought him notoriety, and he decided to devote himself to the solving of problems in crime. Having been wounded on the Somme and invalided out of the Army, I finally took up my quarters with him in London. Since I have a first-hand knowledge of most of his cases, it has been suggested to me that I select some of the most interesting and place them on record. In doing so, I feel that I cannot do better than begin with that strange tangle which aroused such widespread public interest at the time. I refer to the affair at the Victory Ball.

Although perhaps it is not so fully demonstrative of Poirot's peculiar methods as some of the more obscure cases, its sensational features, the well-known people involved, and the tremendous publicity given it by the Press, make it stand out as a *cause célèbre* and I have long felt that it is only fitting that Poirot's connection with the solution should be given to the world.

It was a fine morning in spring, and we were sitting in Poirot's rooms. My little friend, neat and dapper as ever, his egg-shaped head tilted on one side, was delicately applying a new pomade to his moustache. A certain harmless vanity was a characteristic of Poirot's and fell into line with his general love of order and method. The *Daily Newsmonger*, which I had been reading, had slipped to the floor, and I was deep in a brown study when Poirot's voice recalled me.

'Of what are you thinking so deeply, *mon ami*?'

'To tell you the truth,' I replied, 'I was puzzling over this unaccountable affair at the Victory Ball. The papers are full of it.' I tapped the sheet with my finger as I spoke.

'Yes?'

'The more one reads of it, the more shrouded in mystery the whole thing becomes!' I warmed to my subject. 'Who killed Lord Cronshaw? Was Coco Courtenay's death on the same night a mere coincidence? Was it an accident? Or did she deliberately take an overdose of cocaine?' I stopped, and then added dramatically: 'These are the questions I ask myself.'

Poirot, somewhat to my annoyance, did not play up. He was peering into the glass, and merely murmured: 'Decidedly, this new pomade, it is a marvel for the moustaches!' Catching my eye, however, he added hastily: 'Quite so—and how do you reply to your questions?'

But before I could answer, the door opened, and our landlady announced Inspector Japp.

The Scotland Yard man was an old friend of ours and we greeted him warmly.

'Ah, my good Japp,' cried Poirot, 'and what brings you to see us?'

'Well, Monsieur Poirot,' said Japp, seating himself and nodding to me, 'I'm on a case that strikes me as being very much in your line, and I came along to know whether you'd care to have a finger in the pie?'

Poirot had a good opinion of Japp's abilities, though deploring his lamentable lack of method, but I, for my part, considered that the detective's highest talent lay in the gentle art of seeking favours under the guise of conferring them!

'It's the Victory Ball,' said Japp persuasively. 'Come, now, you'd like to have a hand in that.'

Poirot smiled at me.

'My friend Hastings would, at all events. He was just holding forth on the subject, *n'est-ce pas, mon ami?*'

'Well, sir,' said Japp condescendingly, 'you shall be in it too. I can tell you, it's something of a feather in your cap to have inside knowledge of a case like this. Well, here's to business. You know the main facts of the case, I suppose, Monsieur Poirot?'

'From the papers only—and the imagination of the journalist is sometimes misleading. Recount the whole story to me.'

Japp crossed his legs comfortably and began.

'As all the world and his wife knows, on Tuesday last a grand Victory Ball was held. Every twopenny-halfpenny hop calls itself that nowadays, but this was the real thing, held at the Colossus Hall, and all London at it—including your Lord Cronshaw and his party.'

'His *dossier?*' interrupted Poirot. 'I should say his bioscope—no, how do you call it—biograph?'

3

'Viscount Cronshaw was fifth viscount, twenty-five years of age, rich, unmarried, and very fond of the theatrical world. There were rumours of his being engaged to Miss Courtenay of the Albany Theatre, who was known to her friends as "Coco" and who was, by all accounts, a very fascinating young lady.'

'Good. *Continuez*!'

'Lord Cronshaw's party consisted of six people: he himself, his uncle, the Honourable Eustace Beltane, a pretty American widow, Mrs Mallaby, a young actor, Chris Davidson, his wife, and last but not least, Miss Coco Courtenay. It was a fancy dress ball, as you know, and the Cronshaw party represented the old Italian Comedy—whatever that may be.'

'The *Commedia dell' Arte*,' murmured Poirot. 'I know.'

'Anyway, the costumes were copied from a set of china figures forming part of Eustace Beltane's collection. Lord Cronshaw was Harlequin; Beltane was Punchinello; Mrs Mallaby matched him as Pulcinella; the Davidsons were Pierrot and Pierette; and Miss Courtenay, of course, was Columbine. Now, quite early in the evening it was apparent that there was something wrong. Lord Cronshaw was moody and strange in his manner. When the party met together for supper in a small private room engaged by the host, everyone noticed that he and Miss Courtenay were no longer on speaking terms. She had obviously been crying, and seemed on the verge of hysterics. The meal was an uncomfortable one, and as they all left the supper-room, she turned to Chris Davidson and requested him audibly to take her home, as she was "sick of the ball". The young actor hesitated, glancing at Lord Cronshaw, and finally drew them both back to the supper-room.

'But all his efforts to secure a reconciliation were unavailing, and he accordingly got a taxi and escorted the now weeping Miss Courtenay back to her flat. Although obviously very much upset, she did not confide in him, merely reiterating again and again that she would "make old Cronch sorry for this!" That is the only hint we have that her death might not have been accidental, and it's precious little to go upon. By the time Davidson had quieted her down somewhat, it was too late to return to the Colossus Hall, and Davidson accordingly went straight home to his flat in Chelsea, where his wife arrived shortly afterwards, bearing the news of the terrible tragedy that had occurred after his departure.

'Lord Cronshaw, it seems, became more and more moody as the ball went on. He kept away from his party, and they hardly saw him during the rest of the evening. It was about one-thirty a.m., just before the grand cotillion when everyone was to unmask, that Captain Digby, a brother officer who knew his disguise, noticed him standing in a box gazing down on the scene.

'"Hullo, Cronch!" he called. "Come down and be sociable! What are you moping about up there for like a boiled owl? Come along; there's a good old rag coming on now."

'"Right!" responded Cronshaw. "Wait for me, or I'll never find you in the crowd."

'He turned and left the box as he spoke. Captain Digby, who had Mrs Davidson with him, waited. The minutes passed, but Lord Cronshaw did not appear. Finally Digby grew impatient.

'"Does the fellow think we're going to wait all night for him?" he exclaimed.

'At that moment Mrs Mallaby joined them, and they explained the situation.

'"Say, now," cried the pretty widow vivaciously, "he's like a bear with a sore head tonight. Let's go right away and rout him out."

'The search commenced, but met with no success until it occurred to Mrs Mallaby that he might possibly be found in the room where they had supped an hour earlier. They made their way there. What a sight met their eyes! There was Harlequin, sure enough, but stretched on the ground with a table-knife in his heart!'

Japp stopped, and Poirot nodded, and said with the relish of the specialist: '*Une belle affaire*! And there was no clue as to the perpetrator of the deed? But how should there be!'

'Well,' continued the inspector, 'you know the rest. The tragedy was a double one. Next day there were headlines in all the papers, and a brief statement to the effect that Miss Courtenay, the popular actress, had been discovered dead in her bed, and that her death was due to an overdose of cocaine. Now, was it accident or suicide? Her maid, who was called upon to give evidence, admitted that Miss Courtenay was a confirmed taker of the drug, and a verdict of accidental death was returned. Nevertheless we can't leave the possibility of suicide out of account. Her death is particularly unfortunate, since it leaves us no clue now to the cause of the quarrel the preceding night. By the way, a small enamel box was found on the dead man. It had *Coco* written across it in diamonds, and was half full of cocaine. It was identified by Miss Courtenay's maid as belonging to her mistress, who nearly always carried it about with her, since it contained her supply of the drug to which she was fast becoming a slave.'

'Was Lord Cronshaw himself addicted to the drug?'

'Very far from it. He held unusually strong views on the subject of dope.'

Poirot nodded thoughtfully.

'But since the box was in his possession, he knew that Miss Courtenay took it. Suggestive, that, is it not, my good Japp?'

'Ah!' said Japp rather vaguely.

I smiled.

'Well,' said Japp, 'that's the case. What do you think of it?'

'You found no clue of any kind that has not been reported?'

'Yes, there was this.' Japp took a small object from his pocket and handed it over to Poirot. It was a small pompon of emerald green silk, with some ragged threads hanging from it, as though it had been wrenched violently away.

'We found it in the dead man's hand, which was tightly clenched over it,' explained the inspector.

Poirot handed it back without any comment and asked: 'Had Lord Cronshaw any enemies?'

'None that anyone knows of. He seemed a popular young fellow.'

'Who benefits by his death?'

'His uncle, the Honourable Eustace Beltane, comes into the title and estates. There are one or two suspicious facts against him. Several people declare that they heard a violent altercation going on in the little supper-room, and that Eustace Beltane was one of the disputants. You see, the table-knife being snatched up off the table would fit in with the murder being done in the heat of a quarrel.'

'What does Mr Beltane say about the matter?'

'Declares one of the waiters was the worse for liquor, and that he was giving him a dressing down. Also that it was nearer to one than half past. You see, Captain Digby's evidence fixes the time pretty accurately. Only about ten minutes elapsed between his speaking to Cronshaw and the finding of the body.'

'And in any case I suppose Mr Beltane, as Punchinello, was wearing a hump and a ruffle?'

'I don't know the exact details of the costumes,' said Japp, looking curiously at Poirot. 'And anyway, I don't quite see what that has got to do with it?'

'No?' There was a hint of mockery in Poirot's smile. He continued quietly, his eyes shining with the green light I had learned to recognize so well: 'There was a curtain in this little supper-room, was there not?'

'Yes, but—'

'With a space behind it sufficient to conceal a man?'

'Yes—in fact, there's a small recess, but how you knew about it—you haven't been to the place, have you, Monsieur Poirot?'

8

'No, my good Japp, I supplied the curtain from my brain. Without it, the drama is not reasonable. And always one must be reasonable. But tell me, did they not send for a doctor?'

'At once, of course. But there was nothing to be done. Death must have been instantaneous.'

Poirot nodded rather impatiently.

'Yes, yes, I understand. This doctor, now, he gave evidence at the inquest?'

'Yes.'

'Did he say nothing of any unusual symptom—was there nothing about the appearance of the body which struck him as being abnormal?'

Japp stared hard at the little man.

'Yes, Monsieur Poirot. I don't know what you're getting at, but he did mention that there was a tension and stiffness about the limbs which he was quite at a loss to account for.'

'Aha!' said Poirot. 'Aha! *Mon Dieu*! Japp, that gives one to think, does it not?'

I saw that it had certainly not given Japp to think.

'If you're thinking of poison, monsieur, who on earth would poison a man first and then stick a knife into him?'

'In truth that would be ridiculous,' agreed Poirot placidly.

'Now is there anything you want to see, monsieur? If you'd like to examine the room where the body was found—'

Poirot waved his hand.

'Not in the least. You have told me the only thing that interests me—Lord Cronshaw's views on the subject of drug-taking.'

'Then there's nothing you want to see?'

'Just one thing.'

'What is that?'

'The set of china figures from which the costumes were copied.'

Japp stared.

'Well, you're a funny one!'

'You can manage that for me?'

'Come round to Berkeley Square now if you like. Mr Beltane—or His Lordship, as I should say now—won't object.'

We set off at once in a taxi. The new Lord Cronshaw was not at home, but at Japp's request we were shown into the 'china room', where the gems of the collection were kept. Japp looked round him rather helplessly.

'I don't see how you'll ever find the ones you want, monsieur.'

But Poirot had already drawn a chair in front of the mantelpiece and was hopping up upon it like a nimble robin. Above the mirror, on a small shelf to themselves, stood six china figures. Poirot examined them minutely, making a few comments to us as he did so.

'*Les voilà!* The old Italian Comedy. Three pairs! Harlequin and Columbine, Pierrot and Pierrette—very dainty in white and green—and Punchinello and Pulcinella in mauve and yellow. Very elaborate, the costume of Punchinello—ruffles and frills, a hump, a high hat. Yes, as I thought, very elaborate.'

He replaced the figures carefully, and jumped down.

Japp looked unsatisfied, but as Poirot had clearly no intention of explaining anything, the detective put the best face he could upon the matter. As we were preparing to leave, the master of the house came in, and Japp performed the necessary introductions.

The sixth Viscount Cronshaw was a man of about fifty, suave in manner, with a handsome, dissolute face. Evidently an elderly roué, with the languid manner of a poseur. I took an instant dislike to him. He greeted us graciously enough, declaring he had heard great accounts of Poirot's skill, and placing himself at our disposal in every way.

'The police are doing all they can, I know,' Poirot said.

'But I much fear the mystery of my nephew's death will never be cleared up. The whole thing seems utterly mysterious.'

Poirot was watching him keenly. 'Your nephew had no enemies that you know of?'

'None whatever. I am sure of that.' He paused, and then went on: 'If there are any questions you would like to ask—'

'Only one.' Poirot's voice was serious. 'The costumes— they were reproduced *exactly* from your figurines?'

'To the smallest detail.'

'Thank you, milor'. That is all I wanted to be sure of. I wish you good day.'

'And what next?' inquired Japp as we hurried down the street. 'I've got to report at the Yard, you know.'

'*Bien*! I will not detain you. I have one other little matter to attend to, and then—'

'Yes?'

'The case will be complete.'

'What? You don't mean it! You know who killed Lord Cronshaw?'

'*Parfaitement.*'

'Who was it? Eustace Beltane?'

'Ah, *mon ami*, you know my little weakness! Always I have a desire to keep the threads in my own hands up to the last minute. But have no fear. I will reveal all when the time comes. I want no credit—the affair shall be yours, on the condition that you permit me to play out the *dénouement* my own way.'

'That's fair enough,' said Japp. 'That is, if the *dénouement* ever comes! But I say, you *are* an oyster, aren't you?' Poirot smiled. 'Well, so long. I'm off to the Yard.'

He strode off down the steet, and Poirot hailed a passing taxi.

'Where are we going now?' I asked in lively curiosity.

'To Chelsea to see the Davidsons.'

He gave the address to the driver.

'What do you think of the new Lord Cronshaw?' I asked.

'What says my good friend Hastings?'

'I distrust him instinctively.'

'You think he is the "wicked uncle" of the story-books, eh?'

'Don't you?'

'Me, I think he was most amiable towards us,' said Poirot noncommittally.

'Because he had his reasons!'

Poirot looked at me, shook his head sadly, and murmured something that sounded like: 'No method.'

The Davidsons lived on the third floor of a block of 'mansion' flats. Mr Davidson was out, we were told, but

Mrs Davidson was at home. We were ushered into a long, low room with garish Oriental hangings. The air felt close and oppressive, and there was an overpowering fragrance of joss-sticks. Mrs Davidson came to us almost immediately, a small, fair creature whose fragility would have seemed pathetic and appealing had it not been for the rather shrewd and calculating gleam in her light blue eyes.

Poirot explained our connection with the case, and she shook her head sadly.

'Poor Cronch—and poor Coco too! We were both so fond of her, and her death has been a terrible grief to us. What is it you want to ask me? Must I really go over all that dreadful evening again?'

'Oh, madame, believe me, I would not harass your feelings unnecessarily. Indeed, Inspector Japp has told me all that is needful. I only wish to see the constume you wore at the ball that night.'

The lady looked somewhat surprised, and Poirot continued smoothly: 'You comprehend, madame, that I work on the system of my country. There we always "reconstruct" the crime. It is possible that I may have an actual *représentation*, and if so, you understand, the costumes would be important.'

Mrs Davidson still looked a bit doubtful.

'I've heard of reconstructing a crime, of course,' she said. 'But I didn't know you were so particular about details. But I'll fetch the dress now.'

She left the room and returned almost immediately with a dainty wisp of white satin and green. Poirot took it from her and examined it, handing it back with a bow.

'*Merci, madame*! I see you have had the misfortune to lose one of your green pompons, the one on the shoulder here.'

'Yes, it got torn off at the ball. I picked it up and gave it to poor Lord Cronshaw to keep for me.'

'That was after supper?'

'Yes.'

'Not long before the tragedy, perhaps?'

A faint look of alarm came into Mrs Davidson's pale eyes, and she replied quickly: 'Oh no—long before that. Quite soon after supper, in fact.'

'I see. Well, that is all. I will not derange you further. *Bonjour, madame*.'

'Well,' I said as we emerged from the building, 'that explains the mystery of the green pompon.'

'I wonder.'

'Why, what do you mean?'

'You saw me examine the dress, Hastings?'

'Yes?'

'*Eh bien*, the pompon that was missing had not been wrenched off, as the lady said. On the contrary, it had been *cut* off, my friend, cut off with scissors. The threads were all quite even.'

'Dear me!' I exclaimed. 'This becomes more and more involved.'

'On the contrary,' replied Poirot placidly, 'it becomes more and more simple.'

'Poirot,' I cried, 'one day I shall murder you! Your habit of finding everything perfectly simple is aggravating to the last degree!'

'But when I explain, *mon ami*, is it not always perfectly simple?'

'Yes; that is the annoying part of it! I feel then that I could have done it myself.'

'And so you could, Hastings, so you could. If you would but take the trouble of arranging your ideas! Without method—'

'Yes, yes,' I said hastily, for I knew Poirot's eloquence when started on his favourite theme only too well. 'Tell me, what do we do next? Are you really going to reconstruct the crime?'

'Hardly that. Shall we say that the drama is over, but that I propose to add a—harlequinade?'

The following Tuesday was fixed upon by Poirot as the day for this mysterious performance. The preparations greatly intrigued me. A white screen was erected at one side of the room, flanked by heavy curtains at either side. A man with some lighting apparatus arrived next, and finally a group of members of the theatrical profession, who disappeared into Poirot's bedroom, which had been rigged up as a temporary dressing-room.

Shortly before eight, Japp arrived, in no very cheerful mood. I gathered that the official detective hardly approved of Poirot's plan.

'Bit melodramatic, like all his ideas. But there, it can do no harm, and as he says, it might save us a good bit of trouble. He's been very smart over the case. I was on the same scent myself, of course—' I felt instinctively that Japp was straining the truth here—'but there, I promised to let him play the thing out his own way. Ah! Here is the crowd.'

His Lordship arrived first, escorting Mrs Mallaby, whom I had not as yet seen. She was a pretty, dark-haired woman, and appeared perceptibly nervous. The Davidsons followed. Chris Davidson also I saw for the first time. He was handsome enough in a rather obvious style, tall and dark, with the easy grace of the actor.

Poirot had arranged seats for the party facing the screen. This was illuminated by a bright light. Poirot switched out the other lights so that the room was in darkness except for the screen. Poirot's voice rose out of the gloom.

'Messieurs, mesdames, a word of explanation. Six figures in turn will pass across the screen. They are familiar to you. Pierrot and his Pierrette; Punchinello the buffoon, and elegant Pulcinella; beautiful Columbine, lightly dancing, Harlequin, the sprite, invisible to man!'

With these words of introduction, the show began. In turn each figure that Poirot had mentioned bounded before the screen, stayed there a moment poised, and then vanished. The lights went up, and a sigh of relief went round. Everyone had been nervous, fearing they knew not what. It seemed to me that the proceedings had gone singularly flat. If the criminal was among us, and Poirot expected him to break down at the mere sight of a familiar figure the device had failed signally—as it was almost bound to do. Poirot, however, appeared not a whit discomposed. He stepped forward, beaming.

'Now, messieurs and mesdames, will you be so good as to tell me, one at a time, what it is that we have just seen? Will you begin, milor'?'

The gentleman looked rather puzzled. 'I'm afraid I don't quite understand.'

'Just tell me what we have been seeing.'

'I—er—well, I should say we have seen six figures passing in front of a screen and dressed to represent the personages in the old Italian Comedy, or—er—ourselves the other night.'

'Never mind the other night, milor',' broke in Poirot. 'The first part of your speech was what I wanted. Madame, you agree with Milor' Cronshaw?'

He had turned as he spoke to Mrs Mallaby.

'I—er—yes, of course.'

'You agree that you have seen six figures representing the Italian Comedy?'

'Why, certainly.'

'Monsieur Davidson? You too?'

'Yes.'

'Madame?'

'Yes.'

'Hastings? Japp? Yes? You are all in accord?'

He looked around upon us; his face grew rather pale, and his eyes were green as any cat's.

'And yet—*you are all wrong*! Your eyes have lied to you—as they lied to you on the night of the Victory Ball. To "see things with your eyes", as they say, is not always to see the truth. One must see with the eyes of the mind; one must employ the little cells of grey! Know, then, that

17

tonight and on the night of the Victory Ball, you saw not *six* figures but *five*! See!'

The lights went out again. A figure bounded in front of the screen—Pierrot!

'Who is that?' demanded Poirot. 'Is it Pierrot?'

'Yes,' we all cried.

'Look again!'

With a swift movement the man divested himself of his loose Pierrot garb. There in the limelight stood glittering Harlequin! At the same moment there was a cry and an overturned chair.

'Curse you,' snarled Davidson's voice. 'Curse you! How did you guess?'

Then came the clink of handcuffs and Japp's calm official voice. 'I arrest you, Christopher Davidson—charge of murdering Viscount Cronshaw—anything you say will be used in evidence against you.'

It was a quarter of an hour later. A recherché little supper had appeared; and Poirot, beaming all over his face, was dispensing hospitality and answering our eager questions.

'It was all very simple. The circumstances in which the green pompon was found suggested at once that it had been torn from the costume of the murderer. I dismissed Pierrette from my mind (since it takes considerable strength to drive a table-knife home) and fixed upon Pierrot as the criminal. But Pierrot left the ball nearly two hours before the murder was committed. So he must either have returned to the ball later to kill Lord Cronshaw, or—*eh bien*, he must have killed him before he left! Was that impossible? Who had seen Lord Cronshaw after supper that evening? Only Mrs Davidson, whose statement, I suspected, was a deliberate fabrication uttered with the object of accounting for the missing pompon, which, of course, she cut from her own dress to replace the one missing on her husband's costume. But then, Harlequin, who was seen in the box at one-thirty, must have been an impersonation. For a moment, earlier, I had considered the possibility of Mr Beltane being the guilty party. But with his elaborate costume, it was clearly impossible that he could have doubled the roles of Punchinello and Harlequin. On the other hand, to Davidson, a young man of about the same height as the murdered man and an actor by profession, the thing was simplicity itself.

'But one thing worried me. Surely a doctor could not fail to perceive the difference between a man who had been dead two hours and one who had been dead ten minutes! *Eh bien*, the doctor *did* perceive it! But he was not taken to the body and asked, 'How long has this man been dead?' On the contrary, he was informed that the man had been seen alive ten minutes ago, and so he merely commented at the inquest on the abnormal stiffening of the limbs for which he was quite unable to account!

'All was now marching famously for my theory. Davidson had killed Lord Cronshaw immediately after supper, when, as you remember, he was seen to draw him back into the supper-room. Then he departed with Miss Courtenay, left her at the door of her flat (instead of going in and trying to pacify her as he affirmed) and returned post-haste to the Colossus—but as Harlequin, not Pierrot—a simple transformation effected by removing his outer costume.'

The uncle of the dead man leaned forward, his eyes perplexed.

'But if so, he must have come to the ball prepared to kill his victim. What earthly motive could he have had? The motive, that's what I can't get.'

'Ah! There we come to the second tragedy—that of Miss Courtenay. There was one simple point which everyone overlooked. Miss Courtenay died of cocaine poisoning—but her supply of the drug was in the enamel box which was found on Lord Cronshaw's body. Where, then, did she obtain the dose which killed her? Only one person could have supplied her with it—Davidson. And that explains everything. It accounts for her friendship with the Davidsons and her demand that Davidson should escort her home. Lord Cronshaw, who was almost fanatically opposed to drug-taking, discovered that she was addicted to cocaine, and suspected that Davidson supplied her with it. Davidson doubtless denied this, but Lord Cronshaw determined to get the truth from Miss Courtenay at the ball. He could forgive the wretched girl, but he would certainly have no mercy on the man who made a living by trafficking in drugs. Exposure and ruin confronted Davidson. He went to the ball determined that Cronshaw's silence must be obtained at any cost.'

'Was Coco's death an accident, then?'

'I suspect that it was an accident cleverly engineered by Davidson. She was furiously angry with Cronshaw, first for his reproaches, and secondly for taking her cocaine from her. Davidson supplied her with more, and probably suggested her augmenting the dose as a defiance to "old Cronch"!'

'One other thing,' I said. 'The recess and the curtain? How did you know about them?'

'Why, *mon ami*, that was the most simple of all. Waiters had been in and out of that little room, so, obviously, the body could not have been lying where it was found on the floor. There must be some place in the room where it could be hidden. I deduced a curtain and a recess behind it. Davidson dragged the body there, and later, after drawing attention to himself in the box, he dragged it out again before finally leaving the Hall. It was one of his best moves. He is a clever fellow!'

But in Poirot's green eyes I read unmistakably the unspoken remark: 'But not quite so clever as Hercule Poirot!'

The Adventure of the Clapham Cook

At the time that I was sharing rooms with my friend Hercule Poirot, it was my custom to read aloud to him the headlines in the morning newspaper, the *Daily Blare*.

The *Daily Blare* was a paper that made the most of any opportunity for sensationalism. Robberies and murders did not lurk obscurely in its back pages. Instead they hit you in the eye in large type on the front page.

ABSCONDING BANK CLERK DISAPPEARS WITH
FIFTY THOUSAND POUNDS' WORTH OF
NEGOTIABLE SECURITIES.
HUSBAND PUTS HIS HEAD IN GAS-OVEN.
UNHAPPY HOME LIFE. MISSING TYPIST. PRETTY
GIRL OF TWENTY-ONE. WHERE IS EDNA FIELD?

'There you are, Poirot, plenty to choose from. An absconding bank clerk, a mysterious suicide, a missing typist—which will you have?'

My friend was in a placid mood. He quietly shook his head.

'I am not greatly attracted to any of them, *mon ami*. Today I feel inclined for the life of ease. It would have to be

22

a very interesting problem to tempt me from my chair. See you, I have affairs of importance of my own to attend to.'

'Such as?'

'My wardrobe, Hastings. If I mistake not, there is on my new grey suit the spot of grease—only the unique spot, but it is sufficient to trouble me. Then there is my winter overcoat—I must lay him aside in the powder of Keatings. And I think—yes, I think—the moment is ripe for the trimmings of my moustaches—and afterwards I must apply the pomade.'

'Well,' I said, strolling to the window, 'I doubt if you'll be able to carry out this delirious programme. That was a ring at the bell. You have a client.'

'Unless the affair is one of national importance, I touch it not,' declared Poirot with dignity.

A moment later our privacy was invaded by a stout red-faced lady who panted audibly as a result of her rapid ascent of the stairs.

'You're M. Poirot?' she demanded, as she sank into a chair.

'I am Hercule Poirot, yes, madame.'

'You're not a bit like what I thought you'd be,' said the lady, eyeing him with some disfavour. 'Did you pay for the bit in the paper saying what a clever detective you were, or did they put it in themselves?'

'Madame!' said Poirot, drawing himself up.

'I'm sorry, I'm sure, but you know what these papers are nowadays. You begin reading a nice article: "What a bride said to her plain unmarried friend", and it's all about a simple thing you buy at the chemist's and shampoo your hair with. Nothing but puff. But no offence taken, I hope? I'll tell you what I want you to do for me. I want you to find my cook.'

Poirot stared at her; for once his ready tongue failed him. I turned aside to hide the broadening smile I could not control.

'It's all this wicked dole,' continued the lady. 'Putting ideas into servants' heads, wanting to be typists and what nots. Stop the dole, that's what I say. I'd like to know what *my* servants have to complain of—afternoon and evening off a week, alternate Sundays, washing put out, same food as we have—and never a bit of margarine in the house, nothing but the very best butter.'

She paused for want of breath and Poirot seized his opportunity. He spoke in his haughtiest manner, rising to his feet as he did so.

'I fear you are making a mistake, madame. I am not holding an inquiry into the conditions of domestic service. I am a private detective.'

'I know that,' said our visitor. 'Didn't I tell you I wanted you to find my cook for me? Walked out of the house on Wednesday, without so much as a word to me, and never came back.'

'I am sorry, madame, but I do not touch this particular kind of business. I wish you good morning.'

Our visitor snorted with indignation.

'That's it, is it, my fine fellow? Too proud, eh? Only deal with Government secrets and countesses' jewels? Let me tell you a servant's every bit as important as a tiara to a woman in my position. We can't all be fine ladies going out in our motors with our diamonds and our pearls. A good cook's a good cook—and when you lose her, it's as much to you as her pearls are to some fine lady.'

For a moment or two it appeared to be a toss up between Poirot's dignity and his sense of humour. Finally he laughed and sat down again.

'Madame, you are in the right, and I am in the wrong. Your remarks are just and intelligent. This case will be a novelty. Never yet have I hunted a missing domestic. Truly here is the problem of national importance that I was demanding of fate just before your arrival. *En avant*! You say this jewel of a cook went out on Wednesday and did not return. That is the day before yesterday.'

'Yes, it was her day out.'

'But probably, madame, she has met with some accident. Have you inquired at any of the hospitals?'

'That's exactly what I thought yesterday, but this morning, if you please, she sent for her box. And not so much as a line to me! If I'd been at home, I'd not have let it go—treating me like that! But I'd just stepped out to the butcher.'

'Will you describe her to me?'

'She was middle-aged, stout, black hair turning grey—most respectable. She'd been ten years in her last place. Eliza Dunn, her name was.'

'And you had had—no disagreement with her on the Wednesday?'

'None whatever. That's what makes it all so queer.'

'How many servants do you keep, madame?'

'Two. The house-parlourmaid, Annie, is a very nice girl. A bit forgetful and her head full of young men, but a good servant if you keep her up to her work.'

'Did she and the cook get on well together?'

'They had their ups and downs, of course—but on the whole, very well.'

'And the girl can throw no light on the mystery?'

'She says not—but you know what servants are—they all hang together.'

'Well, well, we must look into this. Where did you say you resided, madame?'

'At Clapham; 88 Prince Albert Road.'

'*Bien*, madame, I will wish you good morning, and you may count upon seeing me at your residence during the course of the day.'

Mrs Todd, for such was our new friend's name, then took her departure. Poirot looked at me somewhat ruefully.

'Well, well, Hastings, this is a novel affair that we have here. The Disappearance of the Clapham Cook! Never, *never*, must our friend Inspector Japp get to hear of this!'

He then proceeded to heat an iron and carefully removed the grease spot from his grey suit by means of a piece of blotting-paper. His moustaches he regretfully postponed to another day, and we set out for Clapham.

Prince Albert Road proved to be a street of small prim houses, all exactly alike, with neat lace curtains veiling the windows, and well-polished brass knockers on the doors.

We rang the bell at No. 88, and the door was opened by a neat maid with a pretty face. Mrs Todd came out in the hall to greet us.

'Don't go, Annie,' she cried. 'This gentleman's a detective and he'll want to ask you some questions.'

Annie's face displayed a struggle between alarm and a pleasurable excitement.

'I thank you, madame,' said Poirot bowing. 'I would like to question your maid now—and to see her alone, if I may.'

We were shown into a small drawing-room, and when Mrs Todd, with obvious reluctance, had left the room, Poirot commenced his cross-examination.

'*Voyons, Mademoiselle Annie*, all that you shall tell us will be of the greatest importance. You alone can shed any light on the case. Without your assistance I can do nothing.'

The alarm vanished from the girl's face and the pleasurable excitement became more strongly marked.

'I'm sure, sir,' she said, 'I'll tell you anything I can.'

'That is good.' Poirot beamed approval on her. 'Now, first of all what is your own idea? You are a girl of remarkable intelligence. That can be seen at once! What is your own explanation of Eliza's disappearance?'

Thus encouraged, Annie fairly flowed into excited speech.

'White slavers, sir, I've said so all along! Cook was always warning me against them. "Don't you sniff no scent, or eat any sweets—no matter how gentlemanly the fellow!" Those were her words to me. And now they've got her! I'm sure of it. As likely as not, she's been shipped to Turkey or one of them Eastern places where I've heard they like them fat!'

27

Poirot preserved an admirable gravity.

'But in that case—and it is indeed an idea!—would she have sent for her trunk?'

'Well, I don't know, sir. She'd want her things—even in those foreign places.'

'Who came for the trunk—a man?'

'It was Carter Paterson, sir.'

'Did you pack it?'

'No, sir, it was already packed and corded.'

'Ah! That's interesting. That shows that when she left the house on Wednesday, she had already determined not to return. You see that, do you not?'

'Yes, sir.' Annie looked slightly taken aback. 'I hadn't thought of that. But it might still have been white slavers, mightn't it, sir? she added wistfully.

'Undoubtedly!' said Poirot gravely. He went on: 'Did you both occupy the same bedroom?'

'No, sir, we had separate rooms.'

'And had Eliza expressed any dissatisfaction with her present post to you at all? Were you both happy here?'

'She'd never mentioned leaving. The place is all right—' The girl hesitated.

'Speak freely,' said Poirot kindly. 'I shall not tell your mistress.'

'Well, of course, sir, she's a caution, Missus is. But the food's good. Plenty of it, and no stinting. Something hot for supper, good outings, and as much frying-fat as you like. And anyway, if Eliza did want to make a change, she'd never have gone off this way, I'm sure. She'd have stayed her month. Why, Missus could have a month's wages out of her for doing this!'

'And the work, it is not too hard?'

'Well, she's particular—always poking round in corners and looking for dust. And then there's the lodger, or paying guest as he's always called. But that's only breakfast and dinner, same as Master. They're out all day in the City.'

'You like your master?'

'He's all right—very quiet and a bit on the stingy side.'

'You can't remember, I suppose, the last thing Eliza said before she went out?'

'Yes, I can. "If there's any stewed peaches over from the dining-room," she says, "we'll have them for supper, and a bit of bacon and some fried potatoes." Mad over stewed peaches, she was. I shouldn't wonder if they didn't get her that way.'

'Was Wednesday her regular day out?'

'Yes, she had Wednesdays and I had Thursdays.'

Poirot asked a few more questions, then declared himself satisfied. Annie departed, and Mrs Todd hurried in, her face alight with curiosity. She had, I felt certain, bitterly resented her exclusion from the room during our conversation with Annie. Poirot, however, was careful to soothe her feelings tactfully.

'It is difficult,' he explained, 'for a woman of exceptional intelligence such as yourself, madame, to bear patiently the roundabout methods we poor detectives are forced to use. To have patience with stupidity is difficult for the quick-witted.'

Having thus charmed away any little resentment on Mrs Todd's part, he brought the conversation round to her

Agatha Christie

husband and elicited the information that he worked with a firm in the City and would not be home until after six.

'Doubtless he is very disturbed and worried by this unaccountable business, eh? It is not so?'

'He's never worried,' declared Mrs Todd. '"Well, well, get another, my dear." That's all *he* said! He's so calm that it drives me to distraction sometimes. "An ungrateful woman," he said. "We are well rid of her."'

'What about the other inmates of the house, madame?'

'You mean Mr Simpson, our paying guest? Well, as long as he gets his breakfast and his evening meal all right, *he* doesn't worry.'

'What is his profession, madame?'

'He works in a bank.' She mentioned its name, and I started slightly, remembering my perusal of the *Daily Blare*.

'A young man?'

'Twenty-eight, I believe. Nice quiet young fellow.'

'I should like to have a few words with him, and also with your husband, if I may. I will return for that purpose this evening. I venture to suggest that you should repose yourself a little, madame, you look fatigued.'

'I should just think I am! First the worry about Eliza, and then I was at the sales practically all yesterday, and you know what *that* is, M. Poirot, and what with one thing and another and a lot to do in the house, because of course Annie can't do it all—and very likely she'll give notice anyway, being unsettled in this way—well, what with it all, I'm tired out!'

Poirot murmured sympathetically, and we took our leave.

30

'It's a curious coincidence,' I said, 'but that absconding clerk, Davis, was from the same bank as Simpson. Can there be any connection, do you think?'

Poirot smiled.

'At the one end, a defaulting clerk, at the other a vanishing cook. It is hard to see any relation between the two, unless possibly Davis visited Simpson, fell in love with the cook, and persuaded her to accompany him on his flight!'

I laughed. But Poirot remained grave.

'He might have done worse,' he said reprovingly. 'Remember, Hastings, if you are going into exile, a good cook may be of more comfort than a pretty face!' He paused for a moment and then went on. 'It is a curious case, full of contradictory features. I am interested—yes, I am distinctly interested.'

That evening we returned to 88 Prince Albert Road and interviewed both Todd and Simpson. The former was a melancholy lantern-jawed man of forty-odd.

'Oh! Yes, yes,' he said vaguely. 'Eliza. Yes. A good cook, I believe. And economical. I make a strong point of economy.'

'Can you imagine any reason for her leaving you so suddenly?'

'Oh, well,' said Mr Todd vaguely. 'Servants, you know. My wife worries too much. Worn out from always worrying. The whole problem's quite simple really. "Get another, my dear," I say. "Get another." That's all there is to it. No good crying over spilt milk.'

Mr Simpson was equally unhelpful. He was a quiet inconspicuous young man with spectacles.

'I must have seen her, I suppose,' he said. 'Elderly woman, wasn't she? Of course, it's the other one I see always, Annie. Nice girl. Very obliging.'

'Were those two on good terms with each other?'

Mr Simpson said he couldn't say, he was sure. He supposed so.

'Well, we get nothing of interest there, *mon ami*,' said Poirot as we left the house. Our departure had been delayed by a burst of vociferous repetition from Mrs Todd, who repeated everything she had said that morning at rather greater length.

'Are you disappointed?' I asked. 'Did you expect to hear something?'

Poirot shook his head.

'There was a possibility, of course,' he said. 'But I hardly thought it likely.'

The next development was a letter which Poirot received on the following morning. He read it, turned purple with indignation, and handed it to me.

Mrs Todd regrets that after all she will not avail herself of Mr Poirot's services. After talking the matter over with her husband she sees that it is foolish to call in a detective about a purely domestic affair. Mrs Todd encloses a guinea for consultation fee.

'Aha!' cried Poirot angrily. 'And they think to get rid of Hercule Poirot like that! As a favour—a great favour—I consent to investigate their miserable little twopenny-halfpenny affair—and they dismiss me *comme ça*! Here, I mistake not, is the hand of Mr Todd. But I say no!—thirty-six times no! I will spend my own guineas, thirty-six hundred of them if need be, but I will get to the bottom of this matter!'

'Yes,' I said. 'But how?'

Poirot calmed down a little.

'*D'abord*,' he said, 'we will advertise in the papers. Let me see—yes—something like this: "If Eliza Dunn will communicate with this address, she will hear of something to her advantage." Put it in all the papers you can think of, Hastings. Then I will make some little inquiries of my own. Go, go—all must be done as quickly as possible!'

I did not see him again until the evening, when he condescended to tell me what he had been doing.

'I have made inquiries at the firm of Mr Todd. He was not absent on Wednesday, and he bears a good character—so much for him. Then Simpson, on Thursday he was ill and did not come to the bank, but he was there on Wednesday. He was moderately friendly with Davis. Nothing out of the common. There does not seem to be anything there. No. We must place our reliance on the advertisement.'

The advertisement duly appeared in all the principal daily papers. By Poirot's orders it was to be continued every day for a week. His eagerness over this uninteresting matter of a defaulting cook was extraordinary, but I realized that he considered it a point of honour to persevere until he finally succeeded. Several extremely interesting cases were brought to him about this time, but he declined them all.

Agatha Christie

Every morning he would rush at his letters, scrutinize them earnestly and then lay them down with a sigh.

But our patience was rewarded at last. On the Wednesday following Mrs Todd's visit, our landlady informed us that a person of the name of Eliza Dunn had called.

'*Enfin!*' cried Poirot. 'But make her mount then! At once. Immediately.'

Thus admonished, our landlady hurried out and returned a moment or two later, ushering in Miss Dunn. Our quarry was much as described: tall, stout, and eminently respectable.

'I came in answer to the advertisement,' she explained. 'I thought there must be some muddle or other, and that perhaps you didn't know I'd already got my legacy.'

Poirot was studying her attentively. He drew forward a chair with a flourish.

'The truth of the matter is,' he explained, 'that your late mistress, Mrs Todd, was much concerned about you. She feared some accident might have befallen you.'

Eliza Dunn seemed very much surprised.

'Didn't she get my letter then?'

'She got no word of any kind.' He paused, and then said persuasively: 'Recount to me the whole story, will you not?'

Eliza Dunn needed no encouragement. She plunged at once into a lengthy narrative.

'I was just coming home on Wednesday night and had nearly got to the house, when a gentleman stopped me. A tall gentleman he was, with a beard and a big hat. "Miss Eliza Dunn?" he said. "Yes," I said. "I've been inquiring for you at No. 88," he said. "They told me I might meet you

34

coming along here. Miss Dunn, I have come from Australia specially to find you. Do you happen to know the maiden name of your maternal grandmother?" "Jane Emmott," I said. "Exactly," he said. "Now, Miss Dunn, although you may never have heard of the fact, your grandmother had a great friend, Eliza Leech. This friend went to Australia where she married a very wealthy settler. Her two children died in infancy, and she inherited all her husband's property. She died a few months ago, and by her will you inherit a house in this country and a considerable sum of money."

'You could have knocked me down with a feather,' continued Miss Dunn. 'For a minute, I was suspicious, and he must have seen it, for he smiled. "Quite right to be on your guard, Miss Dunn," he said. "Here are my credentials." He handed me a letter from some lawyers in Melbourne, Hurst and Crotchet, and a card. He was Mr Crotchet. "There are one or two conditions," he said. "Our client was a little eccentric, you know. The bequest is conditional on your taking possession of the house (it is in Cumberland) before twelve o'clock tomorrow. The other condition is of no importance—it is merely a stipulation that you should not be in domestic service." My face fell. "Oh, Mr Crotchet," I said. "I'm a cook. Didn't they tell you at the house?" "Dear, dear," he said. "I had no idea of such a thing. I thought you might possibly be a companion or governess there. This is very unfortunate—very unfortunate indeed."

'"Shall I have to lose all the money?" I said, anxious like. He thought for a minute or two. "There are always ways of getting round the law, Miss Dunn," he said at last. "We lawyers know that. The way out here is for you to have left your employment this afternoon." "But my month?" I said. "My dear Miss Dunn," he said with a smile. "You can leave an employer any minute by forfeiting a month's wages. Your mistress will understand in view of the circumstances. The difficulty is *time*! It is imperative that you should catch the 11.05 from King's Cross to the north. I can advance you ten pounds or so for the fare, and you can write a note at the station to your employer. I will take it to her myself and explain the whole circumstances." I agreed, of course, and an hour later I was in the train, so flustered that I didn't know whether I was on my head or heels. Indeed by the time I got to Carlisle, I was half inclined to think the whole thing was one of those confidence tricks you read about. But I went to the address he had given me—solicitors they were, and it was all right. A nice little house, and an income of three hundred a year. These lawyers knew very little, they'd just got a letter from a gentleman in London instructing them to hand over the house to me and £150 for the first six months. Mr Crotchet sent up my things to me, but there was no word from Missus. I supposed she was angry and grudged me my bit of luck. She kept back my box too, and sent my clothes in paper parcels. But there, of course if she never had my letter, she might think it a bit cool of me.'

Poirot had listened attentively to this long history. Now he nodded his head as though completely satisfied.

'Thank you, mademoiselle. There had been, as you say, a little muddle. Permit me to recompense you for your trouble.'

He handed her an envelope. 'You return to Cumberland immediately? A little word in your ear. *Do not forget how to cook*. It is always useful to have something to fall back upon in case things go wrong.'

'Credulous,' he murmured, as our visitor departed, 'but perhaps not more than most of her class.' His face grew grave. 'Come, Hastings, there is no time to be lost. Get a taxi while I write a note to Japp.'

Poirot was waiting on the doorstep when I returned with the taxi.

'Where are we going?' I asked anxiously.

'First, to despatch this note by special messenger.'

This was done, and re-entering the taxi Poirot gave the address to the driver.

'Eighty-eight Prince Albert Road, Clapham.'

'So we are going there?'

'*Mais oui*. Though frankly I fear we shall be too late. Our bird will have flown, Hastings.'

'Who is our bird?'

Poirot smiled.

'The inconspicuous Mr Simpson.'

'What?' I exclaimed.

'Oh, come now, Hastings, do not tell me that all is not clear to you now!'

'The cook was got out of the way, I realize that,' I said, slightly piqued. 'But why? *Why* should Simpson wish to get her out of the house? Did she know something about him?'

'Nothing whatever.'

'Well, then—'

'But he wanted something that she had.'

'Money? The Australian legacy?'

'No, my friend—something quite different.' He paused a moment and then said gravely: '*A battered tin trunk...*'

I looked sideways at him. His statement seemed so fantastic that I suspected him of pulling my leg, but he was perfectly grave and serious.

'Surely he could buy a trunk if he wanted one,' I cried.

'He did not want a new trunk. He wanted a trunk of pedigree. A trunk of assured respectability.'

'Look here, Poirot,' I cried, 'this really is a bit thick. You're pulling my leg.'

He looked at me.

'You lack the brains and the imagination of Mr Simpson, Hastings. See here: On Wednesday evening, Simpson decoys away the cook. A printed card and a printed sheet of note-paper are simple matters to obtain, and he is willing to pay £150 and a year's house rent to assure the success of his plan. Miss Dunn does not recognize him—the beard and the hat and the slight colonial accent completely deceive her. That is the end of Wednesday—except for the trifling fact that Simpson has helped himself to fifty thousand pounds' worth of negotiable securities.'

'*Simpson*—but it was *Davis*—'

'If you will kindly permit me to continue, Hastings! Simpson knows that the theft will be discovered on Thursday afternoon. He does not go to the bank on Thursday, but he lies in wait for Davis when he comes out to lunch. Perhaps he admits the theft and tells Davis he will return the securities to him—anyhow he succeeds in getting Davis to come to Clapham with him. It is the maid's day out, and Mrs Todd was at the sales, so there is no one in the house. When the theft is discovered and Davis is missing, the implication will be overwhelming. Davis is the thief! Mr Simpson will be perfectly safe, and can return to work on the morrow like the honest clerk they think him.'

'And Davis?'

Poirot made an expressive gesture, and slowly shook his head.

'It seems too cold-blooded to be believed, and yet what other explanation can there be, *mon ami*. The one difficulty for a murderer is the disposal of the body—and Simpson had planned that out beforehand. I was struck at once by the fact that although Eliza Dunn obviously meant to return that night when she went out (witness her remark about the stewed peaches) *yet her trunk was all ready packed when they came for it.* It was Simpson who sent word to Carter Paterson to call on Friday and it was Simpson who corded up the box on Thursday afternoon. What suspicion could possibly arise? A maid leaves and sends for her box, it is labelled and addressed ready in her name, probably to a railway station within easy reach of London. On Saturday afternoon, Simpson, in his Australian disguise, claims it, he affixes a new label and address and redespatches it somewhere else, again "to be left till called for". When the authorities get suspicious, for excellent reasons, and open it, all that can be elicited will be that a bearded colonial despatched it from some junction near London. There will be nothing to connect it with 88 Prince Albert Road. Ah! Here we are.'

Poirot's prognostications had been correct. Simpson had left days previously. But he was not to escape the consequences of his crime. By the aid of wireless, he was discovered on the *Olympia*, en route to America.

A tin trunk, addressed to Mr Henry Wintergreen, attracted the attention of railway officials at Glasgow. It was opened and found to contain the body of the unfortunate Davis.

Mrs Todd's cheque for a guinea was never cashed. Instead Poirot had it framed and hung on the all of our sitting-room.

'It is to me a little reminder, Hastings. Never to despise the trivial—the undignified. A disappearing domestic at one end—a cold-blooded murder at the other. To me, one of the most interesting of my cases.'

The Cornish Mystery

'Mrs Pengelley,' announced our landlady, and withdrew discreetly.

Many unlikely people came to consult Poirot, but to my mind, the woman who stood nervously just inside the door, fingering her feather neck-piece, was the most unlikely of all. She was so extraordinarily commonplace—a thin, faded woman of about fifty, dressed in a braided coat and skirt, some gold jewellery at her neck, and with her grey hair surmounted by a singularly unbecoming hat. In a country town you pass a hundred Mrs Pengelleys in the street every day.

Poirot came forward and greeted her pleasantly, perceiving her obvious embarrassment.

'Madame! Take a chair, I beg of you. My colleague, Captain Hastings.'

The lady sat down, murmuring uncertainly: 'You are M. Poirot, the detective?'

'At your service, madame.'

But our guest was still tongue-tied. She sighed, twisted her fingers, and grew steadily redder and redder.

'There is something I can do for you, eh, madame?'

'Well, I thought—that is—you see—'

'Proceed, madame, I beg of you—proceed.'

Mrs Pengelley, thus encouraged, took a grip on herself.

'It's this way, M. Poirot—I don't want to have anything to do with the police. No, I wouldn't go to the police for anything! But all the same, I'm sorely troubled about something. And yet I don't know if I ought—' She stopped abruptly.

'Me, I have nothing to do with the police. My investigations are strictly private.'

Mrs Pengelley caught at the word.

'Private—that's what I want. I don't want any talk or fuss, or things in the papers. Wicked it is, the way they write things, until the family could never hold up their heads again. And it isn't as though I was even sure—it's just a dreadful idea that's come to me, and put it out of my head I can't.' She paused for breath. 'And all the time I may be wickedly wronging poor Edward. It's a terrible thought for any wife to have. But you do read of such dreadful things nowadays.'

'Permit me—it is of your husband you speak?'

'Yes.'

'And you suspect him of—what?'

'I don't like even to say it, M. Poirot. But you *do* read of such things happening—and the poor souls suspecting nothing.'

I was beginning to despair of the lady's ever coming to the point, but Poirot's patience was equal to the demand made upon it.

'Speak without fear, madame. Think what joy will be yours if we are able to prove your suspicions unfounded.'

'That's true—anything's better than this wearing uncertainty. Oh, M. Poirot, I'm dreadfully afraid I'm being *poisoned*.'

'What makes you think so?'

Mrs Pengelley, her reticence leaving her, plunged into a full recital more suited to the ears of her medical attendant.

'Pain and sickness after food, eh?' said Poirot thoughtfully. 'You have a doctor attending you, madame? What does he say?'

'He says it's acute gastritis, M. Poirot. But I can see that he's puzzled and uneasy, and he's always altering the medicine, but nothing does any good.'

'You have spoken of your—fears, to him?'

'No, indeed, M. Poirot. It might get about in the town. And perhaps it *is* gastritis. All the same, it's very odd that whenever Edward is away for the weekend, I'm quite all right again. Even Freda notices that—my niece, M. Poirot. And then there's that bottle of weed-killer, never used, the gardener says, and yet it's half-empty.'

She looked appealingly at Poirot. He smiled reassuringly at her, and reached for a pencil and notebook.

'Let us be business-like, madame. Now, then, you and your husband reside—where?'

'Polgarwith, a small market town in Cornwall.'

'You have lived there long?'

'Fourteen years.'

'And your household consists of you and your husband. Any children?'

'No.'

'But a niece, I think you said?'

'Yes, Freda Stanton, the child of my husband's only sister. She has lived with us for the last eight years—that is, until a week ago.'

'Oh, and what happened a week ago?'

'Things hadn't been very pleasant for some time; I don't know what had come over Freda. She was so rude and impertinent, and her temper something shocking, and in the end she flared up one day, and out she walked and took rooms of her own in the town. I've not seen her since. Better leave her to come to her senses, so Mr Radnor says.'

'Who is Mr Radnor?'

Some of Mrs Pengelley's initial embarrassment returned.

'Oh, he's—he's just a friend. Very pleasant young fellow.'

'Anything between him and your niece?'

'Nothing whatever,' said Mrs Pengelley emphatically.

Poirot shifted his ground.

'You and your husband are, I presume, in comfortable circumstances?'

'Yes, we're very nicely off.'

'The money, is it yours or your husband's?'

'Oh, it's all Edward's. I've nothing of my own.'

'You see, madame, to be business-like, we must be brutal. We must seek for a motive. Your husband, he would not poison you just *pour passer le temps*! Do you know of any reason why he should wish you out of the way?'

'There's the yellow-haired hussy who works for him,' said Mrs Pengelley, with a flash of temper. 'My husband's a dentist, M. Poirot, and nothing would do but he must have a smart girl, as he said, with bobbed hair and a white overall, to make his appointments and mix his fillings for him. It's come to my ears that there have been fine goings-on, though of course he swears it's all right.'

'This bottle of weed-killer, madame, who ordered it?'

'My husband—about a year ago.'

'Your niece, now, has she any money of her own?'

'About fifty pounds a year, I should say. She'd be glad enough to come back and keep house for Edward if I left him.'

'You have contemplated leaving him, then?'

'I don't intend to let him have it all his own way. Women aren't the downtrodden slaves they were in the old days, M. Poirot.'

'I congratulate you on your independent spirit, madame; but let us be practical. You return to Polgarwith today?'

'Yes, I came up by an excursion. Six this morning the train started, and the train goes back at five this afternoon.'

'*Bien*! I have nothing of great moment on hand. I can devote myself to your little affair. Tomorrow I shall be in Polgarwith. Shall we say that Hastings, here, is a distant relative of yours, the son of your second cousin? Me, I am his eccentric foreign friend. In the meantime, eat only what is prepared by your own hands, or under your eye. You have a maid whom you trust?'

'Jessie is a very good girl, I am sure.'

'Till tomorrow then, madame, and be of good courage.'

Poirot bowed the lady out, and returned thoughtfully to his chair. His absorption was not so great, however, that he failed to see two minute strands of feather scarf wrenched off by the lady's agitated fingers. He collected them carefully and consigned them to the wastepaper basket.

'What do you make of the case, Hastings?'

'A nasty business, I should say.'

'Yes, if what the lady suspects be true. But is it? Woe betide any husband who orders a bottle of weed-killer nowadays. If his wife suffers from gastritis, and is inclined to be of a hysterical temperament, the fat is in the fire.'

'You think that is all there is to it?'

'Ah—*voilà*—I do not know, Hastings. But the case interests me—it interests me enormously. For, you see, it has positively no new features. Hence the hysterical theory, and yet Mrs Pengelley did not strike me as being a hysterical woman. Yes, if I mistake not, we have here a very poignant human drama. Tell me, Hastings, what do you consider Mrs Pengelley's feelings towards her husband to be?'

'Loyalty struggling with fear,' I suggested.

'Yet, ordinarily, a woman will accuse anyone in the world—but not her husband. She will stick to her belief in him through thick and thin.'

'The "other woman" complicates the matter.'

'Yes, affection may turn to hate, under the stimulus of jealousy. But hate would take her to the police—not to me. She would want an outcry—a scandal. No, no, let us exercise our little grey cells. Why did she come to me? To have her suspicions proved wrong? Or—to have them *proved right*? Ah, we have here something I do not understand—an unknown factor. Is she a superb actress, our Mrs Pengelley? No, she was genuine, I would swear that she was genuine, and therefore I am interested. Look up the trains to Polgarwith, I pray you.'

The best train of the day was the one-fifty from Paddington which reached Polgarwith just after seven o'clock. The journey was uneventful, and I had to rouse myself from a pleasant nap to alight upon the platform of the bleak little station. We took our bags to the Duchy Hotel, and after a light meal, Poirot suggested our stepping round to pay an after-dinner call on my so-called cousin.

The Pengelleys' house stood a little way back from the road with an old-fashioned cottage garden in front. The smell of stocks and mignonette came sweetly wafted on the evening breeze. It seemed impossible to associate thoughts of violence with this Old World charm. Poirot rang and knocked. As the summons was not answered, he rang again. This time, after a little pause, the door was opened by a dishevelled-looking servant. Her eyes were red, and she was sniffing violently.

'We wish to see Mrs Pengelley,' explained Poirot. 'May we enter?'

The maid stared. Then, with unusual directness, she answered: 'Haven't you heard, then? She's dead. Died this evening—about half an hour ago.'

We stood staring at her, stunned.

'What did she die of?' I asked at last.

'There's some as could tell.' She gave a quick glance over her shoulder. 'If it wasn't that somebody ought to be in the house with the missus, I'd pack my box and go tonight. But

I'll not leave her dead with no one to watch by her. It's not my place to say anything, and I'm not going to say anything—but everybody knows. It's all over the town. And if Mr Radnor don't write to the 'Ome Secretary, someone else will. The doctor may say what he likes. Didn't I see the master with my own eyes a-lifting down of the weed-killer from the shelf this very evening? And didn't he jump when he turned round and saw me watching of him? And the missus' gruel there on the table, all ready to take to her? Not another bit of food passes my lips while I am in this house! Not if I dies for it.'

'Where does the doctor live who attended your mistress?'

'Dr Adams. Round the corner in High Street. The second house.'

Poirot turned away abruptly. He was very pale.

'For a girl who was not going to say anything, that girl said a lot,' I remarked dryly.

Poirot struck his clenched hand into his palm.

'An imbecile, a criminal imbecile, that is what I have been, Hastings. I have boasted of my little grey cells, and now I have lost a human life, a life that came to me to be saved. Never did I dream that anything would happen so soon. May the good God forgive me, but I never believed anything would happen at all. Her story seemed to me artificial. Here we are at the doctor's. Let us see what he can tell us.'

Dr Adams was the typical genial red-faced country doctor of fiction. He received us politely enough, but at a hint of our errand, his red face became purple.

'Damned nonsense! Damned nonsense, every word of it! Wasn't I in attendance on the case? Gastritis—gastritis pure and simple. This town's a hotbed of gossip—a lot of scandal-mongering old women get together and invent God knows what. They read these scurrilous rags of newspapers, and nothing will suit them but that someone in their town shall get poisoned too. They see a bottle of weed-killer on a shelf—and hey presto!—away goes their imagination with the bit between its teeth. I know Edward Pengelley—he wouldn't poison his grandmother's dog. And why should he poison his wife? Tell me that?'

'There is one thing, M. le Docteur, that perhaps you do not know.'

And, very briefly, Poirot outlined the main facts of Mrs Pengelley's visit to him. No one could have been more astonished than Dr Adams. His eyes almost started out of his head.

'God bless my soul!' he ejaculated. 'The poor woman must have been mad. Why didn't she speak to me? That was the proper thing to do.'

'And have her fears ridiculed?'

'Not at all, not at all. I hope I've got an open mind.'

Poirot looked at him and smiled. The physician was evidently more perturbed than he cared to admit. As we left the house, Poirot broke into a laugh.

'He is as obstinate as a pig, that one. He has said it is gastritis; therefore it is gastritis! All the same, he has the mind uneasy.'

'What's our next step?'

'A return to the inn, and a night of horror upon one of your English provincial beds, *mon ami*. It is a thing to make pity, the cheap English bed!'

'And tomorrow?'

'*Rien à faire*. We must return to town and await developments.'

'That's very tame,' I said, disappointed. 'Suppose there are none?'

'There will be! I can promise you that. Our old doctor may give as many certificates as he pleases. He cannot stop several hundred tongues from wagging. And they will wag to some purpose, I can tell you that!'

Our train for town left at eleven the following morning. Before we started for the station, Poirot expressed a wish to see Miss Freda Stanton, the niece mentioned to us by the dead woman. We found the house where she was lodging easily enough. With her was a tall, dark young man whom she introduced in some confusion as Mr Jacob Radnor.

Miss Freda Stanton was an extremely pretty girl of the old Cornish type—dark hair and eyes and rosy cheeks. There was a flash in those same dark eyes which told of a temper that it would not be wise to provoke.

'Poor Auntie,' she said, when Poirot had introduced himself, and explained his business. 'It's terribly sad. I've been wishing all the morning that I'd been kinder and more patient.'

'You stood a great deal, Freda,' interrupted Radnor.

'Yes, Jacob, but I've got a sharp temper, I know. After all, it was only silliness on Auntie's part. I ought to have just laughed and not minded. Of course, it's all nonsense her thinking that Uncle was poisoning her. She *was* worse after any food he gave her—but I'm sure it was only from thinking about it. She made up her mind she would be, and then she was.'

'What was the actual cause of your disagreement, mademoiselle?'

Miss Stanton hesitated, looking at Radnor. That young gentleman was quick to take the hint.

'I must be getting along, Freda. See you this evening. Goodbye, gentlemen; you're on your way to the station, I suppose?'

Poirot replied that we were, and Radnor departed.

'You are affianced, is it not so?' demanded Poirot, with a sly smile.

Freda Stanton blushed and admitted that such was the case.

'And that was really the whole trouble with Auntie,' she added.

'She did not approve of the match for you?'

'Oh, it wasn't that so much. But you see, she—' The girl came to a stop.

'Yes?' encouraged Poirot gently.

'It seems rather a horrid thing to say about her—now she's dead. But you'll never understand unless I tell you. Auntie was absolutely infatuated with Jacob.'

'Indeed?'

'Yes, wasn't it absurd? She was over fifty, and he's not quite thirty! But there it was. She was silly about him! I had to tell her at last that it was me he was after—and she carried on dreadfully. She wouldn't believe a word of it, and was so rude and insulting that it's no wonder I lost my temper. I talked it over with Jacob, and we agreed that the best thing to do was for me to clear out for a bit till she came to her senses. Poor Auntie—I suppose she was in a queer state altogether.'

'It would certainly seem so. Thank you, mademoiselle, for making things so clear to me.'

A little to my surprise, Radnor was waiting for us in the street below.

'I can guess pretty well what Freda has been telling you,' he remarked. 'It was a most unfortunate thing to happen, and very awkward for me, as you can imagine. I need hardly say that it was none of my doing. I was pleased at first, because I imagined the old woman was helping on things with Freda. The whole thing was absurd—but extremely unpleasant.'

'When are you and Miss Stanton going to be married?'

'Soon, I hope. Now, M. Poirot, I'm going to be candid with you. I know a bit more than Freda does. She believes her uncle to be innocent. I'm not so sure. But I can tell you one thing: I'm going to keep my mouth shut about what I do know. Let sleeping dogs lie. I don't want my wife's uncle tried and hanged for murder.'

'Why do you tell me all this?'

'Because I've heard of you, and I know you're a clever man. It's quite possible that you might ferret out a case against him. But I put it to you—what good is that? The poor woman is past help, and she'd have been the last person to want a scandal—why, she'd turn in her grave at the mere thought of it.'

'You are probably right there. You want me to—hush it up, then?'

'That's my idea. I'll admit frankly that I'm selfish about it. I've got my way to make—and I'm building up a good little business as a tailor and outfitter.'

'Most of us are selfish, Mr Radnor. Not all of us admit it so freely. I will do what you ask—but I tell you frankly you will not succeed in hushing it up.'

'Why not?'

Poirot held up a finger. It was market day, and we were passing the market—a busy hum came from within.

'The voice of the people—that is why, Mr Radnor. Ah, we must run, or we shall miss our train.'

'Very interesting, is it not, Hastings?' said Poirot, as the train steamed out of the station.

He had taken out a small comb from his pocket, also a microscopic mirror, and was carefully arranging his moustache, the symmetry of which had become slightly impaired during our brisk run.

'You seem to find it so,' I replied. 'To me, it is all rather sordid and unpleasant. There's hardly any mystery about it.'

'I agree with you; there is no mystery whatever.'

'I suppose we can accept the girl's rather extraordinary story of her aunt's infatuation? That seemed the only fishy part to me. She was such a nice, respectable woman.'

'There is nothing extraordinary about that—it is completely ordinary. If you read the papers carefully, you will find that often a nice respectable woman of that age leaves a husband she has lived with for twenty years, and sometimes a whole family of children as well, in order to link her life with that of a young man considerably her junior. You admire *les femmes*, Hastings; you prostrate yourself before all of them who are good-looking and have the good taste to smile upon you; but psychologically you know nothing whatever about them. In the autumn of a woman's life, there comes always one mad moment when she longs for romance, for adventure—before it is too late. It comes none the less surely to a woman because she is the wife of a respectable dentist in a country town!'

'And you think—'

'That a clever man might take advantage of such a moment.'

'I shouldn't call Pengelley so clever,' I mused. 'He's got the whole town by the ears. And yet I suppose you're right. The only two men who know anything, Radnor and the doctor, both want to hush it up. He's managed that somehow. I wish we'd seen the fellow.'

'You can indulge your wish. Return by the next train and invent an aching molar.'

I looked at him keenly.

'I wish I knew what you considered so interesting about the case.'

'My interest is very aptly summed up by a remark of yours, Hastings. After interviewing the maid, you observed

54

that for someone who was not going to say a word, she had said a good deal.'

'Oh!' I said doubtfully; then I harped back to my original criticism: 'I wonder why you made no attempt to see Pengelley?'

'*Mon ami*, I give him just three months. Then I shall see him for as long as I please—in the dock.'

For once I thought Poirot's prognostications were going to be proved wrong. The time went by, and nothing transpired as to our Cornish case. Other matters occupied us, and I had nearly forgotten the Pengelley tragedy when it was suddenly recalled to me by a short paragraph in the paper which stated that an order to exhume the body of Mrs Pengelley had been obtained from the Home Secretary.

A few days later, and 'The Cornish Mystery' was the topic of every paper. It seemed that gossip had never entirely died down, and when the engagement of the widower to Miss Marks, his secretary, was announced, the tongues burst out again louder than ever. Finally a petition was sent to the Home Secretary; the body was exhumed; large quantities of arsenic were discovered; and Mr Pengelley was arrested and charged with the murder of his wife.

Poirot and I attended the preliminary proceedings. The evidence was much as might have been expected. Dr Adams admitted that the symptoms of arsenical poisoning might easily be mistaken for those of gastritis. The Home Office expert gave his evidence; the maid Jessie poured out a flood of voluble information, most of which was rejected, but which certainly strengthened the case against the prisoner. Freda Stanton gave evidence as to her aunt's being worse whenever she ate food prepared by her husband. Jacob Radnor told how he had dropped in unexpectedly on the day of Mrs Pengelley's death, and found Pengelley replacing the bottle of weed-killer on the pantry shelf, Mrs Pengelley's gruel being on the table close by. Then Miss Marks, the fair-haired secretary, was called, and wept and went into hysterics and admitted that there had been 'passages' between her and her employer, and that he had promised to marry her in the event of anything happening to his wife. Pengelley reserved his defence and was sent for trial.

Jacob Radnor walked back with us to our lodgings.

'You see, Mr Radnor,' said Poirot, 'I was right. The voice of the people spoke—and with no uncertain voice. There was to be no hushing up of this case.'

'You were quite right,' sighed Radnor. 'Do you see any chance of his getting off?'

'Well, he has reserved his defence. He may have something—up the sleeve, as you English say. Come in with us, will you not?'

Radnor accepted the invitation. I ordered two whiskies and sodas and a cup of chocolate. The last order caused consternation, and I much doubted whether it would ever put in an appearance.

56

'Of course,' continued Poirot, 'I have a good deal of experience in matters of this kind. And I see only one loophole of escape for our friend.'

'What is it?'

'That you should sign this paper.'

With the suddenness of a conjuror, he produced a sheet of paper covered with writing.

'What is it?'

'A confession that *you* murdered Mrs Pengelley.'

There was a moment's pause; then Radnor laughed.

'You must be mad!'

'No, no, my friend, I am not mad. You came here; you started a little business; you were short of money. Mr Pengelley was a man very well-to-do. You met his niece; she was inclined to smile upon you. But the small allowance that Pengelley might have given her upon her marriage was not enough for you. You must get rid of both the uncle and the aunt; then the money would come to her, since she was the only relative. How cleverly you set about it! You made love to that plain middle-aged woman until she was your slave. You implanted in her doubts of her husband. She discovered first that he was deceiving her—then, under your guidance, that he was trying to poison her. You were often at the house; you had opportunities to introduce the arsenic into her food. But you were careful never to do so when her husband was away. Being a woman, she did not keep her suspicions to herself. She talked to her niece; doubtless she talked to other women friends. Your only difficulty was keeping up separate relations with the two women, and even that was not so difficult as it looked. You explained to the aunt that, to allay the suspicions of her husband, you had to pretend to pay court to the niece. And the younger lady needed little convincing—she would never seriously consider her aunt as a rival.

'But then Mrs Pengelley made up her mind, without saying anything to you, to consult *me*. If she could be really assured, beyond any possible doubt, that her husband was trying to poison her, she would feel justified in leaving him, and linking her life with yours—which is what she imagined you wanted her to do. But that did not suit your book at all. You did not want a detective prying around. A favourable minute occurs. You are in the house when Mr Pengelley is getting some gruel for his wife, and you introduce the fatal dose. The rest is easy. Apparently anxious to hush matters up, you secretly foment them. But you reckoned without Hercule Poirot, my intelligent young friend.'

Radnor was deadly pale, but he still endeavoured to carry off matters with a high hand.

'Very interesting and ingenious, but why tell me all this?'

'Because, monsieur, I represent—not the law, but Mrs Pengelley. For her sake, I give you a chance of escape. Sign this paper, and you shall have twenty-four hours' start—twenty-four hours before I place it in the hands of the police.'

Radnor hesitated.

'You can't prove anything.'

'Can't I? I am Hercule Poirot. Look out of the window, monsieur. There are two men in the street. They have orders not to lose sight of you.'

58

Radnor strode across to the window and pulled aside the blind, then shrank back with an oath.

'You see, monsieur? Sign—it is your best chance.'

'What guarantee have I—'

'That I shall keep faith? The word of Hercule Poirot. You will sign? Good. Hastings, be so kind as to pull that left-hand blind half-way up. That is the signal that Mr Radnor may leave unmolested.'

White, muttering oaths, Radnor hurried from the room. Poirot nodded gently.

'A coward! I always knew it.'

'It seems to me, Poirot, that you've acted in a criminal manner,' I cried angrily. 'You always preach against sentiment. And here you are letting a dangerous criminal escape out of sheer sentimentality.'

'That was not sentiment—that was business,' replied Poirot. 'Do you not see, my friend, that we have no shadow of proof against him? Shall I get up and say to twelve stolid Cornishmen that *I*, Hercule Poirot, *know*? They would laugh at me. The only chance was to frighten him and get a confession that way. Those two loafers that I noticed outside came in very useful. Pull down the blind again, will you, Hastings. Not that there was any reason for raising it. It was part of our *mise en scène*.

'Well, well, we must keep our word. Twenty-four hours, did I say? So much longer for poor Mr Pengelley—and it is not more than he deserves; for mark you, he deceived his wife. I am very strong on the family life, as you know. Ah, well, twenty-four hours—and then? I have great faith in Scotland Yard. They will get him, *mon ami*; they will get him.'

The Adventure of Johnnie Waverly

'You can understand the feelings of a mother,' said Mrs Waverly for perhaps the sixth time.

She looked appealingly at Poirot. My little friend, always sympathetic to motherhood in distress, gesticulated reassuringly.

'But yes, but yes, I comprehend perfectly. Have faith in Papa Poirot.'

'The police—' began Mr Waverly.

His wife waved the interruption aside. 'I won't have anything more to do with the police. We trusted to them and look what happened! But I'd heard so much of M. Poirot and the wonderful things he'd done, that I felt he might possibly be able to help us. A mother's feelings—'

Poirot hastily stemmed the reiteration with an eloquent gesture. Mrs Waverly's emotion was obviously genuine, but it assorted strangely with her shrewd, rather hard type of countenance. When I heard later that she was the daughter of a prominent steel manufacturer of Birmingham who had worked his way up in the world from an office boy to his present eminence, I realized that she had inherited many of the paternal qualities.

Mr Waverly was a big, florid, jovial-looking man. He stood with his legs straddled wide apart and looked the type of the country squire.

'I suppose you know all about this business, M. Poirot?'

The question was almost superfluous. For some days past the papers had been full of the sensational kidnapping of little Johnnie Waverly, the three-year-old son and heir of Marcus Waverly, Esq., of Waverly Court, Surrey, one of the oldest families in England.

'The main facts I know, of course, but recount to me the whole story, monsieur, I beg of you. And in detail if you please.'

'Well, I suppose the beginning of the whole thing was about ten days ago when I got an anonymous letter—beastly things, anyway—that I couldn't make head or tail of. The writer had the impudence to demand that I should pay him twenty-five thousand pounds—twenty-five thousand pounds, M. Poirot! Failing my agreement, he threatened to kidnap Johnnie. Of course I threw the thing into the wastepaper basket without more ado. Thought it was some silly joke. Five days later I got another letter. "Unless you pay, your son will be kidnapped on the twenty-ninth." That was on the twenty-seventh. Ada was worried, but I couldn't bring myself to treat the matter seriously. Damn it all, we're in England. Nobody goes about kidnapping children and holding them up to ransom.'

'It is not a common practice, certainly,' said Poirot. 'Proceed, monsieur.'

'Well, Ada gave me no peace, so—feeling a bit of a fool—I laid the matter before Scotland Yard. They didn't seem to take the thing very seriously—inclined to my view that it was some silly joke. On the twenty-eighth I got a third letter. "You have not paid. Your son will be taken from you at twelve o'clock noon tomorrow, the twenty-ninth. It will cost you fifty thousand pounds to recover him." Up I drove to Scotland Yard again. This time they were more impressed. They inclined to the view that the letters were written by a lunatic, and that in all probability an attempt of some kind would be made at the hour stated. They assured me that they would take all due precautions. Inspector McNeil and a sufficient force would come down to Waverly on the morrow and take charge.

'I went home much relieved in mind. Yet we already had the feeling of being in a state of siege. I gave orders that no stranger was to be admitted, and that no one was to leave the house. The evening passed off without any untoward incident, but on the following morning my wife was seriously unwell. Alarmed by her condition, I sent for Doctor Dakers. Her symptoms appeared to puzzle him. While hesitating to suggest that she had been poisoned, I could see that was what was in his mind. There was no danger, he assured me, but it would be a day or two before she would be able to get about again. Returning to my own room, I was startled and amazed to find a note pinned to my pillow. It was in the same handwriting as the others and contained just three words: "At twelve o'clock".

'I admit, M. Poirot, that then I saw red! Someone in the house was in this—one of the servants. I had them all up, blackguarded them right and left. They never split on each other; it was Miss Collins, my wife's companion, who informed me that she had seen Johnnie's nurse slip down the drive early that morning. I taxed her with it, and she broke down. She had left the child with the nursery maid and stolen out to meet a friend of hers—a man! Pretty goings on! She denied having pinned the note to my pillow—she may have been speaking the truth, I don't know. I felt I couldn't take the risk of the child's own nurse being in the plot. One of the servants was implicated—of that I was sure. Finally I lost my temper and sacked the whole bunch, nurse and all. I gave them an hour to pack their boxes and get out of the house.'

Mr Waverly's face was quite two shades redder as he remembered his just wrath.

'Was not that a little injudicious, monsieur?' suggested Poirot. 'For all you know, you might have been playing into the enemy's hands.'

Mr Waverly stared at him. 'I don't see that. Send the whole lot packing, that was my idea. I wired to London for a fresh lot to be sent down that evening. In the meantime, there'd be only people I could trust in the house: my wife's secretary, Miss Collins, and Tredwell, the butler, who has been with me since I was a boy.'

'And this Miss Collins, how long has she been with you?'

'Just a year,' said Mrs Waverly. 'She has been invaluable to me as a secretary-companion, and is also a very efficient housekeeper.'

'The nurse?'

'She has been with me six months. She came to me with excellent references. All the same, I never really liked her, although Johnnie was quite devoted to her.'

'Still, I gather she had already left when the catastrophe occurred. Perhaps, Monsieur Waverly, you will be so kind as to continue.'

Mr Waverly resumed his narrative.

'Inspector McNeil arrived about ten-thirty. The servants had all left by then. He declared himself quite satisfied with the internal arrangements. He had various men posted in the park outside, guarding all the approaches to the house, and he assured me that if the whole thing were not a hoax, we should undoubtedly catch my mysterious correspondent.

'I had Johnnie with me, and he and I and the inspector went together into a room we call the council chamber. The inspector locked the door. There is a big grandfather clock there, and as the hands drew near to twelve I don't mind confessing that I was as nervous as a cat. There was a whirring sound, and the clock began to strike. I clutched at Johnnie. I had a feeling a man might drop from the skies. The last stroke sounded, and as it did so, there was a great commotion outside—shouting and running. The inspector flung up the window, and a constable came running up.

'"We've got him sir," he panted. "He was sneaking up through the bushes. He's got a whole dope outfit on him."

'We hurried out on the terrace where two constables were holding a ruffianly-looking fellow in shabby clothes, who was twisting and turning in a vain endeavour to escape. One of the policemen held out an unrolled parcel which they had wrested from their captive. It contained a pad of cotton wool and a bottle of chloroform. It made my blood boil to see it. There was a note, too, addressed to me. I tore it open. It bore the following words: "You should have paid up. To ransom your son will now cost you fifty thousand. In spite of all your precautions he has been abducted on the twenty-ninth as I said."

'I gave a great laugh, the laugh of relief, but as I did so I heard the hum of a motor and a shout. I turned my head. Racing down the drive towards the south lodge at a furious speed was a low, long grey car. It was the man who drove it who shouted, but that was not what gave me a shock of horror. It was the sight of Johnnie's flaxen curls. The child was in the car beside him.

'The inspector ripped out an oath. "The child was here not a minute ago," he cried. His eyes swept over us. We were all there: myself, Tredwell, Miss Collins. "When did you last see him, Mr Waverly?"

'I cast my mind back, trying to remember. When the constable had called us, I had run out with the inspector, forgetting all about Johnnie.

'And then there came a sound that startled us, the chiming of a church clock from the village. With an exclamation the inspector pulled out his watch. It was exactly twelve o'clock. With one common accord we ran to the council chamber; the clock there marked the hour as ten minutes past. Someone must have deliberately tampered with it, for I have never known it gain or lose before. It is a perfect timekeeper.'

Mr Waverly paused. Poirot smiled to himself and straightened a little mat which the anxious father had pushed askew.

'A pleasing little problem, obscure and charming,' murmured Poirot. 'I will investigate it for you with pleasure. Truly it was planned *à merveille*.'

Mrs Waverly looked at him reproachfully. 'But my boy,' she wailed.

Poirot hastily composed his face and looked the picture of earnest sympathy again. 'He is safe, madame, he is unharmed. Rest assured, these miscreants will take the greatest care of him. Is he not to them the turkey—no, the goose—that lays the golden eggs?'

'M. Poirot, I'm sure there's only one thing to be done—pay up. I was all against it at first—but now! A mother's feelings—'

'But we have interrupted monsieur in his history,' cried Poirot hastily.

'I expect you know the rest pretty well from the papers,' said Mr Waverly. 'Of course, Inspector McNeil got on to the telephone immediately. A description of the car and the man was circulated all round, and it looked at first as though everything was going to turn out all right. A car, answering to the description, with a man and a small boy, had passed through various villages, apparently making for London. At one place they had stopped, and it was noticed that the child was crying and obviously afraid of his companion. When Inspector McNeil announced that the car had been stopped and the man and boy detained, I was almost ill with relief. You know the sequel. The boy was not Johnnie, and the man was an ardent motorist, fond of children, who had picked up a small child playing in the streets of Edenswell, a village about fifteen miles from us, and was kindly giving him a ride. Thanks to the cocksure blundering of the police, all traces have disappeared. Had they not persistently followed the wrong car, they might by now have found the boy.'

'Calm yourself, monsieur. The police are a brave and intelligent force of men. Their mistake was a very natural one. And altogether it was a clever scheme. As to the man they caught in the grounds, I understand that his defence has consisted all along of a persistent denial. He declares that the note and parcel were given to him to deliver at Waverly Court. The man who gave them to him handed him a ten-shilling note and promised him another if it were delivered at exactly ten minutes to twelve. He was to approach the house through the grounds and knock at the side door.'

'I don't believe a word of it,' declared Mrs Waverly hotly. 'It's all a parcel of lies.'

'*En verité*, it is a thin story,' said Poirot reflectively. 'But so far they have not shaken it. I understand, also, that he made a certain accusation?'

His glance interrogated Mr Waverly. The latter got rather red again.

'The fellow had the impertinence to pretend that he recognized in Tredwell the man who gave him the parcel. "Only the bloke has shaved off his moustache." Tredwell, who was born on the estate!'

Poirot smiled a little at the country gentleman's indignation. 'Yet you yourself suspect an inmate of the house to have been accessory to the abduction.'

'Yes, but not Tredwell.'

'And you, madame?' asked Poirot, suddenly turning to her.

'It could not have been Tredwell who gave this tramp the letter and parcel—if anybody ever did, which I don't believe. It was given him at ten o'clock, he says. At ten o'clock Tredwell was with my husband in the smoking-room.'

'Were you able to see the face of the man in the car, monsieur? Did it resemble that of Tredwell in any way?'

'It was too far away for me to see his face.'

'Has Tredwell a brother, do you know?'

'He had several, but they are all dead. The last one was killed in the war.'

'I am not yet clear as to the grounds of Waverly Court. The car was heading for the south lodge. Is there another entrance?'

'Yes, what we call the east lodge. It can be seen from the other side of the house.'

'It seems to me strange that nobody saw the car entering the grounds.'

'There is a right of way through, and access to a small chapel. A good many cars pass through. The man must have stopped the car in a convenient place and run up to the house just as the alarm was given and attention attracted elsewhere.'

'Unless he was already inside the house,' mused Poirot. 'Is there any place where he could have hidden?'

'Well, we certainly didn't make a thorough search of the house beforehand. There seemed no need. I suppose he might have hidden himself somewhere, but who would have let him in?'

'We shall come to that later. One thing at a time—let us be methodical. There is no special hiding-place in the house? Waverly Court is an old place, and there are sometimes "priests' holes", as they call them.'

'By gad, there *is* a priest's hole. It opens from one of the panels in the hall.'

'Near the council chamber?'

'Just outside the door.'

'*Voilà!*'

'But nobody knows of its existence except my wife and myself.'

'Tredwell?'

'Well—he might have heard of it.'

'Miss Collins?'

'I have never mentioned it to her.'

Poirot reflected for a minute.

'Well, monsieur, the next thing is for me to come down to Waverly Court. If I arrive this afternoon, will it suit you?'

'Oh, as soon as possible, please, Monsieur Poirot!' cried Mrs Waverly. 'Read this once more.'

She thrust into his hands the last missive from the enemy which had reached the Waverlys that morning and which had sent her post-haste to Poirot. It gave clever and explicit directions for the paying over of the money, and ended with a threat that the boy's life would pay for any treachery. It was clear that a love of money warred with the essential mother love of Mrs Waverly, and that the latter was at last gaining the day.

Poirot detained Mrs Waverly for a minute behind her husband.

'Madame, the truth, if you please. Do you share your husband's faith in the butler, Tredwell?'

'I have nothing against him, Monsieur Poirot, I cannot see how he can have been concerned in this, but—well, I have never liked him—never!'

'One other thing, madame, can you give me the address of the child's nurse?'

'149 Netherall Road, Hammersmith. You don't imagine—'

'Never do I imagine. Only—I employ the little grey cells. And sometimes, just sometimes, I have a little idea.'

Poirot came back to me as the door closed.

'So madame has never liked the butler. It is interesting, that, eh, Hastings?'

I refused to be drawn. Poirot has deceived me so often that I now go warily. There is always a catch somewhere.

After completing an elaborate outdoor toilet, we set off for Netherall Road. We were fortunate enough to find Miss Jessie Withers at home. She was a pleasant-faced woman of thirty-five, capable and superior. I could not believe that she could be mixed up in the affair. She was bitterly resentful of the way she had been dismissed, but admitted that she had been in the wrong. She was engaged to be married to a painter and decorator who happened to be in the neighbourhood, and she had run out to meet him. The thing seemed natural enough. I could not quite understand Poirot. All his questions seemed to me quite irrelevant. They were concerned mainly with the daily routine of her life at Waverly Court. I was frankly bored and glad when Poirot took his departure.

'Kidnapping is an easy job, *mon ami*,' he observed, as he hailed a taxi in the Hammersmith Road and ordered it to drive to Waterloo. 'That child could have been abducted with the greatest ease any day for the last three years.'

'I don't see that that advances us much,' I remarked coldly.

'*Au contraire*, it advances us enormously, but enormously! If you must wear a tie pin, Hastings, at least let it be in the exact centre of your tie. At present it is at least a sixteenth of an inch too much to the right.'

Waverly Court was a fine old place and had recently been restored with taste and care. Mr Waverly showed us the council chamber, the terrace, and all the various spots connected with the case. Finally, at Poirot's request, he pressed a spring in the wall, a panel slid aside, and a short passage led us into the priest's hole.

'You see,' said Waverly. 'There is nothing here.'

The tiny room was bare enough, there was not even the mark of a footstep on the floor. I joined Poirot where he was bending attentively over a mark in the corner.

'What do you make of this, my friend?'

There were four imprints close together.

'A dog,' I cried.

'A very small dog, Hastings.'

'A Pom.'

'Smaller than a Pom.'

'A griffon?' I suggested doubtfully.

'Smaller even than a griffon. A species unknown to the Kennel Club.'

I looked at him. His face was alight with excitement and satisfaction.

'I was right,' he murmured. 'I knew I was right. Come, Hastings.'

As we stepped out into the hall and the panel closed behind us, a young lady came out of a door farther down the passage. Mr Waverly presented her to us.

'Miss Collins.'

Miss Collins was about thirty years of age, brisk and alert in manner. She had fair, rather dull hair, and wore pince-nez.

At Poirot's request, we passed into a small morning-room, and he questioned her closely as to the servants and particularly as to Tredwell. She admitted that she did not like the butler.

'He gives himself airs,' she explained.

They then went into the question of the food eaten by Mrs Waverly on the night of the 28th. Miss Collins declared that she had partaken of the same dishes upstairs in her sitting-room and had felt no ill effects. As she was departing I nudged Poirot.

'The dog,' I whispered.

'Ah, yes, the dog!' He smiled broadly. 'Is there a dog kept here by any chance, mademoiselle?'

'There are two retrievers in the kennels outside.'

'No, I mean a small dog, a toy dog.'

'No—nothing of the kind.'

Poirot permitted her to depart. Then, pressing the bell, he remarked to me, 'She lies, that Mademoiselle Collins. Possibly I should, also, in her place. Now for the butler.'

Tredwell was a dignified individual. He told his story with perfect aplomb, and it was essentially the same as that of Mr Waverly. He admitted that he knew the secret of the priest's hole.

When he finally withdrew, pontifical to the last, I met Poirot's quizzical eyes.

'What do you make of it all, Hastings?'

'What do you?' I parried.

'How cautious you become. Never, never will the grey cells function unless you stimulate them. Ah, but I will not tease you! Let us make our deductions together. What points strike us specially as being difficult?'

'There is one thing that strikes me,' I said. 'Why did the man who kidnapped the child go out by the south lodge instead of by the east lodge where no one would see him?'

'That is a very good point, Hastings, an excellent one. I will match it with another. Why warn the Waverlys beforehand? Why not simply kidnap the child and hold him to ransom?'

'Because they hoped to get the money without being forced to action.'

'Surely it was very unlikely that the money would be paid on a mere threat?'

'Also they wanted to focus attention on twelve o'clock, so that when the tramp man was seized, the other could emerge from his hiding-place and get away with the child unnoticed.'

'That does not alter the fact that they were making a thing difficult that was perfectly easy. If they do not specify

73

Agatha Christie

a time or date, nothing would be easier than to wait their chance, and carry off the child in a motor one day when he is out with his nurse.'

'Ye—es,' I admitted doubtfully.

'In fact, there is a deliberate playing of the farce! Now let us approach the question from another side. Everything goes to show that there was an accomplice inside the house. Point number one, the mysterious poisoning of Mrs Waverly. Point number two, the letter pinned to the pillow. Point number three, the putting on of the clock ten minutes—all inside jobs. And an additional fact that you may not have noticed. There was no dust in the priest's hole. It had been swept out with a broom.

'Now then, we have four people in the house. We can exclude the nurse, since she could not have swept out the priest's hole, though she could have attended to the other three points. Four people, Mr and Mrs Waverly, Tredwell, the butler, and Miss Collins. We will take Miss Collins first. We have nothing much against her, except that we know very little about her, that she is obviously an intelligent young woman, and that she has only been here a year.'

'She lied about the dog, you said,' I reminded him.

'Ah, yes, the dog.' Poirot gave a peculiar smile. 'Now let us pass to Tredwell. There are several suspicious facts against him. For one thing, the tramp declares that it was Tredwell who gave him the parcel in the village.'

'But Tredwell can prove an alibi on that point.'

'Even then, he could have poisoned Mrs Waverly, pinned the note to the pillow, put on the clock, and swept out the priest's hole. On the other hand, he has been born and bred in the service of the Waverlys. It seems unlikely in the last degree that he should connive at the abduction of the son of the house. It is not in the picture!'

'Well, then?'

'We must proceed logically—however absurd it may seem. We will briefly consider Mrs Waverly. But she is rich, the money is hers. It is her money which has restored this impoverished estate. There would be no reason for her to kidnap her son and pay over her money to herself. Her husband, now, is in a different position. He has a rich wife. It is not the same thing as being rich himself—in fact I have a little idea that the lady is not very fond of parting with her money, except on a very good pretext. But Mr Waverly, you can see at once, he is a *bon viveur*.'

'Impossible,' I spluttered.

'Not at all. Who sends away the servants? Mr Waverly. He can write the notes, drug his wife, put on the hands of the clock, and establish an excellent alibi for his faithful retainer Tredwell. Tredwell has never liked Mrs Waverly. He is devoted to his master and is willing to obey his orders implicitly. There were three of them in it. Waverly, Tredwell, and some friend of Waverly. That is the mistake the police made, they made no further inquiries about the man who drove the grey car with the wrong child in it. He was the third man. He picks up a child in a village near by, a boy with flaxen curls. He drives in through the east lodge and passes out through the south lodge just at the right moment, waving his hand and shouting. They cannot see his face or the number of the car, so obviously they cannot see the child's face, either. Then he lays a false trail to London. In the meantime, Tredwell has done his part in arranging for the parcel and note to be delivered by a rough-looking gentleman. His master can provide an alibi in the unlikely case of the man recognizing him, in spite of the false moustache he wore. As for Mr Waverly, as soon as the hullabaloo occurs outside, and the inspector rushes out, he quickly hides the child in the priest's hole, and follows him out. Later in the day, when the inspector is gone and Miss Collins is out of the way, it will be easy enough to drive him off to some safe place in his own car.'

'But what about the dog?' I asked. 'And Miss Collins lying?'

'That was my little joke. I asked her if there were any toy dogs in the house, and she said no—but doubtless there are some—in the nursery! You see, Mr Waverly placed some toys in the priest's hole to keep Johnnie amused and quiet.'

'M. Poirot—' Mr Waverly entered the room—'have you discovered anything? Have you any clue to where the boy has been taken?'

Poirot handed him a piece of paper. 'Here is the address.'

'But this is a blank sheet.'

'Because I am waiting for you to write it down for me.'

'What the—' Mr Waverly's face turned purple.

'I know everything, monsieur. I give you twenty-four hours to return the boy. Your ingenuity will be equal to the task of explaining his reappearance. Otherwise, Mrs Waverly will be informed of the exact sequence of events.'

Mr Waverly sank down in a chair and buried his face in his hands. 'He is with my old nurse, ten miles away. He is happy and well cared for.'

'I have no doubt of that. If I did not believe you to be a good father at heart, I should not be willing to give you another chance.'

'The scandal—'

'Exactly. Your name is an old and honoured one. Do not jeopardize it again. Good evening, Mr Waverly. Ah, by the way, one word of advice. Always sweep in the corners!'

The Double Clue

'But above everything—no publicity,' said Mr Marcus Hardman for perhaps the fourteenth time.

The word *publicity* occurred throughout his conversation with the regularity of a leitmotif. Mr Hardman was a small man, delicately plump, with exquisitely manicured hands and a plaintive tenor voice. In his way, he was somewhat of a celebrity and the fashionable life was his profession. He was rich, but not remarkably so, and he spent his money zealously in the pursuit of social pleasure. His hobby was collecting. He had the collector's soul. Old lace, old fans, antique jewellery—nothing crude or modern for Marcus Hardman.

Poirot and I, obeying an urgent summons, had arrived to find the little man writhing in an agony of indecision. Under the circumstances, to call in the police was abhorrent to him. On the other hand, not to call them in was to acquiesce in the loss of some of the gems of his collection. He hit upon Poirot as a compromise.

'My rubies, Monsieur Poirot, and the emerald necklace—said to have belonged to Catherine de' Medici. Oh, the emerald necklace!'

'If you will recount to me the circumstances of their disappearance?' suggested Poirot gently.

'I am endeavouring to do so. Yesterday afternoon I had a little tea party—quite an informal affair, some half a dozen people or so. I have given one or two of them during the season, and though perhaps I should not say so, they have been quite a success. Some good music—Nacora, the pianist, and Katherine Bird, the Australian contralto—in the big studio. Well, early in the afternoon, I was showing my guests my collection of medieval jewels. I keep them in the small wall safe over there. It is arranged like a cabinet inside, with coloured velvet background, to display the stones. Afterwards we inspected the fans—in the case on the wall. Then we all went to the studio for music. It was not until after everyone had gone that I discovered the safe rifled! I must have failed to shut it properly, and someone had seized the opportunity to denude it of its contents. The rubies, Monsieur Poirot, the emerald necklace—the collection of a lifetime! What would I not give to recover them! But there must be no publicity! You fully understand that, do you not, Monsieur Poirot? My own guests, my personal friends! It would be a horrible scandal!'

'Who was the last person to leave this room when you went to the studio?'

'Mr Johnston. You may know him? The South African millionaire. He has just rented the Abbotburys' house in Park Lane. He lingered behind a few moments, I remember. But surely, oh, surely it could not be he!'

'Did any of your guests return to this room during the afternoon on any pretext?'

'I was prepared for that question, Monsieur Poirot. Three of them did so. Countess Vera Rossakoff, Mr Bernard Parker, and Lady Runcorn.'

'Let us hear about them.'

'The Countess Rossakoff is a very charming Russian lady, a member of the old régime. She has recently come to this country. She had bade me goodbye, and I was therefore somewhat surprised to find her in this room apparently gazing in rapture at my cabinet of fans. You know, Monsieur Poirot, the more I think of it, the more suspicious it seems to me. Don't you agree?'

'Extremely suspicious; but let us hear about the others.'

'Well, Parker simply came here to fetch a case of miniatures that I was anxious to show to Lady Runcorn.'

'And Lady Runcorn herself?'

'As I dare say you know, Lady Runcorn is a middle-aged woman of considerable force of character who devotes most of her time to various charitable committees. She simply returned to fetch a handbag she had laid down somewhere.'

'*Bien*, monsieur. So we have four possible suspects. The Russian countess, the English *grande dame*, the South African millionaire, and Mr Bernard Parker. Who *is* Mr Parker, by the way?'

The question appeared to embarrass Mr Hardman considerably.

'He is—er—he is a young fellow. Well, in fact, a young fellow I know.'

'I had already deduced as much,' replied Poirot gravely. 'What does he do, this Mr Parker?'

'He is a young man about town—not, perhaps, quite in the swim, if I may so express myself.'

'How did he come to be a friend of yours, may I ask?'

'Well—er—on one or two occasions he has—performed certain little commissions for me.'

'Continue, monsieur,' said Poirot.

Hardman looked piteously at him. Evidently the last thing he wanted to do was to continue. But as Poirot maintained an inexorable silence, he capitulated.

'You see, Monsieur Poirot—it is well known that I am interested in antique jewels. Sometimes there is a family heirloom to be disposed of—which, mind you, would never be sold in the open market or to a dealer. But a private sale to me is a very different matter. Parker arranges the details of such things, he is in touch with both sides, and thus any little embarrassment is avoided. He brings anything of that kind to my notice. For instance, the Countess Rossakoff has brought some family jewels with her from Russia. She is anxious to sell them. Bernard Parker was to have arranged the transaction.'

'I see,' said Poirot thoughtfully. 'And you trust him implicitly?'

'I have had no reason to do otherwise.'

'Mr Hardman, of these four people, which do you yourself suspect?'

'Oh, Monsieur Poirot, what a question! They are my friends, as I told you. I suspect none of them—or all of them, whichever way you like to put it.'

'I do not agree. You suspect one of those four. It is not Countess Rossakoff. It is not Mr Parker. Is it Lady Runcorn or Mr Johnston?'

'You drive me into a corner, Monsieur Poirot, you do indeed. I am most anxious to have no scandal. Lady Runcorn belongs to one of the oldest families in England; but it is true, it is most unfortunately true, that her aunt, Lady Caroline, suffered from a most melancholy affliction. It was understood, of course, by all her friends, and her maid returned the teaspoons, or whatever it was, as promptly as possible. You see my predicament!'

'So Lady Runcorn had an aunt who was a kleptomaniac? Very interesting. You permit that I examine the safe?'

Mr Hardman assenting, Poirot pushed back the door of the safe and examined the interior. The empty velvet-lined shelves gaped at us.

'Even now the door does not shut properly,' murmured Poirot, as he swung it to and fro. 'I wonder why? Ah, what have we here? A glove, caught in the hinge. A man's glove.'

He held it out to Mr Hardman.

'That's not one of my gloves,' the latter declared.

'Aha! Something more!' Poirot bent deftly and picked up a small object from the floor of the safe. It was a flat cigarette case made of black moiré.

'My cigarette case!' cried Mr Hardman.

'Yours? Surely not, monsieur. Those are not your initials.'

He pointed to an entwined monogram of two letters executed in platinum.

Hardman took it in his hand.

'You are right,' he declared. 'It is very like mine, but the initials are different. A "*B*" and a "*P*". Good heavens—Parker!'

'It would seem so,' said Poirot. 'A somewhat carless

young man—especially if the glove is his also. That would be a double clue, would it not?'

'Bernard Parker!' murmured Hardman. 'What a relief! Well, Monsieur Poirot, I leave it to you to recover the jewels. Place the matter in the hands of the police if you think fit—that is, if you are quite sure that it is he who is guilty.'

'See you, my friend,' said Poirot to me, as we left the house together, 'he has one law for the titled, and another law for the plain, this Mr Hardman. Me, I have not yet been ennobled, so I am on the side of the plain. I have sympathy for this young man. The whole thing was a little curious, was it not? There was Hardman suspecting Lady Runcorn; there was I, suspecting the Countess and Johnston; and all the time, the obscure Mr Parker was our man.'

'Why did you suspect the other two?'

'*Parbleu*! It is such a simple thing to be a Russian refugee or a South African millionaire. Any woman can call herself a Russian countess; anyone can buy a house in Park Lane and call himself a South African millionaire. Who is going to contradict them? But I observe that we are passing through Bury Street. Our careless young friend lives here. Let us, as you say, strike while the iron is in the fire.'

Mr Bernard Parker was at home. We found him reclining on some cushions, clad in an amazing dressing-gown of purple and orange. I have seldom taken a greater dislike to anyone than I did to this particular young man with his white, effeminate face and affected lisping speech.

'Good morning, monsieur,' said Poirot briskly. 'I come from Mr Hardman. Yesterday, at the party, somebody has stolen all his jewels. Permit me to ask you, monsieur—is this your glove?'

Mr Parker's mental processes did not seem very rapid. He stared at the glove, as though gathering his wits together.

'Where did you find it?' he asked at last.

'Is it your glove, monsieur?'

Mr Parker appeared to make up his mind.

'No, it isn't,' he declared.

'And this cigarette case, is that yours?'

'Certainly not. I always carry a silver one.'

'Very well, monsieur. I go to put matters in the hands of the police.'

'Oh, I say, I wouldn't do that if I were you,' cried Mr Parker in some concern. 'Beastly unsympathetic people, the police. Wait a bit. I'll go round and see old Hardman. Look here—oh, stop a minute.'

But Poirot beat a determined retreat.

'We have given him something to think about, have we not?' he chuckled. 'Tomorrow we will observe what has occurred.'

But we were destined to have a reminder of the Hardman case that afternoon. Without the least warning the door flew open, and a whirlwind in human form invaded our privacy, bringing with her a swirl of sables (it was as cold as only an English June day can be) and a hat rampant with slaughtered ospreys. Countess Vera Rossakoff was a somewhat disturbing personality.

'You are Monsieur Poirot? What is this that you have done? You accuse that poor boy! It is infamous. It is scandalous. I know him. He is a chicken, a lamb—never would he steal. He has done everything for me. Will I stand by and see him martyred and butchered?'

'Tell me, madame, is this his cigarette case?' Poirot held out the black moiré case.

The Countess paused for a moment while she inspected it.

'Yes, it is his. I know it well. What of it? Did you find it in the room? We were all there; he dropped it then, I suppose. Ah, you policemen, you are worse than the Red Guards—'

'And is this his glove?'

'How should I know? One glove is like another. Do not try to stop me—he must be set free. His character must be cleared. You shall do it. I will sell my jewels and give you much money.'

'Madame—'

'It is agreed, then? No, no, do not argue. The poor boy! He came to me, the tears in his eyes. "I will save you," I said. "I will go to this man—this ogre, this monster! Leave it to Vera." Now it is settled, I go.'

With as little ceremony as she had come, she swept from the room, leaving an overpowering perfume of an exotic nature behind her.

'What a woman!' I exclaimed. 'And what furs!'

'Ah, yes, *they* were genuine enough. Could a spurious countess have real furs? My little joke, Hastings... No, she is truly Russian, I fancy. Well, well, so Master Bernard went bleating to her.'

'The cigarette case is his. I wonder if the glove is also—'

With a smile Poirot drew from his pocket a second glove and placed it by the first. There was no doubt of their being a pair.

'Where did you get the second one, Poirot?'

'It was thrown down with a stick on the table in the hall in Bury Street. Truly, a very careless young man, Monsieur Parker. Well, well, *mon ami*—we must be thorough. Just for the form of the thing, I will make a little visit to Park Lane.'

Needless to say, I accompanied my friend. Johnston was out, but we saw his private secretary. It transpired that Johnston had only recently arrived from South Africa. He had never been in England before.

'He is interested in precious stones, is he not?' hazarded Poirot.

'Gold mining is nearer the mark,' laughed the secretary.

Poirot came away from the interview thoughtful. Late that evening, to my utter surprise, I found him earnestly studying a Russian grammar.

'Good heavens, Poirot!' I cried. 'Are you learning Russian in order to converse with the Countess in her own language?'

'She certainly would not listen to my English, my friend!'

'But surely, Poirot, well-born Russians invariably speak French?'

'You are a mine of information, Hastings! I will cease puzzling over the intricacies of the Russian alphabet.'

He threw the book from him with a dramatic gesture. I was not entirely satisfied. There was a twinkle in his eye which I knew of old. It was an invariable sign that Hercule Poirot was pleased with himself.

'Perhaps,' I said sapiently, 'you doubt her being really a Russian. You are going to test her?'

'Ah, no, no, she is Russian all right.'

'Well, then—'

'If you really want to distinguish yourself over this case, Hastings, I recommend *First Steps in Russian* as an invaluable aid.'

Then he laughed and would say no more. I picked up the book from the floor and dipped into it curiously, but could make neither head nor tail of Poirot's remarks.

The following morning brought us no news of any kind, but that did not seem to worry my little friend. At breakfast, he announced his intention of calling upon Mr Hardman early in the day. We found the elderly social butterfly at home, and seemingly a little calmer than on the previous day.

'Well, Monsieur Poirot, any news?' he demanded eagerly.

Poirot handed him a slip of paper.

'That is the person who took the jewels, monsieur. Shall I put matters in the hands of the police? Or would you prefer me to recover the jewels without bringing the police into the matter?'

Mr Hardman was staring at the paper. At last he found his voice.

'Most astonishing. I should infinitely prefer to have no scandal in the matter. I give you *carte blanche*, Monsieur Poirot. I am sure you will be discreet.'

Our next procedure was to hail a taxi, which Poirot ordered to drive to the Carlton. There he inquired for Countess Rossakoff. In a few minutes we were ushered up into the lady's suite. She came to meet us with outstretched hands, arrayed in a marvellous negligée of barbaric design.

'Monsieur Poirot!' she cried. 'You have succeeded? You have cleared that poor infant?'

'Madame la Comtesse, your friend Mr Parker is perfectly safe from arrest.'

'Ah, but you are the clever little man! Superb! And so quickly too.'

'On the other hand, I have promised Mr Hardman that the jewels shall be returned to him today.'

'So?'

'Therefore, madame, I should be extremely obliged if you would place them in my hands without delay. I am sorry to hurry you, but I am keeping a taxi—in case it should be necessary for me to go on to Scotland Yard; and we Belgians, madame, we practise the thrift.'

The Countess had lighted a cigarette. For some seconds she sat perfectly still, blowing smoke rings, and gazing steadily at Poirot. Then she burst into a laugh, and rose. She went across to the bureau, opened a drawer, and took out a black silk handbag. She tossed it lightly to Poirot. Her tone, when she spoke, was perfectly light and unmoved.

'We Russians, on the contrary, practise prodigality,' she said. 'And to do that, unfortunately, one must have money. You need not look inside. They are all there.'

Poirot arose.

'I congratulate you, madame, on your quick intelligence and your promptitude.'

'Ah! But since you were keeping your taxi waiting, what else could I do?'

'You are too amiable, madame. You are remaining long in London?'

'I am afraid no—owing to you.'

'Accept my apologies.'

'We shall meet again elsewhere, perhaps.'

'I hope so.'

'And I—do not!' exclaimed the Countess with a laugh. 'It is a great compliment that I pay you there—there are very few men in the world whom I fear. Goodbye, Monsieur Poirot.'

'Goodbye, Madame la Comtesse. Ah—pardon me, I forgot! Allow me to return you your cigarette case.'

And with a bow he handed to her the little black moiré case we had found in the safe. She accepted it without any change of expression—just a lifted eyebrow and a murmured: 'I see!'

'What a woman!' cried Poirot enthusiastically as we descended the stairs. '*Mon Dieu, quelle femme*! Not a word of argument—of protestation, of bluff! One quick glance, and she had sized up the position correctly. I tell you, Hastings, a woman who can accept defeat like that—with a careless smile—will go far! She is dangerous, she has the nerves of steel; she—' He tripped heavily.

'If you can manage to moderate your transports and look where you're going, it might be as well,' I suggested. 'When did you first suspect the Countess?'

'*Mon ami*, it was the glove *and* the cigarette case—the double clue, shall we say—that worried me. Bernard Parker might easily have dropped one or the other—but hardly both. Ah, no, that would have been *too* careless! In the same way, if someone else had placed them there to incriminate Parker, one would have been sufficient—the cigarette case *or* the glove—again not both. So I was forced to the conclusion that one of the two things did *not* belong to Parker. I imagined at first that the case was his, and that the glove was not. But when I discovered the fellow to the glove, I saw that it was the other way about. Whose, then, was the cigarette case? Clearly, it could not belong to Lady Runcorn. The initials were wrong. Mr Johnston? Only if he were here under a false name. I interviewed his secretary, and it was apparent at once that everything was clear and above board. There was no reticence about Mr Johnston's past. The Countess, then? She was supposed to have brought jewels with her from Russia; she had only to take the stones from their settings, and it was extremely doubtful if they could ever be identified. What could be easier for her than to pick up one of Parker's gloves from the hall that day and thrust it into the safe? But, *bien sûr*, she did not intend to drop her own cigarette case.'

'But if the case was hers, why did it have "*B.P.*" on it? The Countess's initials are *V.R.*'

Poirot smiled gently upon me.

'Exactly, *mon ami*; but in the Russian alphabet, *B* is *V* and *P* is *R*.'

'Well, you couldn't expect me to guess that. I don't know Russian.'

'Neither do I, Hastings. That is why I bought my little book—and urged it on your attention.'

He sighed.

'A remarkable woman. I have a feeling, my friend—a very decided feeling—I shall meet her again. Where, I wonder?'

The King of Clubs

'Truth,' I observed, laying aside the *Daily Newsmonger*, 'is stranger than fiction!'

The remark was not, perhaps, an original one. It appeared to incense my friend. Tilting his egg-shaped head on one side, the little man carefully flicked an imaginary fleck of dust from his carefully creased trousers, and observed: 'How profound! What a thinker is my friend Hastings!'

Without displaying any annoyance at this quite uncalled-for gibe, I tapped the sheet I had laid aside.

'You've read this morning's paper?'

'I have. And after reading it, I folded it anew symmetrically. I did not cast it on the floor as you have done, with your so lamentable absence of order and method.'

(That is the worst of Poirot. Order and Method are his gods. He goes so far as to attribute all his success to them.)

'Then you saw the account of the murder of Henry Reedburn, the impresario? It was that which prompted my remark. Not only is truth stranger than fiction—it is more dramatic. Think of that solid middle-class English family, the Oglanders. Father and mother, son and daughter, typical of thousands of families all over this country. The men of the family go to the city every day; the women look after the house. Their lives are perfectly peaceful, and utterly monotonous. Last night they were sitting in their neat suburban drawing-room at Daisymead, Streatham, playing bridge. Suddenly, without any warning, the french window bursts open, and a woman staggers into the room. Her grey satin frock is marked with a crimson stain. She utters one word, "Murder!" before she sinks to the ground insensible. It is possible that they recognize her from her pictures as Valerie Saintclair, the famous dancer who has lately taken London by storm!'

'Is this your eloquence, or that of the *Daily Newsmonger*?' inquired Poirot.

'The *Daily Newsmonger* was in a hurry to go to press, and contented itself with bare facts. But the dramatic possibilities of the story struck me at once.'

Poirot nodded thoughtfully. 'Wherever there is human nature, there is drama. *But*—it is not always just where you think it is. Remember that. Still, I too am interested in the case, since it is likely that I shall be connected with it.'

'Indeed?'

'Yes. A gentleman rang me up this morning, and made an appointment with me on behalf of Prince Paul of Maurania.'

'But what has that to do with it?'

'You do not read your pretty little English scandal-papers. The ones with the funny stories, and "a little mouse has heard—" or "a little bird would like to know—" See here.'

I followed his short stubby finger along the paragraph: '—whether the foreign prince and the famous dancer are *really* affinities! And if the lady likes her new diamond ring!'

'And now to resume your so dramatic narrative,' said Poirot. 'Mademoiselle Saintclair had just fainted on the drawing-room carpet at Daisymead, you remember.'

I shrugged. 'As a result of Mademoiselle's first murmured words when she came round, the two male Oglanders stepped out, one to fetch a doctor to attend to the lady, who was evidently suffering terribly from shock, and the other to the police-station—whence after telling his story, he accompanied the police to Mon Désir, Mr Reedburn's magnificent villa, which is situated at no great distance from Daisymead. There they found the great man, who by the way suffers from a somewhat unsavoury reputation, lying in the library with the back of his head cracked open like an eggshell.'

'I have cramped your style,' said Poirot kindly. 'Forgive me, I pray… Ah, here is M. le Prince!'

Our distinguished visitor was announced under the title of Count Feodor. He was a strange-looking youth, tall, eager, with a weak chin, the famous Mauranberg mouth, and the dark fiery eyes of a fanatic.

'M. Poirot?'

My friend bowed.

'Monsieur, I am in terrible trouble, greater than I can well express—'

Poirot waved his hand. 'I comprehend your anxiety. Mademoiselle Saintclair is a very dear friend, is it not so?'

The prince replied simply: 'I hope to make her my wife.'

Poirot sat up in his chair, and his eyes opened.

The prince continued: 'I should not be the first of my family to make a morganatic marriage. My brother Alexander has also defied the Emperor. We are living now in more enlightened days, free from the old caste-prejudice. Besides, Mademoiselle Saintclair, in actual fact, is quite my equal in rank. You have heard hints as to her history?'

'There are many romantic stories of her origin—not an uncommon thing with famous dancers. I have heard that she is the daughter of an Irish charwoman, also the story which makes her mother a Russian grand duchess.'

'The first story is, of course, nonsense,' said the young man. 'But the second is true. Valerie, though bound to secrecy, has let me guess as much. Besides, she proves it unconsciously in a thousand ways. I believe in heredity, M. Poirot.'

'I too believe in heredity,' said Poirot thoughtfully. 'I have seen some strange things in connection with it—*moi qui vous parle*... But to business, M. le Prince. What do you want of me? What do you fear? I may speak freely, may I not? Is there anything to connect Mademoiselle Saintclair with the crime? She knew Reedburn of course?'

'Yes. He professed to be in love with her.'

'And she?'

'She would have nothing to say to him.'

Poirot looked at him keenly. 'Had she any reason to fear him?'

The young man hesitated. 'There was an incident. You know Zara, the clairvoyant?'

'No.'

'She is wonderful. You should consult her some time. Valerie and I went to see her last week. She read the cards for us. She spoke to Valerie of trouble—of gathering clouds; then she turned up the last card—the covering card, they call it. It was the king of clubs. She said to Valerie: "Beware. There is a man who holds you in his power. You fear him—you are in great danger through him. You know whom I mean?" Valerie was white to the lips. She nodded and said: "Yes, yes, I know." Shortly afterwards we left. Zara's last words to Valerie were: "Beware of the king of clubs. Danger threatens you!" I questioned Valerie. She would tell me nothing—assured me that all was well. But now, after last night, I am more sure than ever that in the king of clubs Valerie saw Reedburn, and that he was the man she feared.'

The Prince paused abruptly. 'Now you understand my agitation when I opened the paper this morning. Supposing Valerie, in a fit of madness—oh, it is impossible!'

Poirot rose from his seat, and patted the young man kindly on the shoulder. 'Do not distress yourself, I beg of you. Leave it in my hands.'

'You will go to Streatham? I gather she is still there, at Daisymead—prostrated by the shock.'

'I will go at once.'

'I have arranged matters—through the embassy. You will be allowed access everywhere.'

'Then we will depart—Hastings, you will accompany me? Au revoir, M. le Prince.'

Mon Désir was an exceptionally fine villa, thoroughly modern and comfortable. A short carriage-drive led up to it from the road, and beautiful gardens extended behind the house for some acres.

On mentioning Prince Paul's name, the butler who answered the door at once took us to the scene of the tragedy. The library was a magnificent room, running from back to front of the whole building, with a window at either end, one giving on the front carriage-drive, and the other on the garden. It was in the recess of the latter that the body had lain. It had been removed not long before, the police having concluded their examination.

'That is annoying,' I murmured to Poirot. 'Who knows what clues they may have destroyed?'

My little friend smiled. 'Eh—Eh! How often must I tell you that clues come from *within*? In the little grey cells of the brain lies the solution of every mystery.'

He turned to the butler. 'I suppose, except for the removal of the body, the room has not been touched?'

'No, sir. It's just as it was when the police came up last night.'

'These curtains, now. I see they pull right across the window recess. They are the same in the other window. Were they drawn last night?'

'Yes, sir, I draw them every night.'

'Then Reedburn must have drawn them back himself?'

'I suppose so, sir.'

'Did you know your master expected a visitor last night?'

'He did not say so, sir. But he gave orders he was not to be disturbed after dinner. You see, sir, there is a door leading out of the library on to the terrace at the side of the house. He could have admitted anyone that way.'

'Was he in the habit of doing that?'

The butler coughed discreetly. 'I believe so, sir.'

Poirot strode to the door in question. It was unlocked. He stepped through it on to the terrace which joined the drive on the right; on the left it led up to a red brick wall.

'The fruit garden, sir. There is a door leading into it farther along, but it was always locked at six o'clock.'

Poirot nodded, and re-entered the library, the butler following.

'Did you hear nothing of last night's events?'

'Well, sir, we heard voices in the library, a little before nine. But that wasn't unusual, especially being a lady's voice. But of course, once we were all in the servants' hall, right the other side, we didn't hear anything at all. And then, about eleven o'clock, the police came.'

'How many voices did you hear?'

'I couldn't say, sir. I only noticed the lady's.'

'Ah!'

'I beg pardon, sir, but Dr Ryan is still in the house, if you would care to see him.'

We jumped at the suggestion, and in a few minutes the doctor, a cheery, middle-aged man, joined us, and gave Poirot all the information he required. Reedburn had been lying near the window, his head by the marble window-seat. There were two wounds, one between the eyes, and the other, the fatal one, on the back of the head.

'He was lying on his back?'

'Yes. There is the mark.' He pointed to a small dark stain on the floor.

'Could not the blow on the back of the head have been caused by his striking the floor?'

'Impossible. Whatever the weapon was, it penetrated some distance into the skull.'

Poirot looked thoughtfully in front of him. In the embrasure of each window was a carved marble seat, the arms being fashioned in the form of a lion's head. A light came into Poirot's eyes. 'Supposing he had fallen backwards on this projecting lion's head, and slipped from there to the ground. Would not that cause a wound such as you describe?'

'Yes, it would. But the angle at which he was lying makes that theory impossible. And besides there could not fail to be traces of blood on the marble of the seat.'

'Unless they were washed away?'

The doctor shrugged his shoulders. 'That is hardly likely. It would be to no one's advantage to give an accident the appearance of murder.'

'Quite so,' acquiesced Poirot. 'Could either of the blows have been struck by a woman, do you think?'

'Oh, quite out of the question, I should say. You are thinking of Mademoiselle Saintclair, I suppose?'

'I think of no one in particular until I am sure,' said Poirot gently.

He turned his attention to the open french window, and the doctor continued:

'It is through here that Mademoiselle Saintclair fled. You can just catch a glimpse of Daisymead between the trees. Of course, there are many houses nearer to the front of the house on the road, but as it happens, Daisymead, though some distance away, is the only house visible this side.'

'Thank you for your amiability, Doctor,' said Poirot. 'Come, Hastings, we will follow the footsteps of Mademoiselle.'

Poirot led the way down through the garden, out through an iron gate, across a short stretch of green and in through the garden gate of Daisymead, which was an unpretentious little house in about half an acre of ground. There was a small flight of steps leading up to a french window. Poirot nodded in their direction.

'That is the way Mademoiselle Saintclair went. For us, who have not her urgency to plead, it will be better to go round to the front door.'

A maid admitted us and took us into the drawing-room, then went in search of Mrs Oglander. The room had evidently not been touched since the night before. The ashes were still in the grate, and the bridge-table was still in the centre of the room, with a dummy exposed, and the hands thrown down. The place was somewhat overloaded with gimcrack ornaments, and a good many family portraits of surpassing ugliness adorned the walls.

Poirot gazed at them more leniently than I did, and straightened one or two that were hanging a shade askew. '*La famille*, it is a strong tie, is it not? Sentiment, it takes the place of beauty.'

I agreed, my eyes being fixed on a family group comprising a gentleman with whiskers, a lady with a high 'front' of hair, a solid, thick-set boy, and two little girls tied up with a good many unnecessary bows of ribbon. I took this to be the Oglander family in earlier days, and studied it with interest.

The door opened, and a young woman came in. Her dark hair was neatly arranged, and she wore a drab-coloured sportscoat and a tweed skirt.

She looked at us inquiringly. Poirot stepped forward. 'Miss Oglander? I regret to derange you—especially after all you have been through. The whole affair must have been most disturbing.'

'It has been rather upsetting,' admitted the young lady cautiously. I began to think that the elements of drama were wasted on Miss Oglander, that her lack of imagination rose superior to any tragedy. I was confirmed in this belief as she continued: 'I must apologize for the state this room is in. Servants get so foolishly excited.'

'It was here that you were sitting last night, *n'est-ce pas?*'

'Yes, we were playing bridge after supper, when—'

'Excuse me—how long had you been playing?'

'Well—' Miss Oglander considered. 'I really can't say. I suppose it must have been about ten o'clock. We had had several rubbers, I know.'

'And you yourself were sitting—where?'

'Facing the window. I was playing with my mother and had gone one no trump. Suddenly, without any warning, the window burst open, and Miss Saintclair staggered into the room.'

'You recognized her?'

'I had a vague idea her face was familiar.'

'She is still here, is she not?'

'Yes, but she refuses to see anyone. She is still quite prostrated.'

'I think she will see me. Will you tell her that I am here at the express request of Prince Paul of Maurania?'

I fancied that the mention of a royal prince rather shook Miss Oglander's imperturbable calm. But she left the room on her errand without any further remark, and returned almost immediately to say that Mademoiselle Saintclair would see us in her room.

We followed her upstairs, and into a fair-sized light bedroom. On a couch by the window a woman was lying who turned her head as we entered. The contrast between the two women struck me at once, the more so as in actual features and colouring they were not unalike—but oh, the difference! Not a look, not a gesture of Valerie Saintclair's but expressed drama. She seemed to exhale an atmosphere of romance. A scarlet flannel dressing-gown covered her feet—a homely garment in all conscience; but the charm of her personality invested it with an exotic flavour, and it seemed an Eastern robe of glowing colour.

Her large dark eyes fastened themselves on Poirot.

'You come from Paul?' Her voice matched her appearance—it was full and languid.

'Yes, mademoiselle. I am here to serve him—and you.'

'What do you want to know?'

'Everything that happened last night. *But everything*!'

She smiled rather wearily.

'Do you think I should lie? I am not stupid. I see well enough that there can be no concealment. He held a secret of mine, that man who is dead. He threatened me with it. For Paul's sake, I endeavoured to make terms with him. I could not risk losing Paul... Now that he is dead, I am safe. But for all that, I did not kill him.'

Poirot shook his head with a smile. 'It is not necessary to tell me that, mademoiselle. Now recount to me what happened last night.'

'I offered him money. He appeared to be willing to treat with me. He appointed last night at nine o'clock. I was to go to Mon Désir. I knew the place; I had been there before. I was to go round to the side door into the library, so that the servants should not see me.

'Excuse me, mademoiselle, but were you not afraid to trust yourself alone there at night?'

Was it my fancy, or was there a momentary pause before she answered?

'Perhaps I was. But you see, there was no one I could ask to go with me. And I was desperate. Reedburn admitted me to the library. Oh, that man! I am glad he is dead! He played with me, as a cat does with a mouse. He taunted me. I begged and implored him on my knees. I offered him every jewel I have. All in vain! Then he named his own terms. Perhaps you can guess what they were. I refused. I told him what I thought of him. I raved at him. He remained calmly smiling. And then, as I fell to silence at last, there was a sound—from behind the curtain in the window... He heard it too. He strode to the curtains and flung them wide apart. There was a man there, hiding—a dreadful-looking man, a sort of tramp. He struck at Mr Reedburn—then he struck again, and he went down. The tramp clutched at me with his bloodstained hand. I tore myself free, slipped through the window, and ran for my life. Then I perceived the lights in this house, and made for them. The blinds were up, and I saw some people playing bridge. I almost fell into the room. I just managed to gasp out "Murder!" and then everything went black—'

'Thank you, Mademoiselle. It must have been a great shock to your nervous system. As to this tramp, could you describe him? Do you remember what he was wearing?'

'No—it was all so quick. But I should know the man anywhere. His face is burnt in on my brain.'

'Just one more question, mademoiselle. The curtains of the *other* window, the one giving on the drive, were they drawn?'

For the first time a puzzled expression crept over the dancer's face. She seemed to be trying to remember.

'*Eh bien, mademoiselle?*'

'I think—I am almost sure—yes, quite sure! They were *not* drawn.'

'That is curious, since the other ones were. No matter. It is, I dare say, of no great importance. You are remaining here long, mademoiselle?'

'The doctor thinks I shall be fit to return to town tomorrow.' She looked round the room. Miss Oglander had gone out. 'These people, they are very kind—but they are not of my world. I shock them! And to me—well, I am not fond of the *bourgeoisie*!'

A faint note of bitterness underlay her words.

Poirot nodded. 'I understand. I hope I have not fatigued you unduly with my questions?'

'Not at all, monsieur. I am only too anxious Paul should know all as soon as possible.'

'Then I will wish you good day, mademoiselle.'

As Poirot was leaving the room, he paused, and pounced on a pair of patent-leather slippers. 'Yours, mademoiselle?'

'Yes, monsieur. They have just been cleaned and brought up.'

'Ah!' said Poirot, as we descended the stairs. 'It seems that the domestics are not too excited to clean shoes, though they forget a grate. Well, *mon ami*, at first there appeared to be one or two points of interest, but I fear, I very much fear, that we must regard the case as finished. It all seems straightforward enough.'

'And the murderer?'

'Hercule Poirot does not hunt down tramps,' replied my friend grandiloquently.

Miss Oglander met us in the hall. 'If you will wait in the drawing-room a minute, Mamma would like to speak to you.'

The room was still untouched, and Poirot idly gathered up the cards, shuffling them with his tiny, fastidiously groomed hands.

'Do you know what I think, my friend?'

'No?' I said eagerly.

'I think that Miss Oglander made a mistake in going one no trump. She should have gone three spades.'

'Poirot! You are the limit.'

'*Mon Dieu*, I cannot always be talking blood and thunder!'

105

Suddenly he stiffened: 'Hastings—*Hastings*. See! The king of clubs is missing from the pack!'

'Zara!' I cried.

'Eh?' he did not seem to understand my allusion. Mechanically he stacked the cards and put them away in their cases. His face was very grave.

'Hastings,' he said at last, 'I, Hercule Poirot, have come near to making a big mistake—a very big mistake.'

I gazed at him, impressed, but utterly uncomprehending.

'We must begin again, Hastings. Yes, we must begin again. But this time we shall not err.'

He was interrupted by the entrance of a handsome middle-aged lady. She carried some household books in her hand. Poirot bowed to her.

'Do I understand, sir, that you are a friend of—er—Miss Saintclair's?'

'I come from a friend of hers, madame.'

'Oh, I see. I thought perhaps—'

Poirot suddenly waved brusquely at the window.

'Your blinds were not pulled down last night?'

'No—I suppose that is why Miss Saintclair saw the light so plainly.'

'There was moonlight last night. I wonder that you did not see Mademoiselle Saintclair from your seat here facing the windows?'

'I suppose we were engrossed with our game. Nothing like this has ever happened before to us.'

'I can quite believe that, madame. And I will put your mind at rest. Mademoiselle Saintclair is leaving tomorrow.'

'Oh!' The good lady's face cleared.

'And I will wish you good morning, madame.'

A servant was cleaning the steps as we went out of the front door. Poirot addressed her.

'Was it you who cleaned the shoes of the young lady upstairs?'

The maid shook her head. 'No, sir. I don't think they've been cleaned.'

'Who cleaned them, then?' I inquired of Poirot, as we walked down the road.

'Nobody. They did not need cleaning.'

'I grant that walking on the road or path on a fine night would not soil them. But surely after going through the long grass of the garden, they would have been soiled and stained.'

'Yes,' said Poirot with a curious smile. 'In that case, I agree, they would have been stained.'

'But—'

'Have patience a little half-hour, my friend. We are going back to Mon Désir.'

The butler looked surprised at our reappearance, but offered no objection to our returning to the library.

'Hi, that's the wrong window, Poirot,' I cried as he made for the one overlooking the carriage-drive.

'I think not, my friend. See here.' He pointed to the marble lion's head. On it was a faint discoloured smear. He shifted his finger and pointed to a similar stain on the polished floor.

'Someone struck Reedburn a blow with his clenched fist betwen the eyes. He fell backward on this projecting bit of marble, then slipped to the floor. Afterwards, he was dragged across the floor to the other window, and laid there instead, but not quite at the same angle, as the Doctor's evidence told us.'

'But why? It seems utterly unnecessary.'

'On the contrary, it was essential. Also, it is the key to the murderer's identity—though, by the way, he had no intention of killing Reedburn, and so it is hardly permissible to call him a murderer. He must be a very strong man!'

'Because of having dragged the body across the floor?'

'Not altogether. It has been an interesting case. I nearly made an imbecile of myself, though.'

'Do you mean to say it is over, that you know everything?'

'Yes.'

A remembrance smote me. 'No,' I cried. 'There is one thing you do *not* know!'

'And that?'

'You do not know where the missing king of clubs is!'

'Eh? Oh, that is droll! That is very droll, my friend.'

'Why?'

'*Because it is in my pocket*!' He drew it forth with a flourish.

'Oh!' I said, rather crestfallen. 'Where did you find it? Here?'

'There was nothing sensational about it. It had simply not been taken out with the other cards. It was in the box.'

'H'm! All the same, it gave you an idea, didn't it?'

'Yes, my friend. I present my respects to His Majesty.'

'And to Madame Zara!'

'Ah, yes—to the lady also.'

'Well, what are we going to do now?'

'We are going to return to town. But I must have a few words with a certain lady at Daisymead first.'

The same little maid opened the door to us.

'They're all at lunch now, sir—unless it's Miss Saintclair you want to see, and she's resting.'

'It will do if I can see Mrs Oglander for a few minutes. Will you tell her?'

We were led into the drawing-room to wait. I had a glimpse of the family in the dining-room as we passed, now reinforced by the presence of two heavy, solid-looking men, one with a moustache, the other with a beard also.

In a few minutes Mrs Oglander came into the room, looking inquiringly at Poirot, who bowed.

'Madame, we, in our country, have a great tenderness, a great respect for the mother. The *mère de famille*, she is everything!'

Mrs Oglander looked rather astonished at this opening.

'It is for that reason that I have come—to allay a mother's anxiety. The murderer of Mr Reedburn will not be discovered. Have no fear. I, Hercule Poirot, tell you so. I am right, am I not? Or is it a wife that I must reassure?'

There was a moment's pause. Mrs Oglander seemed searching Poirot with her eyes. At last she said quietly: 'I don't know how you know—but yes, you are right.'

Poirot nodded gravely. 'That is all, madame. But do not be uneasy. Your English policemen have not the eyes of

109

Hercule Poirot.' He tapped the family portrait on the wall with his fingernail.

'You had another daughter once. She is dead, madame?'

Again there was a pause, as she searched him with her eyes. Then she answered: 'Yes, she is dead.'

'Ah!' said Poirot briskly. 'Well, we must return to town. You permit that I return the king of clubs to the pack? It was your only slip. You understand, to have played bridge for an hour or so, with only fifty-one cards—well, no one who knows anything of the game would credit it for a minute! *Bonjour*!'

'And now, my friend,' said Poirot as we stepped towards the station, 'you see it all!'

'I see nothing! Who killed Reedburn?'

'John Oglander, Junior. I was not quite sure if it was the father or the son, but I fixed on the son as being the stronger and younger of the two. It had to be one of them, because of the window.'

'Why?'

'There were four exits from the library—two doors, two windows; but evidently only one would do. Three exits gave on the front, directly or indirectly. The tragedy had to occur in the back window in order to make it appear that Valerie Saintclair came to Daisymead by chance. Really, of course, she fainted, and John Oglander carried her across over his shoulders. That is why I said he must be a strong man.'

'Did they go there together, then?'

'Yes. You remember Valerie's hesitation when I asked her if she was not afraid to go alone? John Oglander went with her—which didn't improve Reedburn's temper, I fancy. They quarrelled, and it was probably some insult levelled at Valerie that made Oglander hit him. The rest, you know.'

'But why the bridge?'

'Bridge presupposes four players. A simple thing like that carries a lot of conviction. Who would have supposed that there had been only three people in that room all the evening?'

I was still puzzled.

'There's one thing I don't understand. What have the Oglanders to do with the dancer Valerie Saintclair?'

'Ah, that I wonder you did not see. And yet you looked long enough at that picture on the wall—longer than I did. Mrs Oglander's other daughter may be dead to her family, but the world knows her as Valerie Saintclair!'

'*What?*'

'Did you not see the resemblance the moment you saw the two sisters together?'

'No,' I confessed. 'I only thought how extraordinarily dissimilar they were.'

'That is because your mind is so open to external romantic impressions, my dear Hastings. The features are almost identical. So is the colouring. The interesting thing is that Valerie is ashamed of her family, and her family is ashamed of her. Nevertheless, in a moment of peril, she turned to her brother for help, and when things went wrong, they all hung together in a remarkable way. Family strength is a marvellous thing. They can all act, that family. That is where Valerie gets her histrionic talent from. I, like Prince

Paul, believe in heredity! They deceived *me*! But for a lucky accident, and test question to Mrs Oglander by which I got her to contradict her daughter's account of how they were sitting, the Oglander family would have put a defeat on Hercule Poirot.'

'What shall you tell the Prince?'

'That Valerie could not possibly have committed the crime, and that I doubt if that tramp will ever be found. Also, to convey my compliments to Zara. A curious coincidence, that! I think I shall call this little affair the Adventure of the King of Clubs. What do you think, my friend?'

The Lemesurier Inheritance

In company with Poirot, I have investigated many strange cases, but none, I think, to compare with that extraordinary series of events which held our interest over a period of many years, and which culminated in the ultimate problem brought to Poirot to solve. Our attention was first drawn to the family history of the Lemesuriers one evening during the war. Poirot and I had but recently come together again, renewing the old days of our acquaintanceship in Belgium. He had been handling some little matter for the War Office—disposing of it to their entire satisfaction; and we had been dining at the Carlton with a Brass Hat who paid Poirot heavy compliments in the intervals of the meal. The Brass Hat had to rush away to keep an appointment with someone, and we finished our coffee in a leisurely fashion before following his example.

As we were leaving the room, I was hailed by a voice which struck a familiar note, and turned to see Captain Vincent Lemesurier, a young fellow whom I had known in France. He was with an older man whose likeness to him proclaimed him to be of the same family. Such proved to be the case, and he was introduced to us as Mr Hugo Lemesurier, uncle of my young friend.

I did not really know Captain Lemesurier at all intimately, but he was a pleasant young fellow, somewhat dreamy in manner, and I remembered hearing that he belonged to an old and exclusive family with a property in Northumberland which dated from before the Reformation. Poirot and I were not in a hurry, and at the younger man's invitation, we sat down at the table with our two new-found friends, and chattered pleasantly enough on various matters. The elder Lemesurier was a man of about forty, with a touch of the scholar in his stooping shoulders; he was engaged at the moment upon some chemical research work for the Government, it appeared.

Our conversation was interrupted by a tall dark young man who strode up to the table, evidently labouring under some agitation of mind.

'Thank goodness I've found you both!' he exclaimed.

'What's the matter, Roger?'

'Your guv'nor, Vincent. Bad fall. Young horse.' The rest trailed off, as he drew the other aside.

In a few minutes our two friends had hurriedly taken leave of us. Vincent Lemesurier's father had had a serious accident while trying a young horse, and was not expected to live until morning. Vincent had gone deadly white, and appeared almost stunned by the news. In a way, I was surprised—for from the few words he had let fall on the subject while in France, I had gathered that he and his father were not on particularly friendly terms, and so his display of filial feeling now rather astonished me.

The dark young man, who had been introduced to us as

a cousin, Mr Roger Lemesurier, remained behind, and we three strolled out together.

'Rather a curious business, this,' observed the young man. 'It would interest M. Poirot, perhaps. I've heard of you, you know, M. Poirot—from Higginson.' (Higginson was our Brass Hat friend.) 'He says you're a whale on psychology.'

'I study the psychology, yes,' admitted my friend cautiously.

'Did you see my cousin's face? He was absolutely bowled over, wasn't he? Do you know why? A good old-fashioned family curse! Would you care to hear about it?'

'It would be most kind of you to recount it to me.'

Roger Lemesurier looked at his watch.

'Lots of time. I'm meeting them at King's Cross. Well, M. Poirot, the Lemesuriers are an old family. Way back in medieval times, a Lemesurier became suspicious of his wife. He found the lady in a compromising situation. She swore that she was innocent, but old Baron Hugo didn't listen. She had one child, a son—and he swore that the boy was no child of his and should never inherit. I forget what he did—some pleasing medieval fancy like walling up the mother and son alive; anyway, he killed them both, and she died protesting her innocence and solemnly cursing the Lemesuriers forever. No first-born son of a Lemesurier should ever inherit—so the curse ran. Well, time passed, and the lady's innocence was established beyond doubt. I believe that Hugo wore a hair shirt and ended up his days on his knees in a monk's cell. But the curious thing is that from that day to this, no first-born son ever has succeeded to the estate. It's gone to brothers, to nephews, to second sons—never to the eldest son. Vincent's father was the second of five sons, the eldest of whom died in infancy. Of course, all through the war, Vincent has been convinced that whoever else was doomed, he certainly was. But strangely enough, his two younger brothers have been killed, and he himself has remained unscathed.'

'An interesting family history,' said Poirot thoughtfully. 'But now his father is dying, and he, as the eldest son, succeeds?'

'Exactly. A curse has gone rusty—unable to stand the strain of modern life.'

Poirot shook his head, as though deprecating the other's jesting tone. Roger Lemesurier looked at his watch again, and declared that he must be off.

The sequel to the story came on the morrow, when we learned of the tragic death of Captain Vincent Lemesurier. He had been travelling north by the Scotch mail-train, and during the night must have opened the door of the compartment and jumped out on the line. The shock of his father's accident coming on top of the shell-shock was deemed to have caused temporary mental aberration. The curious superstition prevalent in the Lemesurier family was mentioned, in connection with the new heir, his father's brother, Ronald Lemesurier, whose only son had died on the Somme.

I suppose our accidental meeting with young Vincent on the last evening of his life quickened our interest in anything that pertained to the Lemesurier family, for we noted with some interest two years later the death of Ronald Lemesurier, who had been a confirmed invalid at the time of his succession to the family estates. His brother John succeeded him, a hale, hearty man with a boy at Eton.

Certainly an evil destiny overshadowed the Lemesuriers. On his very next holiday the boy managed to shoot himself fatally. His father's death, which occurred quite suddenly after being stung by a wasp, gave the estate over to the youngest brother of the five—Hugo, whom we remembered meeting on the fatal night at the Carlton.

Beyond commenting on the extraordinary series of misfortunes which befell the Lemesuriers, we had taken no personal interest in the matter, but the time was now close at hand when we were to take a more active part.

One morning 'Mrs Lemesurier' was announced. She was a tall, active woman, possibly about thirty years of age, who conveyed by her demeanour a great deal of determination and strong common sense. She spoke with a faint transatlantic accent.

'M. Poirot? I am pleased to meet you. My husband, Hugo Lemesurier, met you once many years ago, but you will hardly remember the fact.'

'I recollect it perfectly, madame. It was at the Carlton.'

'That's quite wonderful of you. M. Poirot, I'm very worried.'

'What about, Madame?'

'My elder boy—I've two boys, you know. Ronald's eight, and Gerald's six.'

'Proceed, madame: why should you be worried about little Ronald?'

'M. Poirot, within the last six months he has had three narrow escapes from death: once from drowning—when we were all down at Cornwall this summer; once when he fell from the nursery window; and once from ptomaine poisoning.'

Perhaps Poirot's face expressed rather too eloquently what he thought, for Mrs Lemesurier hurried on with hardly a moment's pause: 'Of course I know you think I'm just a silly fool of a woman, making mountains out of molehills.'

'No, indeed, madame. Any mother might be excused for being upset at such occurrences, but I hardly see where I can be of any assistance to you. I am not *le bon Dieu* to control the waves; for the nursery window I should suggest some iron bars; and for the food—what can equal a mother's care?'

'But why should these things happen to Ronald and not to Gerald?'

'The chance, madame—*le hasard*!'

'You think so?'

'What do you think, madame—you and your husband?'

A shadow crossed Mrs Lemesurier's face.

'It's no good going to Hugo—he won't listen. As perhaps you may have heard, there's supposed to be a curse on the family—no eldest son can succeed. Hugo believes in it. He's wrapped up in the family history, and he's superstitious to the last degree. When I go to him with my fears, he just says it's the curse, and we can't escape it. But I'm from the States, M. Poirot, and over there we don't believe much in curses.

We like them as belonging to a real high-toned old family—it gives a sort of *cachet*, don't you know. I was just a musical comedy actress in a small part when Hugo met me—and I thought his family curse was just too lovely for words. That kind of thing's all right for telling round the fire on a winter's evening, but when it comes to one's own children—I just adore my children, M. Poirot. I'd do anything for them.'

'So you decline to believe in the family legend, madame?'

'Can a legend saw through an ivy stem?'

'What is that you are saying, madame?' cried Poirot, an expression of great astonishment on his face.

'I said, can a legend—or a ghost, if you like to call it that—saw through an ivy stem? I'm not saying anything about Cornwall. Any boy might go out too far and get into difficulties—though Ronald could swim when he was four years old. But the ivy's different. Both the boys were very naughty. They'd discovered they could climb up and down by the ivy. They were always doing it. One day—Gerald was away at the time—Ronald did it once too often, and the ivy gave way and he fell. Fortunately he didn't damage himself seriously. But I went out and examined the ivy: it was cut through, M. Poirot—deliberately cut through.'

'It is very serious what you are telling me there, madame. You say your younger boy was away from home at the moment?'

'Yes.'

'And at the time of the ptomaine poisoning, was he still away?'

'No, they were both there.'

119

'Curious,' murmured Poirot. 'Now, madame, who are the inmates of your establishment?'

'Miss Saunders, the children's governess, and John Gardiner, my husband's secretary—'

Mrs Lemesurier paused, as though slightly embarrassed.

'And who else, madame?'

'Major Roger Lemesurier, whom you also met on that night, I believe, stays with us a good deal.'

'Ah, yes—he is a cousin is he not?'

'A distant cousin. He does not belong to our branch of the family. Still, I suppose now he is my husband's nearest relative. He is a dear fellow, and we are all very fond of him. The boys are devoted to him.'

'It was not he who taught them to climb up the ivy?'

'It might have been. He incites them to mischief often enough.'

'Madame, I apologize for what I said to you earlier. The danger is real, and I believe that I can be of assistance. I propose that you should invite us both to stay with you. Your husband will not object?'

'Oh no. But he will believe it to be all of no use. It makes me furious the way he just sits around and expects the boy to die.'

'Calm yourself, madame. Let us make our arrangements methodically.'

Our arrangements were duly made, and the following day saw us flying northward. Poirot was sunk in a reverie. He came out of it, to remark abruptly: 'It was from a train such as this that Vincent Lemesurier fell?'

He put a slight accent on the 'fell'.

'You don't suspect foul play there, surely?' I asked.

'Has it struck you, Hastings, that some of the Lemesurier deaths were, shall we say, capable of being arranged? Take that of Vincent, for instance. Then the Eton boy—an accident with a gun is always ambiguous. Supposing this child had fallen from the nursery window and been dashed to death—what more natural and unsuspicious? But why only the one child, Hastings? Who profits by the death of the elder child? His younger brother, a child of seven! Absurd!'

'They mean to do away with the other later,' I suggested, though with the vaguest ideas as to who 'they' were.

Poirot shook his head as though dissatisfied.

'Ptomaine poisoning,' he mused. 'Atropine will produce much the same symptoms. Yes, there is need for our presence.'

Mrs Lemesurier welcomed us enthusiastically. Then she took us to her husband's study and left us with him. He had changed a good deal since I saw him last. His shoulders stooped more than ever, and his face had a curious pale grey tinge. He listened while Poirot explained our presence in the house.

'How exactly like Sadie's practical common sense!' he said at last. 'Remain by all means, M. Poirot, and I thank you for coming; but—what is written, is written. The way of the transgressor is hard. We Lemesuriers *know*—none of us can escape the doom.'

Poirot mentioned the sawn-through ivy, but Hugo seemed very little impressed.

'Doubtless some careless gardener—yes, yes, there may be an instrument, but the purpose behind is plain; and I will tell you this, M. Poirot, it cannot be long delayed.'

Poirot looked at him attentively.

'Why do you say that?'

'Because I myself am doomed. I went to a doctor last year. I am suffering from an incurable disease—the end cannot be much longer delayed; but before I die, Ronald will be taken. Gerald will inherit.'

'And if anything were to happen to your second son also?'

'Nothing will happen to him; he is not threatened.'

'But if it did?' persisted Poirot.

'My cousin Roger is the next heir.'

We were interrupted. A tall man with a good figure and crispy curling auburn hair entered with a sheaf of papers.

'Never mind about those now, Gardiner,' said Hugo Lemesurier, then he added: 'My secretary, Mr Gardiner.'

The secretary bowed, uttered a few pleasant words and then went out. In spite of his good looks, there was something repellent about the man. I said so to Poirot shortly afterward when we were walking round the beautiful old grounds together, and rather to my surprise, he agreed.

'Yes, yes, Hastings, you are right. I do not like him. He is too good-looking. He would be one for the soft job always. Ah, here are the children.'

Mrs Lemesurier was advancing towards us, her two children beside her. They were fine-looking boys, the younger dark like his mother, the elder with auburn curls. They shook hands prettily enough, and were soon absolutely devoted to Poirot. We were next introduced to Miss Saunders, a nondescript female, who completed the party.

For some days we had a pleasant, easy existence—ever vigilant, but without result. The boys led a happy normal life and nothing seemed to be amiss. On the fourth day after our arrival Major Roger Lemesurier came down to stay. He was little changed, still care-free and debonair as of old, with the same habit of treating all things lightly. He was evidently a great favourite with the boys, who greeted his arrival with shrieks of delight and immediately dragged him off to play wild Indians in the garden. I noticed that Poirot followed them unobtrusively.

On the following day we were all invited to tea, boys included, with Lady Claygate, whose place adjoined that of the Lemesuriers. Mrs Lemesurier suggested that we also should come, but seemed rather relieved when Poirot refused and declared he would much prefer to remain at home.

Once everyone had started, Poirot got to work. He reminded me of an intelligent terrier. I believe that there was no corner of the house that he left unsearched; yet it was all done so quietly and methodically that no attention was directed to his movements. Clearly, at the end, he remained unsatisfied. We had tea on the terrace with Miss Saunders, who had not been included in the party.

'The boys will enjoy it,' she murmured in her faded way, 'though I hope they will behave nicely, and not damage the flower-beds, or go near the bees—'

Poirot paused in the very act of drinking. He looked like a man who has seen a ghost.

'Bees?' he demanded in a voice of thunder.

'Yes, M. Poirot, bees. Three hives. Lady Claygate is very proud of her bees—'

'Bees?' cried Poirot again. Then he sprang from the table and walked up and down the terrace with his hands to his head. I could not imagine why the little man should be so agitated at the mere mention of bees.

At that moment we heard the car returning. Poirot was on the doorstep as the party alighted.

'Ronald's been stung,' cried Gerald excitedly.

'It's nothing,' said Mrs Lemesurier. 'It hasn't even swollen. We put ammonia on it.'

'Let me see, my little man,' said Poirot. 'Where was it?'

'Here, on the side of my neck,' said Ronald importantly. 'But it doesn't hurt. Father said: "Keep still—there's a bee on you." And I kept still, and he took it off, but it stung me first, though it didn't really hurt, only like a pin, and I didn't cry, because I'm so big and going to school next year.'

Poirot examined the child's neck, then drew away again. He took me by the arm and murmured:

'Tonight, *mon ami*, tonight we have a little affair on! Say nothing—to anyone.'

He refused to be more communicative, and I went through the evening devoured by curiosity. He retired early and I followed his example. As we went upstairs, he caught me by the arm and delivered his instructions:

'Do not undress. Wait a sufficient time, extinguish your light and join me here.'

I obeyed, and found him waiting for me when the time came. He enjoined silence on me with a gesture, and we crept quietly along the nursery wing. Ronald occupied a small room of his own. We entered it and took up our position in the darkest corner. The child's breathing sounded heavy and undisturbed.

'Surely he is sleeping very heavily?' I whispered.

Poirot nodded.

'Drugged,' he murmured.

'Why?'

'So that he should not cry out at—'

'At what?' I asked, as Poirot paused.

'At the prick of the hypodermic needle, *mon ami*! Hush, let us speak no more—not that I expect anything to happen for some time.'

But in this Poirot was wrong. Hardly ten minutes had elapsed before the door opened softly, and someone entered the room. I heard a sound of quick hurried breathing. Footsteps moved to the bed, and then there was a sudden click. The light of a little electric lantern fell on the sleeping child—the holder of it was still invisible in the shadow. The figure laid down the lantern. With the right hand it brought forth a syringe; with the left it touched the boy's neck—

Poirot and I sprang at the same minute. The lantern rolled to the floor, and we struggled with the intruder in the dark. His strength was extraordinary. At last we overcame him.

'The light, Hastings, I must see his face—though I fear I know only too well whose face it will be.'

So did I, I thought as I groped for the lantern. For a moment I had suspected the secretary, egged on by my secret dislike of the man, but I felt assured by now that the man who stood to gain by the death of his two childish cousins was the monster we were tracking.

My foot struck against the lantern. I picked it up and switched on the light. It shone full on the face of—Hugo Lemesurier, the boy's father!

The lantern almost dropped from my hand.

'Impossible,' I murmured hoarsely. 'Impossible!'

Lemesurier was unconscious. Poirot and I between us carried him to his room and laid him on the bed. Poirot bent and gently extricated something from his right hand. He showed it to me. It was a hypodermic syringe. I shuddered.

'What is in it? Poison?'

'Formic acid, I fancy.'

'Formic acid?'

'Yes. Probably obtained by distilling ants. He was a chemist, you remember. Death would have been attributed to the bee sting.'

'My God,' I muttered. 'His own son! And you expected this?'

Poirot nodded gravely.

'Yes. He is insane, of course. I imagine that the family history has become a mania with him. His intense longing to succeed to the estate led him to commit the long series of crimes. Possibly the idea occurred to him first when travelling north that night with Vincent. He couldn't bear the prediction to be falsified. Ronald's son was already dead, and Ronald himself was a dying man—they are a weakly lot. He arranged the accident to the gun, and—which I did not suspect until now—contrived the death of his brother John by this same method of injecting formic acid into the jugular vein. His ambition was realized then, and he became the master of the family acres. But his triumph was short-lived—he found that he was suffering from an incurable disease. And he had the madman's fixed idea—the eldest son of a Lemesurier could not inherit. I suspect that the bathing accident was due to him—he encouraged the child to go out too far. That failing, he sawed through the ivy, and afterwards poisoned the child's food.'

'Diabolical!' I murmured with a shiver. 'And so cleverly planned!'

'Yes, *mon ami*, there is nothing more amazing than the extraordinary sanity of the insane! Unless it is the extraordinary eccentricity of the sane! I imagine that it is only lately that he has completely gone over the borderline, there was method in his madness to begin with.'

'And to think that I suspected Roger—that splendid fellow.'

'It was the natural assumption, *mon ami*. We knew that he also travelled north with Vincent that night. We knew, too, that he was the next heir after Hugo and Hugo's children. But our assumption was not borne out by the facts. The ivy was sawn through when only little Ronald was at home—but it would be to Roger's interest that both children should perish. In the same way, it was only Ronald's food that was poisoned. And today when they came home and I found that there was only his father's word for it that Ronald had been stung, I remembered the other death from a wasp sting—and I knew!'

Hugo Lemesurier died a few months later in the private asylum to which he was removed. His widow was remarried a year later to Mr John Gardiner, the auburn-haired secretary. Ronald inherited the broad acres of his father, and continues to flourish.

'Well, well,' I remarked to Poirot. 'Another illusion gone. You have disposed very successfully of the curse of the Lemesuriers.'

'I wonder,' said Poirot very thoughtfully. 'I wonder very much indeed.'

'What do you mean?'

'*Mon ami*, I will answer you with one significant word—*red*!'

'Blood?' I queried, dropping my voice to an awe-stricken whisper.

'Always you have the imagination melodramatic, Hastings! I refer to something much more prosaic—the colour of little Ronald Lemesurier's hair.'

The Lost Mine

I laid down my bank book with a sigh.

'It is a curious thing,' I observed, 'but my overdraft never seems to grow any less.'

'And it perturbs you not? Me, if I had an overdraft, never should I close my eyes all night,' declared Poirot.

'You deal in comfortable balances, I suppose!' I retorted.

'Four hundred and forty-four pounds, four and fourpence,' said Poirot with some complacency. 'A neat figure, is it not?'

'It must be tact on the part of your bank manager. He is evidently acquainted with your passion for symmetrical details. What about investing, say, three hundred of it in the Porcupine oil-fields? Their prospectus, which is advertised in the papers today, says that they will pay one hundred per cent dividends next year.'

'Not for me,' said Poirot, shaking his head. 'I like not the sensational. For me the safe, the prudent investment—*les rentes*, the consols, the—how do you call it?—the conversion.'

'Have you never made a speculative investment?'

'No, *mon ami*,' replied Poirot severely. 'I have not. And the only shares I own which have not what you call the gilded edge are fourteen thousand shares in the Burma Mines Ltd.'

Poirot paused with an air of waiting to be encouraged to go on.

'Yes?' I prompted.

'And for them I paid no cash—no, they were the reward of the exercise of my little grey cells. You would like to hear the story? Yes?'

'Of course I would.'

'These mines are situated in the interior of Burma about two hundred miles inland from Rangoon. They were discovered by the Chinese in the fifteenth century and worked down to the time of the Mohammedan Rebellion, being finally abandoned in the year 1868. The Chinese extracted the rich lead-silver ore from the upper part of the ore body, smelting it for the silver alone, and leaving large quantities of rich lead-bearing slag. This, of course, was soon discovered when prospecting work was carried out in Burma, but owing to the fact that the old workings had become full of loose filling and water, all attempts to find the source of the ore proved fruitless. Many parties were sent out by syndicates, and they dug over a large area, but this rich prize still eluded them. But a representative of one of the syndicates got on the track of a Chinese family who were supposed to have still kept a record of the situation of the mine. The present head of the family was one Wu Ling.'

'What a fascinating page of commercial romance!' I exclaimed.

'Is it not? Ah, *mon ami*, one can have romance without golden-haired girls of matchless beauty—no, I am wrong; it is auburn hair that so excites you always. You remember—'

'Go on with the story,' I said hastily.

'*Eh bien*, my friend, this Wu Ling was approached. He was an estimable merchant, much respected in the province where he lived. He admitted at once that he owned the documents in question, and was perfectly prepared to negotiate for this sale, but he objected to dealing with anyone other than principals. Finally it was arranged that he should journey to England and meet the directors of an important company.

'Wu Ling made the journey to England in the SS *Assunta*, and the *Assunta* docked at Southampton on a cold, foggy morning in November. One of the directors, Mr Pearson, went down to Southampton to meet the boat, but owing to the fog, the train down was very much delayed, and by the time he arrived, Wu Ling had disembarked and left by special train for London. Mr Pearson returned to town somewhat annoyed, as he had no idea where the Chinaman proposed to stay. Later in the day, however, the offices of the company were rung up on the telephone. Wu Ling was staying at the Russell Square Hotel. He was feeling somewhat unwell after the voyage, but declared himself perfectly able to attend the board meeting on the following day.

'The meeting of the board took place at eleven o'clock. When half past eleven came, and Wu Ling had not put in an appearance, the secretary rang up the Russell Hotel. In answer to his inquiries, he was told that the Chinaman had gone out with a friend about half past ten. It seemed clear that he had started out with the intention of coming to the meeting, but the morning wore away, and he did not appear. It was, of course, possible that he had lost his way, being unacquainted with London, but at a late hour that night he had not returned to the hotel. Thoroughly alarmed now, Mr Pearson put matters in the hands of the police. On the following day, there was still no trace of the missing man, but towards evening of the day after that again, a body was found in the Thames which proved to be that of the ill-fated Chinaman. Neither on the body, nor in the luggage at the hotel, was there any trace of the papers relating to the mine.

'At this juncture, *mon ami*, I was brought into the affair. Mr Pearson called upon me. While profoundly shocked by the death of Wu Ling, his chief anxiety was to recover the papers which were the object of the Chinaman's visit to England. The main anxiety of the police, of course, would be to track down the murderer—the recovery of the papers would be a secondary consideration. What he wanted me to do was to co-operate with the police while acting in the interests of the company.

'I consented readily enough. It was clear that there were two fields of search open to me. On the one hand, I might look among the employees of the company who knew of the Chinaman's coming; on the other, among the passengers on the boat who might have been acquainted with his mission. I started with the second, as being a narrower field of search. In this I coincided with Inspector Miller, who was in charge of the case—a man altogether different from our friend Japp, conceited, ill-mannered and quite insufferable. Together we interviewed the officers of the ship. They had little to tell us. Wu Ling had kept much to himself on the voyage. He had been intimate with but two of the other passengers—one a broken-down European named Dyer who appeared to bear a somewhat unsavoury reputation, the other a young bank clerk named Charles Lester, who was returning from Hong Kong. We were lucky enough to obtain snapshots of both these men. At the moment there seemed little doubt that if either of the two was implicated, Dyer was the man. He was known to be mixed up with a gang of Chinese crooks, and was altogether a most likely suspect.

'Our next step was to visit the Russell Square Hotel. Shown a snapshot of Wu Ling, they recognized him at once. We then showed them the snapshot of Dyer, but to our disappointment, the hall porter declared positively that that was not the man who had come to the hotel on the fatal morning. Almost as an afterthought, I produced the photograph of Lester, and to my surprise the man at once recognized it.

'"Yes, sir," he asserted, "that's the gentleman who came in at half past ten and asked for Mr Wu Ling, and afterwards went out with him."

'The affair was progressing. Our next move was to interview Mr Charles Lester. He met us with the utmost frankness, was desolated to hear of the Chinaman's untimely death, and put himself at our disposal in every way. His story was as follows: By arrangement with Wu Ling, he called for him at the hotel at ten-thirty. Wu Ling, however, did not appear. Instead, his servant came, explained that his master had had to go out, and offered to conduct the young man to where his master now was. Suspecting nothing, Lester agreed, and the Chinaman procured a taxi. They drove for some time in the direction of the docks. Suddenly becoming mistrustful, Lester stopped the taxi and got out, disregarding the servant's protests. That, he assured us, was all he knew.

'Apparently satisfied, we thanked him and took our leave. His story was soon proved to be a somewhat inaccurate one. To begin with, Wu Ling had had no servant with him, either on the boat or at the hotel. In the second place, the taxi driver who had driven the two men on that morning came forward. Far from Lester's having left the taxi en route, he and the Chinese gentleman had driven to a certain unsavoury dwelling-place in Limehouse, right in the heart of Chinatown. The place in question was more or less well known as an opium-den of the lowest description. The two gentlemen had gone in—about an hour later the English gentleman, whom he identified from the photograph, came out alone. He looked very pale and ill, and directed the taxi-man to take him to the nearest underground station.

'Inquiries were made about Charles Lester's standing, and it was found that, though bearing an excellent character, he was heavily in debt, and had a secret passion for gambling. Dyer, of course, was not lost sight of. It seemed just faintly possible that he might have impersonated the other man, but that idea was proved utterly groundless. His alibi for the whole of the day in question was absolutely unimpeachable. Of course, the proprietor of the opium-den denied everything with Oriental stolidity. He had never seen Wu Ling; he had never seen Charles Lester. No two gentlemen had been to the place that morning. In any case, the police were wrong: no opium was ever smoked there.

'His denials, however well meant, did little to help Charles Lester. He was arrested for the murder of Wu Ling. A search of his effects was made, but no papers relating to the mine were discovered. The proprietor of the opium-den was also taken into custody, but a cursory raid of his premises yielded nothing. Not even a stick of opium rewarded the zeal of the police.

'In the meantime my friend Mr Pearson was in a great state of agitation. He strode up and down my room, uttering great lamentations.

'"But you must have some ideas, M. Poirot!" he kept urging. "Surely you must have some ideas!"

'"Certainly I have ideas," I replied cautiously. "That is the trouble—one has too many; therefore they all lead in different directions."

'"For instance?" he suggested.

'"For instance—the taxi-driver. We have only his word for it that he drove the two men to that house. That is one idea. Then—was it really that house they went to? Supposing that they left the taxi there, passed through the house and out by another entrance and went elsewhere?"

'Mr Pearson seemed struck by that.

'"But you do nothing but sit and think? Can't we *do* something?"

'He was of an impatient temperament, you comprehend.

'"Monsieur," I said with dignity, "It is not for Hercule Poirot to run up and down the evil-smelling streets of

Limehouse like a little dog of no breeding. Be calm. My agents are at work."

'On the following day I had news for him. The two men had indeed passed through the house in question, but their real objective was a small eating-house close to the river. They were seen to pass in there, and Lester came out alone.

'And then, figure to yourself, Hastings, an idea of the most unreasonable seized this Mr Pearson! Nothing would suit him but that we should go ourselves to this eating-house and make investigations. I argued and prayed, but he would not listen. He talked of disguising himself—he even suggested that I—*I* should—I hesitate to say it—should shave off my moustache! Yes, *rien que ça*! I pointed out to him that that was an idea ridiculous and absurd. One destroys not a thing of beauty wantonly. Besides, shall not a Belgian gentleman with a moustache desire to see life and smoke opium just as readily as one without a moustache?

'*Eh bien*, he gave in on that, but he still insisted on his project. He turned up that evening—*Mon dieu*, what a figure! He wore what he called the "pea-jacket", his chin, it was dirty and unshaved; he had a scarf of the vilest that offended the nose. And figure to yourself, he was enjoying himself! Truly, the English are mad! He made some changes in my own appearance. I permitted it. Can one argue with a maniac? We started out—after all, could I let him go alone, a child dressed up to act the charades?'

'Of course you couldn't,' I replied.

'To continue—we arrived. Mr Pearson talked English of the strangest. He represented himself to be a man of the sea. He talked of "lubbers" and "focselles" and I know not what. It was a low little room with many Chinese in it. We ate of peculiar dishes. *Ah, Dieu, mon estomac!*' Poirot clasped that portion of his anatomy before continuing. 'Then there came to us the proprietor, a Chinaman with a face of evil smiles.

'"You gentlemen no likee food here," he said. "You come for what you likee better. Piecee pipe, eh?"

'Mr Pearson, he gave me the great kick under the table. (He had on the boots of the sea too!) And he said: "I don't mind if I do, John. Lead ahead."

'The Chinaman smiled, and he took us through a door and to a cellar and through a trapdoor, and down some steps and up again into a room all full of divans and cushions of the most comfortable. We lay down and a Chinese boy took off our boots. It was the best moment of the evening. Then they brought us the opium-pipes and cooked the opium-pills, and we pretended to smoke and then to sleep and dream. But when we were alone, Mr Pearson called softly to me, and immediately he began crawling along the floor. We went into another room where other people were asleep, and so on, until we heard two men talking. We stayed behind a curtain and listened. They were speaking of Wu Ling.

'"What about the papers?" said one.

'"Mr Lester, he takee those," answered the other, who was a Chinaman. "He say, puttee them allee in safee place—where pleeceman no lookee."

'"Ah, but he's nabbed," said the first one.

'"He gettee free. Pleeceman not sure he done it."

'There was more of the same kind of thing, then apparently the two men were coming our way, and we scuttled back to our beds.

'"We'd better get out of here," said Pearson, after a few minutes had elapsed. "This place isn't healthy."

'"You are right, monsieur," I agreed. "We have played the farce long enough."

'We succeeded in getting away, all right, paying handsomely for our smoke. Once clear of Limehouse, Pearson drew a long breath.

'"I'm glad to get out of that," he said. "But it's something to be sure."

'"It is indeed," I agreed. "And I fancy that we shall not have much difficulty in finding what we want—after this evening's masquerade."

'And there was no difficulty whatsoever,' finished Poirot suddenly.

This abrupt ending seemed so extraordinary that I stared at him.

'But—but where were they?' I asked.

'In his pocket—*tout simplement*.'

'But in whose pocket?'

'Mr Pearson's, *parbleu*!' Then, observing my look of bewilderment, he continued gently: 'You do not yet see it? Mr Pearson, like Charles Lester, was in debt. Mr Pearson, like Charles Lester, was fond of gambling. And he conceived the idea of stealing the papers from the Chinaman. He met him all right at Southampton, came up to London with him, and took him straight to Limehouse. It was foggy that day; the Chinaman would not notice where he was going. I fancy Mr Pearson smoked the opium fairly often down there and had some peculiar friends in consequence. I do not think he meant murder. His idea was that one of the Chinamen should impersonate Wu Ling and receive the money for the sale of the document. So far, so good! But, to the Oriental mind, it was infinitely simpler to kill Wu Ling and throw his body into the river, and Pearson's Chinese accomplices followed their own methods without consulting him. Imagine, then, what you would call the "funk *bleu*" of M. Pearson. Someone may have seen him in the train with Wu Ling—murder is a very different thing from simple abduction.

'His salvation lies with the Chinaman who is personating Wu Ling at the Russell Square Hotel. If only the body is not discovered too soon! Probably Wu Ling had told him of the arrangement between him and Charles Lester whereby the latter was to call for him at the hotel. Pearson sees there an excellent way of diverting suspicion from himself. Charles Lester shall be the last person to be seen in company with Wu Ling. The impersonator has orders to represent himself to Lester as the servant of Wu Ling, and to bring him as speedily as possible to Limehouse. There, very likely, he was offered a drink. The drink would be suitably drugged, and when Lester emerged an hour later, he would have a very hazy impression of what had happened. So much was this the case, that as soon as Lester learned of Wu Ling's death, he loses his nerve, and denies that he ever reached Limehouse.

139

Agatha Christie

'By that, of course, he plays right into Pearson's hands. But is Pearson content? No—my manner disquiets him, and he determines to complete the case against Lester. So he arranges an elaborate masquerade. Me, I am to be gulled completely. Did I not say just now that he was as a child acting the charades? *Eh bien*, I play my part. He goes home rejoicing. But in the morning, Inspector Miller arrives on his doorstep. The papers are found on him; the game is up. Bitterly he regrets permitting himself to play the farce with Hercule Poirot! There was only one real difficulty in the affair.'

'What was that?' I demanded curiously.

'Convincing Inspector Miller! What an animal, that! Both obstinate and imbecile. And in the end he took all the credit!'

'Too bad,' I cried.

'Ah, well, I had my compensations. The other directors of the Burma Mines Ltd awarded me fourteen thousand shares as a small recompense for my services. Not so bad, eh? But when investing money, keep, I beg of you, Hastings, strictly to the conservative. The things you read in the paper, they may not be true. The directors of the Porcupine—they may be so many Mr Pearsons!'

140

The Plymouth Express

Alec Simpson, RN, stepped from the platform at Newton Abbot into a first-class compartment of the Plymouth Express. A porter followed him with a heavy suitcase. He was about to swing it up to the rack, but the young sailor stopped him.

'No—leave it on the seat. I'll put it up later. Here you are.'

'Thank you, sir.' The porter, generously tipped, withdrew.

Doors banged; a stentorian voice shouted: 'Plymouth only. Change for Torquay. Plymouth next stop.' Then a whistle blew, and the train drew slowly out of the station.

Lieutenant Simpson had the carriage to himself. The December air was chilly, and he pulled up the window. Then he sniffed vaguely, and frowned. What a smell there was! Reminded him of that time in hospital, and the operation on his leg. Yes, chloroform; that was it!

He let the window down again, changing his seat to one with its back to the engine. He pulled a pipe out of his pocket and lit it. For a little time he sat inactive, looking out into the night and smoking.

At last he roused himself, and opening the suitcase, took out some papers and magazines, then closed the suitcase again and endeavoured to shove it under the opposite seat—without success. Some obstacle resisted it. He shoved harder with rising impatience, but it still stuck out half-way into the carriage.

'Why the devil won't it go in?' he muttered, and hauling it out completely, he stooped down and peered under the seat…

A moment later a cry rang out into the night, and the great train came to an unwilling halt in obedience to the imperative jerking of the communication cord.

'*Mon ami*,' said Poirot, 'you have, I know, been deeply interested in this mystery of the Plymouth Express. Read this.'

I picked up the note he flicked across the table to me. It was brief and to the point.

> Dear Sir,
>   I shall be obliged if you will call upon me at your
> earliest convenience.
>   Yours faithfully,
>   Ebenezer Halliday

The connection was not clear to my mind, and I looked inquiringly at Poirot.

For answer he took up the newspaper and read aloud: '"A sensational discovery was made last night. A young naval officer returning to Plymouth found under the seat of his compartment the body of a woman, stabbed through the heart. The officer at once pulled the communication cord, and the train was brought to a standstill. The woman, who was about thirty years of age, and richly dressed, has not yet been identified."

'And later we have this: "The woman found dead in the Plymouth Express has been identified as the Honourable Mrs Rupert Carrington." You see now, my friend? Or if you do not I will add this—Mrs Rupert Carrington was, before her marriage, Flossie Halliday, daughter of old man Halliday, the steel king of America.'

'And he has sent for you? Splendid!'

'I did him a little service in the past—an affair of bearer bonds. And once, when I was in Paris for a royal visit, I had Mademoiselle Flossie pointed out to me. *La jolie petite pensionnaire*! She had the *joli dot* too! It caused trouble. She nearly made a bad affair.'

'How was that?'

'A certain Count de la Rochefour. *Un bien mauvais sujet*! A bad hat, as you would say. An adventurer pure and simple, who knew how to appeal to a romantic young girl. Luckily her father got wind of it in time. He took her back to America in haste. I heard of her marriage some years later, but I know nothing of her husband.'

'H'm,' I said. 'The Honourable Rupert Carrington is no beauty, by all accounts. He'd pretty well run through his own money on the turf, and I should imagine old man Halliday's dollars came along in the nick of time. I should say that for a good-looking, well-mannered, utterly unscrupulous young scoundrel, it would be hard to find his match!'

'Ah, the poor little lady! *Elle n'est pas bien tombée*!'

'I fancy he made it pretty obvious at once that it was her money, and not she, that had attacted him. I believe they drifted apart almost at once. I have heard rumours lately that there was to be a definite legal separation.'

'Old man Halliday is no fool. He would tie up her money pretty tight.'

'I dare say. Anyway, I know as a fact that the Honourable Rupert is said to be extremely hard up.'

'Aha! I wonder—'

'You wonder what?'

'My good friend, do not jump down my throat like that. You are interested, I see. Suppose you accompany me to see Mr Halliday. There is a taxi-stand at the corner.'

A few minutes sufficed to whirl us to the superb house in Park Lane rented by the American magnate. We were shown into the library, and almost immediately we were joined by a large stout man, with piercing eyes and an aggressive chin.

'M. Poirot?' said Mr Halliday. 'I guess I don't need to tell you what I want you for. You've read the papers, and I'm never one to let the grass grow under my feet. I happened to hear you were in London, and I remembered the good work you did over those bombs. Never forget a name. I've the pick of Scotland Yard, but I'll have my own man as well. Money no object. All the dollars were made for my little girl—and now she's gone, I'll spend my last cent to catch the damned scoundrel that did it! See? So it's up to you to deliver the goods.'

Poirot bowed.

'I accept, monsieur, all the more willingly that I saw your daughter in Paris several times. And now I will ask you to tell me the circumstances of her journey to Plymouth and any other details that seem to you to bear upon the case.'

'Well, to begin with,' responded Halliday, 'she wasn't going to Plymouth. She was going to join a house-party at Avonmead Court, the Duchess of Swansea's place. She left London by the twelve-fourteen from Paddington, arriving at Bristol (where she had to change) at two-fifty. The principal Plymouth expresses, of course, run via Westbury, and do not go near Bristol at all. The twelve-fourteen does a non-stop run to Bristol, afterwards stopping at Weston, Taunton, Exeter and Newton Abbot. My daughter travelled alone in her carriage, which was reserved as far as Bristol, her maid being in a third class carriage in the next coach.'

Poirot nodded, and Mr Halliday went on: 'The party at Avonmead Court was to be a very gay one, with several balls, and in consequence my daughter had with her nearly all her jewels—amounting in value, perhaps, to about a hundred thousand dollars.'

'*Un moment*,' interrupted Poirot. 'Who had charge of the jewels? Your daughter, or the maid?'

'My daughter always took charge of them herself, carrying them in a small blue morocco case.'

'Continue, monsieur.'

'At Bristol the maid, Jane Mason, collected her mistress's dressing-bag and wraps, which were with her, and came to the door of Flossie's compartment. To her intense surprise, my daughter told her that she was not getting out at Bristol, but was going on farther. She directed Mason to get out the luggage and put it in the cloakroom. She could have tea in the refreshment-room, but she was to wait at the station for her mistress, who would return to Bristol by an up-train in the course of the afternoon. The maid, although very much astonished, did as she was told. She put the luggage in the cloakroom and had some tea. But up-train after up-train came in, and her mistress did not appear. After the arrival of the last train, she left the luggage where it was, and went to a hotel near the station for the night. This morning she read of the tragedy, and returned to town by the first available train.'

'Is there nothing to account for your daughter's sudden change of plan?'

'Well there is this: According to Jane Mason, at Bristol, Flossie was no longer alone in her carriage. There was a man in it who stood looking out of the farther window so that she could not see his face.'

'The train was a corridor one, of course?'

'Yes.'

'Which side was the corridor?'

'On the platform side. My daughter was standing in the corridor as she talked to Mason.'

'And there is no doubt in your mind—excuse me!' He got up, and carefully straightened the ink-stand which was a little askew. '*Je vous demande pardon*,' he continued, re-seating himself. 'It affects my nerves to see anything crooked. Strange, is it not? I was saying, monsieur, that there is no doubt in your mind as to this probably unexpected meeting being the cause of your daughter's sudden change of plan?'

'It seems the only reasonable supposition.'

'You have no idea as to who the gentleman in question might be?'

The millionaire hesitated for a moment, and then replied: 'No—I do not know at all.'

'Now—as to the discovery of the body?'

'It was discovered by a young naval officer who at once gave the alarm. There was a doctor on the train. He examined the body. She had been first chloroformed, and then stabbed. He gave it as his opinion that she had been dead about four hours, so it must have been done not long after leaving Bristol—probably between there and Weston, possibly between Weston and Taunton.'

'And the jewel-case?'

'The jewel-case, M. Poirot, was missing.'

'One thing more, monsieur. Your daughter's fortune—to whom does it pass at her death?'

'Flossie made a will soon after her marriage, leaving everything to her husband.' He hesitated for a minute, and then went on: 'I may as well tell you, Monsieur Poirot, that I regard my son-in-law as an unprincipled scoundrel, and that, by my advice, my daughter was on the eve of freeing herself from him by legal means—no difficult matter. I settled her money upon her in such a way that he could not touch it during her lifetime, but although they have lived entirely apart for some years, she had frequently acceded to his demands for money, rather than face an open scandal. However, I was determined to put an end to this. At last Flossie agreed, and my lawyers were instructed to take proceedings.'

'And where is Monsieur Carrington?'

'In town. I believe he was away in the country yesterday, but he returned last night.'

Poirot considered a little while. Then he said: 'I think that is all, monsieur.'

'You would like to see the maid, Jane Mason?'

'If you please.'

Halliday rang the bell, and gave a short order to the footman.

A few minutes later Jane Mason entered the room, a respectable, hard-featured woman, as emotionless in the face of tragedy as only a good servant can be.

'You will permit me to put a few questions? Your mistress, she was quite as usual before starting yesterday morning? Not excited or flurried?'

'Oh no, sir!'

'But at Bristol she was quite different?'

'Yes, sir, regular upset—so nervous she didn't seem to know what she was saying.'

'What did she say exactly?'

'Well, sir, as near as I can remember, she said: "Mason, I've got to alter my plans. Something has happened—I mean, I'm not getting out here after all. I must go on. Get out the luggage and put it in the cloakroom; then have some tea, and wait for me in the station."

'"Wait for you here, ma'am?" I asked.

'"Yes, yes. Don't leave the station. I shall return by a later train. I don't know when. It mayn't be until quite late."'

'"Very well, ma'am," I says. It wasn't my place to ask questions, but I thought it very strange.'

'It was unlike your mistress, eh?'

'Very unlike her, sir.'

'What did you think?'

'Well, sir, I thought it was to do with the gentleman in the carriage. She didn't speak to him, but she turned round once or twice as though to ask him if she was doing right.'

'But you didn't see the gentleman's face?'

'No, sir; he stood with his back to me all the time.'

'Can you describe him at all?'

'He had on a light fawn overcoat, and a travelling-cap. He was tall and slender, like and the back of his head was dark.'

'You didn't know him?'

'Oh no, I don't think so, sir.'

'It was not your master, Mr Carrington, by any chance?'

Mason looked rather startled.

'Oh, I don't think so, sir!'

'But you are not *sure*?'

'It was about the master's build, sir—but I never thought of it being him. We so seldom saw him… I couldn't say it *wasn't* him!'

Poirot picked up a pin from the carpet, and frowned at it severely; then he continued: 'Would it be possible for the man to have entered the train at Bristol before you reached the carriage?'

Mason considered.

'Yes, sir, I think it would. My compartment was very crowded, and it was some minutes before I could get out—and then there was a very large crowd on the platform, and that delayed me too. But he'd only have had a minute or two to speak to the mistress, that way. I took it for granted that he'd come along the corridor.'

'That is more probable, certainly.'

He paused, still frowning.

'You know how the mistress was dressed, sir?'

'The papers give a few details, but I would like you to confirm them.'

'She was wearing a white fox fur toque, sir, with a white spotted veil, and a blue frieze coat and skirt—the shade of blue they call electric.'

'H'm, rather striking.'

'Yes,' remarked Mr Halliday. 'Inspector Japp is in hopes that that may help us to fix the spot where the crime took place. Anyone who saw her would remember her.'

'*Précisément*!—Thank you, mademoiselle.'

The maid left the room.

'Well!' Poirot got up briskly. 'That is all I can do here—except, monsieur, that I would ask you to tell me everything, but *everything*!'

'I have done so.'

'You are sure?'

'Absolutely.'

'Then there is nothing more to be said. I must decline the case.'

'Why?'

'Because you have not been frank with me.'

150

'I assure you—'

'No, you are keeping something back.'

There was a moment's pause, and then Halliday drew a paper from his pocket and handed it to my friend.

'I guess that's what you're after, Monsieur Poirot—though how you know about it fairly gets my goat!'

Poirot smiled, and unfolded the paper. It was a letter written in thin sloping handwriting. Poirot read it aloud.

'Chère Madame,

It is with infinite pleasure that I look forward to the felicity of meeting you again. After your so amiable reply to my letter, I can hardly restrain my impatience. I have never forgotten those days in Paris. It is most cruel that you should be leaving London tomorrow. However, before very long, and perhaps sooner than you think, I shall have the joy of beholding once more the lady whose image has ever reigned supreme in my heart.

Believe, chère madame, all the assurances of my most devoted and unaltered sentiments—

Armand de la Rochefour.'

Poirot handed the letter back to Halliday with a bow.

'I fancy, monsieur, that you did not know that your daughter intended renewing her acquaintance with the Count de la Rochefour?'

'It came as a thunderbolt to me! I found this letter in my daughter's handbag. As you probably know, Monsieur Poirot, this so-called count is an adventurer of the worst type.'

Poirot nodded.

'But I want to know how you knew of the existence of this letter?'

My friend smiled. 'Monsieur, I did not. But to track footmarks and recognize cigarette-ash is not sufficient for a detective. He must also be a good psychologist! I knew that you disliked and mistrusted your son-in-law. He benefits by your daughter's death; the maid's description of the mysterious man bears a sufficient resemblance to him. Yet you are not keen on his track! Why? Surely because your suspicions lie in another direction. Therefore you were keeping something back.'

'You're right, Monsieur Poirot. I was sure of Rupert's guilt until I found this letter. It unsettled me horribly.'

'Yes. The Count says "Before very long, and perhaps sooner than you think." Obviously he would not want to wait until you should get wind of his reappearance. Was it he who travelled down from London by the twelve-fourteen, and came along the corridor to your daughter's compartment? The Count de la Rochefour is also, if I remember rightly, tall and dark!'

The millionaire nodded.

'Well, monsieur, I will wish you good day. Scotland Yard has, I presume, a list of the jewels?'

'Yes, I believe Inspector Japp is here now if you would like to see him.'

Japp was an old friend of ours, and greeted Poirot with a sort of affectionate contempt.

'And how are you, monsieur? No bad feeling between us, though we *have* got our different ways of looking at things. How are the "little grey cells", eh? Going strong?'

Poirot beamed upon him. 'They function, my good Japp; assuredly they do!'

'Then that's all right. Think it was the Honourable Rupert, or a crook? We're keeping an eye on all the regular places, of course. We shall know if the shiners are disposed of, and of course whoever did it isn't going to keep them to admire their sparkle. Not likely! I'm trying to find out where Rupert Carrington was yesterday. Seems a bit of a mystery about it. I've got a man watching him.'

'A great precaution, but perhaps a day late,' suggested Poirot gently.

'You always will have your joke, Monsieur Poirot. Well, I'm off to Paddington. Bristol, Weston, Taunton, that's my beat. So long.'

'You will come round and see me this evening, and tell me the result?'

'Sure thing, if I'm back.'

'The good inspector believes in matter in motion,' murmured Poirot as our friend departed. 'He travels; he measures footprints; he collects mud and cigarette-ash! He is extremely busy! He is zealous beyond words! And if I mentioned psychology to him, do you know what he would do, my friend? He would smile! He would say to himself: "Poor old Poirot! He ages! He grows senile!" Japp is the "younger generation knocking on the door." And *ma foi*! They are so busy knocking that they do not notice that the door is open!'

'And what are you going to do?'

'As we have *carte blanche*, I shall expend threepence in ringing up the Ritz—where you may have noticed our Count is staying. After that, as my feet are a little damp, and I have sneezed twice, I shall return to my rooms and make myself a *tisane* over the spirit lamp!'

I did not see Poirot again until the following morning. I found him placidly finishing his breakfast.

'Well?' I inquired eagerly. 'What has happened?'

'Nothing.'

'But Japp?'

'I have not seen him.'

'The Count?'

'He left the Ritz the day before yesterday.'

'The day of the murder?'

'Yes.'

'Then that settles it! Rupert Carrington is cleared.'

'Because the Count de la Rochefour has left the Ritz? You go too fast, my friend.'

'Anyway, he must be followed, arrested! But what could be his motive?'

'One hundred thousand dollars' worth of jewellery is a very good motive for anyone. No, the question to my mind is: why kill her? Why not simply steal the jewels? She would not prosecute.'

'Why not?'

'Because she is a woman, *mon ami*. She once loved this

man. Therefore she would suffer her loss in silence. And the Count, who is an extremely good psychologist where women are concerned—hence his successes—would know that perfectly well! On the other hand, if Rupert Carrington killed her, why take the jewels which would incriminate him fatally?'

'As a blind.'

'Perhaps you are right, my friend. Ah, here is Japp! I recognize his knock.'

The inspector was beaming good-humouredly.

'Morning, Poirot. Only just got back. I've done some good work! And you?'

'Me, I have arranged my ideas,' replied Poirot placidly.

Japp laughed heartily.

'Old chap's getting on in years,' he observed beneath his breath to me. 'That won't do for us young folk,' he said aloud.

'*Quel dommage?*' Poirot inquired.

'Well, do you want to hear what I've done?'

'You permit me to make a guess? You have found the knife with which the crime was committed, by the side of the line between Weston and Taunton, and you have interviewed the paper-boy who spoke to Mrs Carrington at Weston!'

Japp's jaw fell. 'How on earth did you know? Don't tell me it was those almighty "little grey cells" of yours!'

'I am glad you admit for once that they are *all mighty*! Tell me, did she give the paper-boy a shilling for himself?'

'No, it was half a crown!' Japp had recovered his temper, and grinned. 'Pretty extravagant, these rich Americans!'

'And in consequence the boy did not forget her?'

'Not he. Half-crowns don't come his way every day. She hailed him and bought two magazines. One had a picture of a girl in blue on the cover. "That'll match me," she said. Oh, he remembered her perfectly. Well, that was enough for me. By the doctor's evidence, the crime *must* have been committed before Taunton. I guessed they'd throw the knife away at once, and I walked down the line looking for it; and sure enough, there it was. I made inquiries at Taunton about our man, but of course it's a big station, and it wasn't likely they'd notice him. He probably got back to London by a later train.'

Poirot nodded. 'Very likely.'

'But I found another bit of news when I got back. They're passing the jewels, all right! That large emerald was pawned last night—by one of the regular lot. Who do you think it was?'

'I don't know—except that he was a short man.'

Japp stared. 'Well, you're right there. He's short enough. It was Red Narky.'

'Who is Red Narky?' I asked.

'A particularly sharp jewel-thief, sir. And not one to stick at murder. Usually works with a woman—Gracie Kidd; but she doesn't seem to be in it this time—unless she's got off to Holland with the rest of the swag.'

'You've arrested Narky?'

'Sure thing. But mind you, it's the other man we want—the man who went down with Mrs Carrington in the train. He was the one who planned the job, right enough. But Narky won't squeal on a pal.'

I noticed Poirot's eyes had become very green.

'I think,' he said gently, 'that I can find Narky's pal for you, all right.'

'One of your little ideas, eh?' Japp eyed Poirot sharply. 'Wonderful how you manage to deliver the goods sometimes, at your age and all. Devil's own luck, of course.'

'Perhaps, perhaps,' murmured my friend. 'Hastings, my hat. And the brush. So! My galoshes, if it still rains! We must not undo the good work of that *tisane*. *Au revoir*, Japp!'

'Good luck to you, Poirot.'

Poirot hailed the first taxi we met, and directed the driver to Park Lane.

When we drew up before Halliday's house, he skipped out nimbly, paid the driver and rang the bell. To the footman who opened the door he made a request in a low voice, and we were immediately taken upstairs. We went up to the top of the house, and were shown into a small neat bedroom.

Poirot's eyes roved round the room and fastened themselves on a small black trunk. He knelt in front of it, scrutinized the labels on it, and took a small twist of wire from his pocket.

'Ask Mr Halliday if he will be so kind as to mount to me here,' he said over his shoulder to the footman.

The man departed, and Poirot gently coaxed the lock of the trunk with a practised hand. In a few minutes the lock gave, and he raised the lid of the trunk. Swiftly he began rummaging among the clothes it contained, flinging them out on the floor.

There was a heavy step on the stairs, and Halliday entered the room.

'What in hell are you doing here?' he demanded, staring.

'I was looking, monsieur, for *this*.' Poirot withdrew from the trunk a coat and skirt of bright blue frieze, and a small toque of white fox fur.

'What are you doing with my trunk?' I turned to see that the maid, Jane Mason, had entered the room.

'If you will just shut the door, Hastings. Thank you. Yes, and stand with your back against it. Now, Mr Halliday, let me introduce you to Gracie Kidd, otherwise Jane Mason, who will shortly rejoin her accomplice, Red Narky, under the kind escort of Inspector Japp.'

Poirot waved a deprecating hand. 'It was of the most simple!' He helped himself to more caviar.

'It was the maid's insistence on the clothes that her mistress was wearing that first struck me. Why was she so anxious that our attention should be directed to them? I reflected that we had only the maid's word for the mysterious man in the carriage at Bristol. As far as the doctor's evidence went, Mrs Carrington might easily have been murdered *before* reaching Bristol. But if so, then the maid must be an accomplice. And if she were an accomplice, she would not wish this point to rest on her evidence alone. The clothes Mrs Carrington was wearing were of a striking nature. A maid usually has a good deal of choice as to what her mistress shall wear. Now if, after Bristol, anyone saw a lady in a bright blue coat and skirt, and a fur toque, he will be quite ready to swear he had seen Mrs Carrington.

'I began to reconstruct. The maid would provide herself with duplicate clothes. She and her accomplice chloroform and stab Mrs Carrington between London and Bristol, probably taking advantage of a tunnel. Her body is rolled under the seat; and the maid takes her place. At Weston she must make herself noticed. How? In all probability, a newspaper-boy will be selected. She will insure his remembering her by giving him a large tip. She also drew his attention to the colour of her dress by a remark about one of the magazines. After leaving Weston, she throws the knife out of the window to mark the place where the crime presumably occurred, and changes her clothes, or buttons a long mackintosh over them. At Taunton she leaves the train and returns to Bristol as soon as possible, where her accomplice has duly left the luggage in the cloakroom. He hands over the ticket and himself returns to London. She waits on the platform, carrying out her role, goes to a hotel for the night and returns to town in the morning, exactly as she said.

'When Japp returned from his expedition, he confirmed all my deductions. He also told me that a well-known crook was passing the jewels. I knew that whoever it was would be the exact opposite of the man Jane Mason described. When I heard that it was Red Narky, who always worked with Gracie Kidd—well, I knew just where to find her.'

'And the Count?'

'The more I thought of it, the more I was convinced that he had nothing to do with it. That gentleman is much too careful of his own skin to risk murder. It would be out of keeping with his character.'

Agatha Christie

'Well, Monsieur Poirot,' said Halliday, 'I owe you a big debt. And the cheque I write after lunch won't go near to settling it.'

Poirot smiled modestly, and murmured to me: 'The good Japp, he shall get the official credit, all right, but though he has got his Gracie Kidd, I think that I, as the Americans say, have got his goat!'

The Chocolate Box

It was a wild night. Outside, the wind howled malevolently, and the rain beat against the windows in great gusts.

Poirot and I sat facing the hearth, our legs stretched out to the cheerful blaze. Between us was a small table. On my side of it stood some carefully brewed hot toddy; on Poirot's was a cup of thick, rich chocolate which I would not have drunk for a hundred pounds! Poirot sipped the thick brown mess in the pink china cup, and sighed with contentment.

'*Quelle belle vie*!' he murmured.

'Yes, it's a good old world,' I agreed. 'Here am I with a job, and a good job too! And here are you, famous—'

'Oh, *mon ami*!' protested Poirot.

'But you are. And rightly so! When I think back on your long line of successes, I am positively amazed. I don't believe you know what failure is!'

'He would be a droll kind of original who could say that!'

'No, but seriously, *have* you ever failed?'

'Innumerable times, my friend. What would you? *La bonne chance*, it cannot always be on your side. I have been called in too late. Very often another, working towards the same goal, has arrived there first. Twice have I been stricken

161

down with illness just as I was on the point of success. One must take the downs with the ups, my friend.'

'I didn't quite mean that,' I said. 'I meant, had you ever been completely down and out over a case through your own fault?'

'Ah, I comprehend! You ask if I have ever made the complete prize ass of myself, as you say over here? Once, my friend—' A slow, reflective smile hovered over his face. 'Yes, once I made a fool of myself.'

He sat up suddenly in his chair.

'See here, my friend, you have, I know, kept a record of my little successes. You shall add one more story to the collection, the story of a failure!'

He leaned forward and placed a log on the fire. Then, after carefully wiping his hands on a little duster that hung on a nail by the fireplace, he leaned back and commenced his story.

That of which I tell you (said M. Poirot) took place in Belgium many years ago. It was at the time of the terrible struggle in France between church and state. M. Paul Déroulard was a French deputy of note. It was an open secret that the portfolio of a Minister awaited him. He was among the bitterest of the anti-Catholic party, and it was certain that on his accession to power, he would have to face violent enmity. He was in many ways a peculiar man. Though he neither drank nor smoked, he was nevertheless not so scrupulous in other ways. You comprehend, Hastings, *c'était des femmes—toujours des femmes*!

He had married some years earlier a young lady from Brussels who had brought him a substantial dot. Undoubtedly

162

the money was useful to him in his career, as his family was not rich, though on the other hand he was entitled to call himself M. le Baron if he chose. There were no children of the marriage, and his wife died after two years—the result of a fall downstairs. Among the property which she bequeathed to him was a house on the Avenue Louise in Brussels.

It was in this house that his sudden death took place, the event coinciding with the resignation of the Minister whose portfolio he was to inherit. All the papers printed long notices of his career. His death, which had taken place quite suddenly in the evening after dinner, was attributed to heart-failure.

At that time, *mon ami*, I was, as you know, a member of the Belgian detective force. The death of M. Paul Déroulard was not particularly interesting to me. I am, as you also know, *bon catholique*, and his demise seemed to me fortunate.

It was some three days afterwards, when my vacation had just begun, that I received a visitor at my own apartments—a lady, heavily veiled, but evidently quite young; and I perceived at once that she was a *jeune fille tout à fait comme il faut*.

'You are Monsieur Hercule Poirot?' she asked in a low sweet voice.

I bowed.

'Of the detective service?'

Again I bowed. 'Be seated, I pray of you, mademoiselle,' I said.

She accepted a chair and drew aside her veil. Her face was charming, though marred with tears, and haunted as though with some poignant anxiety.

'Monsieur,' she said, 'I understand that you are now taking a vacation. Therefore you will be free to take up a private case. You understand that I do not wish to call in the police.'

I shook my head. 'I fear what you ask is impossible, mademoiselle. Even though on vacation, I am still of the police.'

She leaned forward. '*Ecoutez, monsieur*. All that I ask of you is to investigate. The result of your investigations you are at perfect liberty to report to the police. If what I believe to be true *is* true, we shall need all the machinery of the law.'

That placed a somewhat different complexion on the matter, and I placed myself at her service without more ado.

A slight colour rose in her cheeks. 'I thank you, monsieur. It is the death of M. Paul Déroulard that I ask you to investigate.'

'*Comment?*' I exclaimed, surprised.

'Monsieur, I have nothing to go upon—nothing but my woman's instinct, but I am convinced—*convinced*, I tell you—that M. Déroulard did not die a natural death!'

'But surely the doctors—'

'Doctors may be mistaken. He was so robust, so strong. Ah, Monsieur Poirot, I beseech of you to help me—'

The poor child was almost beside herself. She would have knelt to me. I soothed her as best I could.

'I will help you, mademoiselle. I feel almost sure that your fears are unfounded, but we will see. First, I will ask you to describe to me the inmates of the house.'

'There are the domestics, of course, Jeannette, Félice, and Denise the cook. She has been there many years; the others are simple country girls. Also there is François, but he too is an old servant. Then there is Monsieur Déroulard's mother who lived with him, and myself. My name is Virginie Mesnard. I am a poor cousin of the late Madame Déroulard, M. Paul's wife, and I have been a member of their ménage for over three years. I have now described to you the household. There were also two guests staying in the house.'

'And they were?'

'M. de Saint Alard, a neighbour of M. Déroulard's in France. Also an English friend, Mr John Wilson.'

'Are they still with you?'

'Mr Wilson, yes, but M. de Saint Alard departed yesterday.'

'And what is your plan, Mademoiselle Mesnard?'

'If you will present yourself at the house in half an hour's time, I will have arranged some story to account for your presence. I had better represent you to be connected with journalism in some way. I shall say you have come from Paris, and that you have brought a card of introduction from M. de Saint Alard. Madame Déroulard is very feeble in health, and will pay little attention to details.'

On mademoiselle's ingenious pretext I was admitted to the house, and after a brief interview with the dead deputy's mother, who was a wonderfully imposing and aristocratic figure though obviously in failing health, I was made free of the premises.

I wonder, my friend (continued Poirot), whether you can possibly figure to yourself the difficulties of my task?

Here was a man whose death had taken place three days previously. If there *had* been foul play, only one possibility was admittable—*poison*! And I had no chance of seeing the body, and there was no possibility of examining, or analysing, any medium in which the poison could have been administered. There were no clues, false or otherwise, to consider. Had the man been poisoned? Had he died a natural death? I, Hercule Poirot, with nothing to help me, had to decide.

First, I interviewed the domestics, and with their aid, I recapitulated the evening. I paid especial notice to the food at dinner, and the method of serving it. The soup had been served by M. Déroulard himself from a tureen. Next a dish of cutlets, then a chicken. Finally, a compote of fruits. And all placed on the table, and served by Monsieur himself. The coffee was brought in a big pot to the dinner-table. Nothing there, *mon ami*—impossible to poison one without poisoning all!

After dinner Madame Déroulard had retired to her own apartments and Mademoiselle Virginie had accompanied her. The three men had adjourned to M. Déroulard's study. Here they had chatted amicably for some time, when suddenly, without any warning, the deputy had fallen heavily to the ground. M. de Saint Alard had rushed out and told François to fetch the doctor immediately. He said it was without doubt an apoplexy, explained the man. But when the doctor arrived, the patient was past help.

Mr John Wilson, to whom I was presented by Mademoiselle Virginie, was what was known in those days as a regular

John Bull Englishman, middle-aged and burly. His account, delivered in very British French, was substantially the same.

'Déroulard went very red in the face, and down he fell.'

There was nothing further to be found out there. Next I went to the scene of the tragedy, the study, and was left alone there at my own request. So far there was nothing to support Mademoiselle Mesnard's theory. I could not but believe that it was a delusion on her part. Evidently she had entertained a romantic passion for the dead man which had not permitted her to take a normal view of the case. Nevertheless, I searched the study with meticulous care. It was just possible that a hypodermic needle might have been introduced into the dead man's chair in such a way as to allow of a fatal injection. The minute puncture it would cause was likely to remain unnoticed. But I could discover no sign to support that theory. I flung myself down in the chair with a gesture of despair.

'*Enfin*, I abandon it!' I said aloud. 'There is not a clue anywhere! Everything is perfectly normal.'

As I said the words, my eyes fell on a large box of chocolates standing on a table near by, and my heart gave a leap. It might not be a clue to M. Déroulard's death, but here at least was something that was *not* normal. I lifted the lid. The box was full, untouched; not a chocolate was missing—but that only made the peculiarity that had caught my eye more striking. For, see you, Hastings, while the box itself was pink, the lid was *blue*. Now, one often sees a blue ribbon on a pink box, and vice versa, but a box of one colour, and a lid of another—no, decidedly—*ça ne se voit jamais*!

I did not as yet see that this little incident was of any use to me, yet I determined to investigate it as being out of the ordinary. I rang the bell for François, and asked him if his late master had been fond of sweets. A faint melancholy smile came to his lips.

'Passionately fond of them, monsieur. He would always have a box of chocolates in the house. He did not drink wine of any kind, you see.'

'Yet this box has not been touched?' I lifted the lid to show him.

'Pardon, monsieur, but that was a new box purchased on the day of his death, the other being nearly finished.'

'Then the other box was finished on the day of his death,' I said slowly.

'Yes, monsieur, I found it empty in the morning and threw it away.'

'Did M. Déroulard eat sweets at all hours of the day?'

'Usually after dinner, monsieur.'

I began to see light.

'François,' I said, 'you can be discreet?'

'If there is need, monsieur.'

'*Bon*! Know, then, that I am of the police. Can you find me that other box?'

'Without doubt, monsieur. It will be in the dustbin.'

He departed, and returned in a few minutes with a dust-covered object. It was the duplicate of the box I held, save for the fact that this time the box was *blue* and the lid was *pink*. I thanked François, recommended him once more to be discreet, and left the house in the Avenue Louise without more ado.

Next I called upon the doctor who had attended M. Déroulard. With him I had a difficult task. He entrenched himself prettily behind a wall of learned phraseology, but I fancied that he was not quite as sure about the case as he would like to be.

'There have been many curious occurrences of the kind,' he observed, when I had managed to disarm him somewhat. 'A sudden fit of anger, a violent emotion—after a heavy dinner, *c'est entendu*—then, with an access of rage, the blood flies to the head, and *pst!*—there you are!'

'But M. Déroulard had had no violent emotion.'

'No? I made sure that he had been having a stormy altercation with M. de Saint Alard.'

'Why should he?'

'*C'est évident*!' The doctor shrugged his shoulders. 'Was not M. de Saint Alard a Catholic of the most fanatical? Their friendship was being ruined by this question of church and state. Not a day passed without discussions. To M. de Saint Alard, Déroulard appeared almost as Antichrist.'

This was unexpected, and gave me food for thought.

'One more question, Doctor: would it be possible to introduce a fatal dose of poison into a chocolate?'

'It would be possible, I suppose,' said the doctor slowly. 'Pure prussic acid would meet the case if there were no chance of evaporation, and a tiny globule of anything might be swallowed unnoticed—but it does not seem a very likely

supposition. A chocolate full of morphine or strychnine—'
He made a wry face. 'You comprehend, M. Poirot—one
bite would be enough! The unwary one would not stand
upon ceremony.'

'Thank you, M. le Docteur.'

I withdrew. Next I made inquiries of the chemists, especially those in the neighbourhood of the Avenue Louise. It
is good to be of the police. I got the information I wanted
without any trouble. Only in one case could I hear of
any poison having been supplied to the house in question.
This was some eye drops of atropine sulphate for Madame
Déroulard. Atropine is a potent poison, and for the moment
I was elated, but the symptoms of atropine poisoning are
closely allied to those of ptomaine, and bear no resemblance
to those I was studying. Besides, the prescription was an
old one. Madame Déroulard had suffered from cataracts
in both eyes for many years.

I was turning away discouraged when the chemist's voice
called me back.

'*Un moment, M. Poirot.* I remember, the girl who brought
that prescription, she said something about having to go on
to the *English* chemist. You might try there.'

I did. Once more enforcing my official status, I got the
information I wanted. On the day before M. Déroulard's
death they had made up a prescription for Mr John Wilson.
Not that there was any making up about it. They were
simply little tablets of trinitrine. I asked if I might see some.
He showed me them, and my heart beat faster—for the tiny
tablets were of *chocolate*.

'Is it a poison?' I asked.

'No, monsieur.'

'Can you describe to me its effect?'

'It lowers the blood-pressure. It is given for some forms of heart trouble—angina pectoris for instance. It relieves the arterial tension. In arteriosclerosis—'

I interrupted him. '*Ma foi*! This rigmarole says nothing to me. Does it cause the face to flush?'

'Certainly it does.'

'And supposing I ate ten—twenty of your little tablets, what then?'

'I should not advise you to attempt it,' he replied drily.

'And yet you say it is not poison?'

'There are many things not called poison which can kill a man,' he replied as before.

I left the shop elated. At last, things had begun to march! I now knew that John Wilson had the means for the crime—but what about the motive? He had come to Belgium on business, and had asked M. Déroulard, whom he knew slightly, to put him up. There was apparently no way in which Déroulard's death could benefit him. Moreover, I discovered by inquiries in England that he had suffered for some years from that painful form of heart disease known as angina. Therefore he had a genuine right to have those tablets in his possession. Nevertheless, I was convinced that someone had gone to the chocolate box, opening the full one first by mistake, and had abstracted the contents of the last chocolate, cramming in instead as many little trinitrine tablets as it would hold. The chocolates were large ones.

Between twenty or thirty tablets, I felt sure, could have been inserted. But who had done this?

There were two guests in the house. John Wilson had the means. Saint Alard had the motive. Remember, he was a fanatic, and there is no fanatic like a religious fanatic. Could he, by any means, have got hold of John Wilson's trinitrine?

Another little idea came to me. Ah, you smile at my little ideas! Why had Wilson run out of trinitrine? Surely he would bring an adequate supply from England. I called once more at the house in the Avenue Louise. Wilson was out, but I saw the girl who did his room, Félice. I demanded of her immediately whether it was not true that M. Wilson had lost a bottle from his washstand some little time ago. The girl responded eagerly. It was quite true. She, Félice, had been blamed for it. The English gentleman had evidently thought that she had broken it, and did not like to say so. Whereas she had never even touched it. Without doubt it was Jeannette—always nosing round where she had no business to be—

I calmed the flow of words, and took my leave. I knew now all that I wanted to know. It remained for me to prove my case. That, I felt, would not be easy. *I* might be sure that Saint Alard had removed the bottle of trinitrine from John Wilson's washstand, but to convince others, I would have to produce evidence. And I had none to produce!

Never mind. I *knew*—that was the great thing. You remember our difficulty in the Styles case, Hastings? There again, I *knew*—but it took me a long time to find the last link which made my chain of evidence against the murderer complete.

I asked for an interview with Mademoiselle Mesnard. She came at once. I demanded of her the address of M. de Saint Alard. A look of trouble came over her face.

'Why do you want it, monsieur?'

'Mademoiselle, it is necessary.'

She seemed doubtful—troubled.

'He can tell you nothing. He is a man whose thoughts are not in this world. He hardly notices what goes on around him.'

'Possibly, mademoiselle. Nevertheless, he was an old friend of M. Déroulard's. There may be things he can tell me—things of the past—old grudges—old love-affairs.'

The girl flushed and bit her lip. 'As you please—but—but I feel sure now that I have been mistaken. It was good of you to accede to my demand, but I was upset—almost distraught at the time. I see now that there is no mystery to solve. Leave it, I beg of you, monsieur.'

I eyed her closely.

'Mademoiselle,' I said, 'it is sometimes difficult for a dog to find a scent, but once he *has* found it, nothing on earth will make him leave it! That is if he is a good dog! And I, mademoiselle, I, Hercule Poirot, am a very good dog.'

Without a word she turned away. A few minutes later she returned with the address written on a sheet of paper. I left the house. François was waiting for me outside. He looked at me anxiously.

'There is no news, monsieur?'

'None as yet, my friend.'

'Ah! *Pauvre* Monsieur Déroulard!' he sighed. 'I too was of his way of thinking. I do not care for priests. Not that I would say so in the house. The women are all devout—a good thing perhaps. *Madame est très pieuse—et Mademoiselle Virginie aussi.*'

Mademoiselle Virginie? Was she '*très pieuse*?' Thinking of the tear-stained passionate face I had seen that first day, I wondered.

Having obtained the address of M. de Saint Alard, I wasted no time. I arrived in the neighbourhood of his château in the Ardennes but it was some days before I could find a pretext for gaining admission to the house. In the end I did—how do you think—as a plumber, *mon ami*! It was the affair of a moment to arrange a neat little gas leak in his bedroom. I departed for my tools, and took care to return with them at an hour when I knew I should have the field pretty well to myself. What I was searching for, I hardly knew. The one thing needful, I could not believe there was any chance of finding. He would never have run the risk of keeping it.

Still when I found the little cupboard above the washstand locked, I could not resist the temptation of seeing what was inside it. The lock was quite a simple one to pick. The door swung open. It was full of old bottles. I took them up one by one with a trembling hand. Suddenly, I uttered a cry. Figure to yourself, my friend, I held in my hand a little phial with an English chemist's label. On it were the words: '*Trinitrine Tablets. One to be taken when required. Mr John Wilson.*'

I controlled my emotion, closed the cupboard, slipped the bottle into my pocket, and continued to repair the gas leak! One must be methodical. Then I left the château, and took train for my own country as soon as possible. I arrived in Brussels late that night. I was writing out a report for the préfet in the morning, when a note was brought to me. It was from old Madame Déroulard, and it summoned me to the house in the Avenue Louise without delay.

François opened the door to me.

'Madame la Baronne is awaiting you.'

He conducted me to her apartments. She sat in state in a large armchair. There was no sign of Mademoiselle Virginie.

'M. Poirot,' said the old lady, 'I have just learned that you are not what you pretend to be. You are a police officer.'

'That is so, madame.'

'You came here to inquire into the circumstances of my son's death?'

Again I replied: 'That is so, madame.'

'I should be glad if you would tell me what progress you have made.'

I hesitated.

'First I would like to know how you have learned all this, madame.'

'From one who is no longer of this world.'

Her words, and the brooding way she uttered them, sent a chill to my heart. I was incapable of speech.

'Therefore, monsieur, I would beg of you most urgently to tell me exactly what progress you have made in your investigation.'

'Madame, my investigation is finished.'

'My son?'

'Was killed deliberately.'

'You know by whom?'

'Yes, madame.'

'Who, then?'

'M. de Saint Alard.'

The old lady shook her head.

'You are wrong. M. de Saint Alard is incapable of such a crime.'

'The proofs are in my hands.'

'I beg of you once more to tell me all.'

This time I obeyed, going over each step that had led me to the discovery of the truth. She listened attentively. At the end she nodded her head.

'Yes, yes, it is all as you say, all but one thing. It was not M. de Saint Alard who killed my son. It was I, his mother.'

I stared at her. She continued to nod her head gently.

'It is well that I sent for you. It is the providence of the good God that Virginie told me before she departed for the convent, what she had done. Listen, M. Poirot! My son was an evil man. He persecuted the church. He led a life of mortal sin. He dragged down other souls beside his own. But there was worse than that. As I came out of my room in this house one morning, I saw my daughter-in-law standing at the head of the stairs. She was reading a letter. I saw my son steal up behind her. One swift push, and she fell, striking her head on the marble steps. When they picked her up she was dead. My son was a murderer, and only I, his mother, knew it.'

She closed her eyes for a moment. 'You cannot conceive, monsieur, of my agony, my despair. What was I to do? Denounce him to the police? I could not bring myself to do it. It was my duty, but my flesh was weak. Besides, would they believe me? My eyesight had been failing for some time—they would say I was mistaken. I kept silence. But my conscience gave me no peace. By keeping silence I too was a murderer. My son inherited his wife's money. He flourished as the green bay tree. And now he was to have a Minister's portfolio. His persecution of the church would be redoubled. And there was Virginie. She, poor child, beautiful, naturally pious, was fascinated by him. He had a strange and terrible power over women. I saw it coming. I was powerless to prevent it. He had no intention of marrying her. The time came when she was ready to yield everything to him.

'Then I saw my path clear. He was my son. I had given him life. I was responsible for him. He had killed one woman's body, now he would kill another's soul! I went to Mr Wilson's room, and took the bottle of tablets. He had once said laughingly that there were enough in it to kill a man! I went into the study and opened the big box of chocolates that always stood on the table. I opened a new box by mistake. The other was on the table also. There was just one chocolate left in it. That simplified things. No one ate chocolates except my son and Virginie. I would keep her with me that night. All went as I had planned—'

She paused, closing her eyes a minute then opened them again.

'M. Poirot, I am in your hands. They tell me I have not many days to live. I am willing to answer for my action before the good God. Must I answer for it on earth also?'

I hesitated. 'But the empty bottle, madame,' I said to gain time. 'How came that into M. de Saint Alard's possession?'

'When he came to say goodbye to me, monsieur, I slipped it into his pocket. I did not know how to get rid of it. I am so infirm that I cannot move about much without help, and finding it empty in my rooms might have caused suspicion. You understand, monsieur—' she drew herself up to her full height—'it was with no idea of casting suspicion on M. de Saint Alard! I never dreamed of such a thing. I thought his valet would find an empty bottle and throw it away without question.'

I bowed my head. 'I comprehend, madame,' I said.

'And your decision, monsieur?'

Her voice was firm and unfaltering, her head held as high as ever.

I rose to my feet.

'Madame,' I said, 'I have the honour to wish you good day. I have made my investigations—and failed! The matter is closed.'

He was silent for a moment, then said quietly: 'She died just a week later. Mademoiselle Virginie passed through her novitiate, and duly took the veil. That, my friend, is the story. I must admit that I do not make a fine figure in it.'

'But that was hardly a failure,' I expostulated. 'What else could you have thought under the circumstances?'

'*Ah, sacré, mon ami,*' cried Poirot, becoming suddenly animated. 'Is it that you do not see? But I was thirty-six times an idiot! My grey cells, they functioned not at all. The whole time I had the clue in my hands.'

'What clue?'

'*The chocolate box*! Do you not see? Would anyone in possession of their full eyesight make such a mistake? I knew Madame Déroulard had cataracts—the atropine drops told me that. There was only one person in the household whose eyesight was such that she could not see which lid to replace. It was the chocolate box that started me on the track, and yet up to the end I failed consistently to perceive its real significance!

'Also my psychology was at fault. Had M. de Saint Alard been the criminal, he would never have kept an incriminating bottle. Finding it was a proof of his innocence. I had learned already from Mademoiselle Virginie that he was absent-minded. Altogether it was a miserable affair that I have recounted to you there! Only to you have I told the story. You comprehend, I do not figure well in it! An old lady commits a crime in such a simple and clever fashion that I, Hercule Poirot, am completely deceived. *Sapristi*! It does not bear thinking of! Forget it. Or no—remember it, and if you think at any time that I am growing conceited—it is not likely, but it might arise.'

I concealed a smile.

'*Eh bien*, my friend, you shall say to me, "Chocolate box". Is it agreed?'

'It's a bargain!'

'After all,' said Poirot reflectively, 'it was an experience! I, who have undoubtedly the finest brain in Europe at present, can afford to be magnanimous!'

'Chocolate box,' I murmured gently.

'*Pardon, mon ami?*'

I looked at Poirot's innocent face, as he bent forward inquiringly, and my heart smote me. I had suffered often at his hands, but I, too, though not possessing the finest brain in Europe, could afford to be magnanimous!

'Nothing,' I lied, and lit another pipe, smiling to myself.

The Submarine Plans

A note had been brought by special messenger. Poirot read it, and a gleam of excitement and interest came into his eyes as he did so. He dismissed the man with a few curt words and then turned to me.

'Pack a bag with all haste, my friend. We're going down to Sharples.'

I started at the mention of the famous country place of Lord Alloway. Head of the newly formed Ministry of Defence, Lord Alloway was a prominent member of the Cabinet. As Sir Ralph Curtis, head of a great engineering firm, he had made his mark in the House of Commons, and he was now freely spoken of as *the* coming man, and the one most likely to be asked to form a ministry should the rumours as to Mr David MacAdam's health prove well founded.

A big Rolls-Royce car was waiting for us below, and as we glided off into the darkness, I plied Poirot with questions.

'What on earth can they want us for at this time of night?' I demanded. It was past eleven.

Poirot shook his head. 'Something of the most urgent, without doubt.'

'I remember,' I said, 'that some years ago there was some rather ugly scandal about Ralph Curtis, as he then was—some jugglery with shares, I believe. In the end, he was completely exonerated; but perhaps something of the kind has arisen again?'

'It would hardly be necessary for him to send for me in the middle of the night, my friend.'

I was forced to agree, and the remainder of the journey was passed in silence. Once out of London, the powerful car forged rapidly ahead, and we arrived at Sharples in a little under the hour.

A pontifical butler conducted us at once to a small study where Lord Alloway was awaiting us. He sprang up to greet us—a tall, spare man who seemed actually to radiate power and vitality.

'M. Poirot, I am delighted to see you. It is the second time the government has demanded your services. I remember only too well what you did for us during the war, when the Prime Minister was kidnapped in that astounding fashion. Your masterly deductions—and may I add, your discretion?—saved the situation.'

Poirot's eyes twinkled a little.

'Do I gather then, milor', that this is another case for—discretion?'

'Most emphatically. Sir Harry and I—oh, let me intoduce you—Admiral Sir Harry Weardale, our First Sea Lord—M. Poirot and—let me see, Captain—'

'Hastings,' I supplied.

'I've often heard of you, M. Poirot,' said Sir Harry, shaking hands. 'This is a most unaccountable business, and if you can solve it, we'll be extremely grateful to you.'

I liked the First Sea Lord immediately, a square, bluff sailor of the good old-fashioned type.

Poirot looked inquiringly at them both, and Alloway took up the tale.

'Of course, you understand that all this is in confidence, M. Poirot. We have had a most serious loss. The plans of the new Z type of submarine have been stolen.'

'When was that?'

'Tonight—less than three hours ago. You can appreciate perhaps, M. Poirot, the magnitude of the disaster. It is essential that the loss should not be made public. I will give you the facts as briefly as possible. My guests over the week-end were the Admiral, here, his wife and son, and Mrs Conrad, a lady well known in London society. The ladies retired to bed early—about ten o'clock; so did Mr Leonard Weardale. Sir Harry is down here partly for the purpose of discussing the construction of this new type of submarine with me. Accordingly, I asked Mr Fitzroy, my secretary, to get out the plans from the safe in the corner there, and to arrange them ready for me, as well as various other documents that bore upon the subject in hand. While he was doing this, the Admiral and I strolled up and down the terrace, smoking cigars and enjoying the warm June air. We finished our smoke and our chat, and decided to get down to business. Just as we turned at the far end of the terrace, I fancied I saw a shadow slip out of the french window here, cross the terrace, and disappear. I paid very little attention, however. I knew Fitzroy to be in this room, and it never entered my head that anything might be amiss. There, of course, I am to blame. Well, we retraced our steps along the terrace and entered this room by the window just as Fitzroy entered it from the hall.

'"Got everything out we are likely to need, Fitzroy?" I asked.

'"I think so, Lord Alloway. The papers are all on your desk," he answered. And then he wished us both good night.

'"Just wait a minute," I said, going to the desk. "I may want something I haven't mentioned."

'I looked quickly through the papers that were lying there.

'"You've forgotten the most important of the lot, Fitzroy," I said. "The actual plans of the submarine!"

'"The plans are right on top, Lord Alloway."

'"Oh no, they're not," I said, turning over the papers.

'"But I put them there not a minute ago!"

'"Well, they're not here now," I said.

'Fitzroy advanced with a bewildered expression on his face. The thing seemed incredible. We turned over the papers on the desk; we hunted through the safe; but at last we had to make up our minds to it that the papers were gone—and gone within the short space of about three minutes while Fitzroy was absent from the room.'

'Why did he leave the room?' asked Poirot quickly.

'Just what I asked him,' exclaimed Sir Harry.

'It appears,' said Lord Alloway, 'that just when he had finished arranging the papers on my desk, he was startled by hearing a woman scream. He dashed out into the hall.

On the stairs he discovered Mrs Conrad's French maid. The girl looked very white and upset, and declared that she had seen a ghost—a tall figure dressed all in white that moved without a sound. Fitzroy laughed at her fears and told her, in more or less polite language, not to be a fool. Then he returned to this room just as we entered from the window.'

'It all seems very clear,' said Poirot thoughtfully. 'The only question is, was the maid an accomplice? Did she scream by arrangement with her confederate lurking outside, or was he merely waiting there in the hope of an opportunity presenting itself? It was a man, I suppose—not a woman you saw?'

'I can't tell you, M. Poirot. It was just a—shadow.'

The admiral gave such a peculiar snort that it could not fail to attract attention.

'M. l'Amiral has something to say, I think,' said Poirot quietly, with a slight smile. 'You saw this shadow, Sir Harry?'

'No, I didn't,' returned the other. 'And neither did Alloway. The branch of a tree flapped, or something, and then afterwards, when we discovered the theft, he leaped to the conclusion that he had seen someone pass across the terrace. His imagination played a trick on him; that's all.'

'I am not usually credited with having much imagination,' said Lord Alloway with a slight smile.

'Nonsense, we've all got imagination. We can all work ourselves up to believe that we've seen more than we have. I've had a lifetime of experience at sea, and I'll back my eyes against those of any landsman. I was looking right down the terrace, and I'd have seen the same if there was anything to see.'

He was quite excited over the matter. Poirot rose and stepped quickly to the window.

'You permit?' he asked. 'We must settle this point if possible.'

He went out upon the terrace, and we followed him. He had taken an electric torch from his pocket, and was playing the light along the edge of the grass that bordered the terrace.

'Where did he cross the terrace, milor'?' he asked.

'About opposite the window, I should say.'

Poirot continued to play the torch for some minutes longer, walking the entire length of the terrace and back. Then he shut it off and straightened himself up.

'Sir Harry is right—and you are wrong, milor', he said quietly. 'It rained heavily earlier this evening. Anyone who passed over that grass could not avoid leaving footmarks. But there are none—none at all.'

His eyes went from one man's face to the other's. Lord Alloway looked bewildered and unconvinced; the Admiral expressed a noisy gratification.

'Knew I couldn't be wrong,' he declared. 'Trust my eyes anywhere.'

He was such a picture of an honest old sea-dog that I could not help smiling.

'So that brings us to the people in the house,' said Poirot smoothly. 'Let us come inside again. Now, milor', while Mr Fitzroy was speaking to the maid on the stairs, could anyone have seized the opportunity to enter the study from the hall?'

Lord Alloway shook his head.

'Quite impossible—they would have had to pass him in order to do so.'

'And Mr Fitzroy himself—you are sure of him, eh?'

Lord Alloway flushed.

'Absolutely, M. Poirot. I will answer confidently for my secretary. It is quite impossible that he should be concerned in the matter in any way.'

'Everything seems to be impossible,' remarked Poirot rather drily. 'Possibly the plans attached to themselves a little pair of wings, and flew away—*comme ça*!' He blew his lips out like a comical cherub.

'The whole thing is impossible,' declared Lord Alloway impatiently. 'But I beg, M. Poirot, that you will not dream of suspecting Fitzroy. Consider for one moment—had he wished to take the plans, what could have been easier for him than to take a tracing of them without going to the trouble of stealing them?'

'There, milor',' said Poirot with approval, 'you make a remark *bien juste*—I see that you have a mind orderly and methodical. *L'Angleterre* is happy in possessing you.'

Lord Alloway looked rather embarrassed by this sudden burst of praise. Poirot returned to the matter in hand.

'The room in which you had been sitting all the evening—'

'The drawing-room? Yes?'

'That also has a window on the terrace, since I remember your saying you went out that way. Would it not be possible for someone to come out by the drawing-room window and in by this one while Mr Fitzroy was out of the room, and return the same way?'

'But we'd have seen them,' objected the Admiral.

'Not if you had your backs turned, walking the other way.'

'Fitzroy was only out of the room a few minutes, the time it would take us to walk to the end and back.'

'No matter—it is a possibility—in fact, the only one as things stand.'

'But there was no one in the drawing-room when we went out,' said the Admiral.

'They may have come there afterwards.'

'You mean,' said Lord Alloway slowly, 'that when Fitzroy heard the maid scream and went out, someone was already concealed in the drawing-room, and that they darted in and out through the windows, and only left the drawing-room when Fitzroy had returned to this room?'

'The methodical mind again,' said Poirot, bowing. 'You express the matter perfectly.'

'One of the servants, perhaps?'

'Or a guest. It was Mrs Conrad's maid who screamed. What exactly can you tell me of Mrs Conrad?'

Lord Alloway considered for a minute.

'I told you that she is a lady well known in society. That is true in the sense that she gives large parties, and goes everywhere. But very little is known as to where she really comes from, and what her past life has been. She is a lady who frequents diplomatic and Foreign Office circles as much as possible. The Secret Service is inclined to ask—why?'

'I see,' said Poirot. 'And she was asked here this week-end—'

'So that—shall we say?—we might observe her at close quarters.'

'*Parfaitement*! It is possible that she has turned the tables on you rather neatly.'

Lord Alloway looked discomfited, and Poirot continued: 'Tell me, milor', was any reference made in her hearing to the subjects you and the Admiral were going to discuss together?'

'Yes,' admitted the other. 'Sir Harry said: "And now for our submarine! To work!" or something of that sort. The others had left the room, but she had come back for a book.'

'I see,' said Poirot thoughtfully. 'Milor', it is very late—but this is an urgent affair. I would like to question the members of this house-party at once if it is possible.'

'It can be managed, of course,' said Lord Alloway. 'The awkward thing is, we don't want to let it get about more than can be helped. Of course, Lady Juliet Weardale and young Leonard are all right—but Mrs Conrad, if she is not guilty, is rather a different proposition. Perhaps you could just state that an important paper is missing, without specifying what it is, or going into any of the circumstances of the disappearance?'

'Exactly what I was about to propose myself,' said Poirot, beaming. 'In fact, in all three cases. Monsieur the Admiral will pardon me, but even the best of wives—'

'No offence,' said Sir Harry. 'All women talk, bless 'em! I wish Juliet would talk a little more and play bridge a little less. But women are like that nowadays, never happy unless they're dancing or gambling. I'll get Juliet and Leonard up, shall I, Alloway?'

'Thank you. I'll call the French maid. M. Poirot will want to see her, and she can rouse her mistress. I'll attend to it now. In the meantime, I'll send Fitzroy along.'

Mr Fitzroy was a pale, thin young man with pince-nez and a frigid expression. His statement was practically word for word what Lord Alloway had already told us.

'What is your own theory, Mr Fitzroy?'

Mr Fitzroy shrugged his shoulders.

'Undoubtedly someone who knew the hang of things was waiting his chance outside. He could see what went on through the window, and he slipped in when I left the room. It's a pity Lord Alloway didn't give chase then and there when he saw the fellow leave.'

Poirot did not undeceive him. Instead he asked: 'Do you believe the story of the French maid—that she had seen a ghost?'

'Well, hardly, M. Poirot!'

'I mean—that she really thought so?'

'Oh, as to that, I can't say. She certainly seemed rather upset. She had her hands to her head.'

'Aha!' cried Poirot with the air of one who has made a discovery. 'Is that so indeed—and she was without doubt a pretty girl?'

'I didn't notice particularly,' said Mr Fitzroy in a repressive voice.

'You did not see her mistress, I suppose?'

'As a matter of fact, I did. She was in the gallery at the top of the steps and was calling her—"Léonie!" Then she saw me—and of course retired.'

'Upstairs,' said Poirot, frowning.

'Of course, I realize that all this is very unpleasant for me— or rather would have been, if Lord Alloway had not chanced to see the man actually leaving. In any case, I should be glad if you would make a point of searching my room—and myself.'

'You really wish that?'

'Certainly I do.'

What Poirot would have replied I do not know, but at that moment Lord Alloway reappeared and informed us that the two ladies and Mr Leonard Weardale were in the drawing-room.

The women were in becoming negligées. Mrs Conrad was a beautiful woman of thirty-five, with golden hair and a slight tendency to *embonpoint*. Lady Juliet Weardale must have been forty, tall and dark, very thin, still beautiful, with exquisite hands and feet, and a restless, haggard manner. Her son was rather an effeminate-looking young man, as great a contrast to his bluff, hearty father as could well be imagined.

Poirot gave forth the little rigmarole we had agreed upon, and then explained that he was anxious to know if anyone had heard or seen anything that night which might assist us.

Turning to Mrs Conrad first, he asked her if she would be so kind as to inform him exactly what her movements had been.

'Let me see… I went upstairs. I rang for my maid. Then, as she did not put in an appearance, I came out and called

191

her. I could hear her talking on the stairs. After she had brushed my hair, I sent her away—she was in a very curious nervous state. I read awhile and then went to bed.'

'And you, Lady Juliet?'

'I went straight upstairs and to bed. I was very tired.'

'What about your book, dear?' asked Mrs Conrad with a sweet smile.

'My book?' Lady Juliet flushed.

'Yes, you know, when I sent Léonie away, you were coming up the stairs. You had been down to the drawing-room for a book, you said.'

'Oh yes, I did go down. I—I forgot.'

Lady Juliet clasped her hands nervously together.

'Did you hear Mrs Conrad's maid scream, milady?'

'No—no, I didn't.'

'How curious—because you must have been in the drawing-room at the time.'

'I heard nothing,' said Lady Juliet in a firmer voice.

Poirot turned to young Leonard.

'Monsieur?'

'Nothing doing. I went straight upstairs and turned in.'

Poirot stroked his chin.

'Alas, I fear there is nothing to help me here. Mesdames and monsieur, I regret—I regret infinitely to have deranged you from your slumbers for so little. Accept my apologies, I pray of you.'

Gesticulating and apologizing, he marshalled them out. He returned with the French maid, a pretty, impudent-looking girl. Alloway and Weardale had gone out with the ladies.

'Now, mademoiselle,' said Poirot in a brisk tone, 'let us have the truth. Recount to me no histories. Why did you scream on the stairs?'

'Ah, monsieur, I saw a tall figure—all in white—'

Poirot arrested her with an energetic shake of his forefinger.

'Did I not say, recount to me no histories? I will make a guess. He kissed you, did he not? M. Leonard Weardale, I mean?'

'*Eh bien, monsieur*, and after all, what is a kiss?'

'Under the circumstances, it is most natural,' replied Poirot gallantly. 'I myself, or Hastings here—but tell me just what occurred.'

'He came up behind me, and caught me. I was startled, and I screamed. If I had known, I would not have screamed—but he came upon me like a cat. Then came M. *le secrêtaire*. M. Leonard flew up the stairs. And what could I say? Especially to a *jeune homme comme ça—tellement comme il faut? Ma foi*, I invent a ghost.'

'And all is explained,' cried Poirot genially. 'You then mounted to the chamber of Madame your mistress. Which is her room, by the way?'

'It is at the end, monsieur. That way.'

'Directly over the study, then. *Bien*, mademoiselle, I will detain you no longer. And *la prochaine fois*, do not scream.'

Handing her out, he came back to me with a smile.

'An interesting case, is it not, Hastings? I begin to have a few little ideas. *Et vous?*'

'What was Leonard Weardale doing on the stairs? I don't like that young man, Poirot. He's a thorough young rake, I should say.'

'I agree with you, *mon ami*.'

'Fitzroy seems an honest fellow.'

'Lord Alloway is certainly insistent on that point.'

'And yet there is something in his manner—'

'That is almost too good to be true? I felt it myself. On the other hand, our friend Mrs Conrad is certainly no good at all.'

'And her room is over the study,' I said musingly, and keeping a sharp eye on Poirot.

He shook his head with a slight smile.

'No, *mon ami*, I cannot bring myself seriously to believe that that immaculate lady swarmed down the chimney, or let herself down from the balcony.'

As he spoke, the door opened, and to my great surprise, Lady Juliet Weardale flitted in.

'M. Poirot,' she said somewhat breathlessly, 'Can I speak to you alone?'

'Milady, Captain Hastings is as my other self. You can speak before him as though he were a thing of no account, not there at all. Be seated, I pray you.'

She sat down, still keeping her eyes fixed on Poirot.

'What I have to say is—rather difficult. You are in charge of this case. If the—papers were to be returned, would that end the matter? I mean, could it be done without questions being asked?'

Poirot stared hard at her.

'Let me understand you, madame. They are to be placed in my hand—is that right? And I am to return them to Lord Alloway on the condition that he asks no questions as to where I got them?'

She bowed her head. 'That is what I mean. But I must be sure there will be no—publicity.'

'I do not think Lord Alloway is particularly anxious for publicity,' said Poirot grimly.

'You accept then?' she cried eagerly in response.

'A little moment, milady. It depends on how soon you can place those papers in my hands.'

'Almost immediately.'

Poirot glanced up at the clock.

'How soon, exactly?'

'Say—ten minutes,' she whispered.

'I accept, milady.'

She hurried from the room. I pursed my mouth up for a whistle.

'Can you sum up the situation for me, Hastings?'

'Bridge,' I replied succinctly.

'Ah, you remember the careless words of Monsieur the Admiral! What a memory! I felicitate you, Hastings.'

We said no more, for Lord Alloway came in, and looked inquiringly at Poirot.

'Have you any further ideas, M. Poirot? I am afraid the answers to your questions have been rather disappointing.'

'Not at all, milor'. They have been quite sufficiently illuminating. It will be unnecessary for me to stay here any longer, and so, with your permission, I will return at once to London.'

Lord Alloway seemed dumbfounded.

'But—but what have you discovered? Do you know who took the plans?'

'Yes, milor', I do. Tell me—in the case of the papers being returned to you anonymously, you would prosecute no further inquiry?'

Lord Alloway stared at him.

'Do you mean on payment of a sum of money?'

'No, milor', returned unconditionally.'

'Of course, the recovery of the plans is the great thing,' said Lord Alloway slowly. He looked puzzled and uncomprehending.

'Then I should seriously recommend you to adopt that course. Only you, the Admiral and your secretary know of the loss. Only they need know of the restitution. And you may count on me to support you in every way—lay the mystery on my shoulders. You asked me to restore the papers—I have done so. You know no more.' He rose and held out his hand. 'Milor', I am glad to have met you. I have faith in you—and your devotion to England. You will guide her destinies with a strong, sure hand.'

'M. Poirot—I swear to you that I will do my best. It may be a fault, or it may be a virtue—but I believe in myself.'

'So does every great man. Me, I am the same!' said Poirot grandiloquently.

The car came round to the door in a few minutes, and Lord Alloway bade us farewell on the steps with renewed cordiality.

'That is a great man, Hastings,' said Poirot as we drove off. 'He has brains, resource, power. He is the strong man that England needs to guide her through these difficult days of reconstruction.'

'I'm quite ready to agree with all you say, Poirot—but what about Lady Juliet? Is she to return the papers straight to Alloway? What will she think when she finds you have gone off without a word?'

'Hastings, I will ask you a little question. Why, when she was talking with me, did she not hand me the plans then and there?'

'She hadn't got them with her.'

'Perfectly. How long would it take her to fetch them from her room? Or from any hiding-place in the house? You need not answer. I will tell you. Probably about two minutes and a half! Yet she asks for ten minutes. Why? Clearly she has to obtain them from some other person, and to reason or argue with that person before they give them up. Now, what person could that be? Not Mrs Conrad, clearly, but a member of her own family, her husband or son. Which is it likely to be? Leonard Weardale said he went straight to bed. We know that to be untrue. Supposing his mother went to his room and found it empty; supposing she came down filled with a nameless dread—he is no beauty that son of hers! She does not find him, but later she hears him deny that he ever left his room. She leaps to the conclusion that he is the thief. Hence her interview with me.

'But, *mon ami*, we know something that Lady Juliet does not. We know that her son could not have been in the study, because he was on the stairs, making love to the pretty French maid. Although she does not know it, Leonard Weardale has an alibi.'

'Well, then, who did steal the papers? We seem to have eliminated everybody—Lady Juliet, her son, Mrs Conrad, the French maid—'

'Exactly. Use your little grey cells, my friend. The solution stares you in the face.'

I shook my head blankly.

'But yes! If you would only persevere! See, then, Fitzroy goes out of the study; he leaves the papers on the desk. A few minutes later Lord Alloway enters the room, goes to the desk, and the papers are gone. Only two things are possible: either Fitzroy did *not* leave the papers on the desk, but put them in his pocket—and that is not reasonable, because, as Alloway pointed out, he could have taken a tracing at his own convenience any time—or else the papers were still on the desk when Lord Alloway went to it—in which case they went into his pocket.'

'Lord Alloway the thief,' I said, dumbfounded. 'But why? Why?'

'Did you not tell me of some scandal in the past? He was exonerated, you said. But suppose, after all, it had been true? In English public life there must be no scandal. If this were raked up and proved against him now—goodbye to his political career. We will suppose that he was being blackmailed, and the price asked was the submarine plans.'

'But the man's a black traitor!' I cried.

'Oh no, he is not. He is clever and resourceful. Supposing, my friend, that he copied those plans, making—for he is a

198

clever engineer—a slight alteration in each part which will render them quite impractible. He hands the faked plans to the enemy's agent—Mrs Conrad, I fancy; but in order that no suspicion of their genuineness may arise, the plans must seem to be stolen. He does his best to throw no suspicion on anyone in the house, by pretending to see a man leaving the window. But there he ran up against the obstinacy of the Admiral. So his next anxiety is that no suspicion shall fall on Fitzroy.'

'This is all guesswork on your part, Poirot,' I objected.

'It is psychology, *mon ami*. A man who had handed over the real plans would not be overscrupulous as to who was likely to fall under suspicion. And why was he so anxious that no details of the robbery should be given to Mrs Conrad? Because he had handed over the faked plans earlier in the evening, and did not want her to know that the theft could only have taken place later.'

'I wonder if you are right,' I said.

'Of course I am right. I spoke to Alloway as one great man to another—and he understood perfectly. You will see.'

One thing is quite certain. On the day when Lord Alloway became Prime Minister, a cheque and a signed photograph arrived; on the photograph were the words: '*To my discreet friend, Hercule Poirot—from Alloway.*'

I believe that the Z type of submarine is causing great exultation in naval circles. They say it will revolutionize modern naval warfare. I have heard that a certain foreign power essayed to construct something of the same kind and the result was a dismal failure. But I still consider that Poirot was guessing. He will do it once too often one of these days.

The Third-Floor Flat

'Bother!' said Pat.

With a deepening frown she rummaged wildly in the silken trifle she called an evening bag. Two young men and another girl watched her anxiously. They were all standing outside the closed door of Patricia Garnett's flat.

'It's no good,' said Pat. 'It's not there. And now what shall we do?'

'What is life without a latchkey?' murmured Jimmy Faulkener.

He was a short, broad-shouldered young man, with good-tempered blue eyes.

Pat turned on him angrily. 'Don't make jokes, Jimmy. This is serious.'

'Look again, Pat,' said Donovan Bailey. 'It must be there somewhere.'

He had a lazy, pleasant voice that matched his lean, dark figure.

'If you ever brought it out,' said the other girl, Mildred Hope.

'Of course I brought it out,' said Pat. 'I believe I gave it to one of you two.' She turned on the men accusingly. 'I told Donovan to take it for me.'

But she was not to find a scapegoat so easily. Donovan put in a firm disclaimer, and Jimmy backed him up.

'I saw you put it in your bag, myself,' said Jimmy.

'Well, then, one of you dropped it out when you picked up my bag. I've dropped it once or twice.'

'Once or twice!' said Donovan. 'You've dropped it a dozen times at least, besides leaving it behind on every possible occasion.'

'I can't see why everything on earth doesn't drop out of it the whole time,' said Jimmy.

'The point is—how are we going to get in?' said Mildred.

She was a sensible girl, who kept to the point, but she was not nearly so attractive as the impulsive and troublesome Pat.

All four of them regarded the closed door blankly.

'Couldn't the porter help?' suggested Jimmy. 'Hasn't he got a master key or something of that kind?'

Pat shook her head. There were only two keys. One was inside the flat hung up in the kitchen and the other was—or should be—in the maligned bag.

'If only the flat were on the ground floor,' wailed Pat. 'We could have broken open a window or something. Donovan, you wouldn't like to be a cat burglar, would you?'

Donovan declined firmly but politely to be a cat burglar.

'A flat on the fourth floor is a bit of an undertaking,' said Jimmy.

'How about a fire-escape?' suggested Donovan.

'There isn't one.'

'There should be,' said Jimmy. 'A building five storeys high ought to have a fire escape.'

'I dare say,' said Pat. 'But what should be doesn't help us. How am I ever to get into my flat?'

'Isn't there a sort of thingummybob?' said Donovan. 'A thing the tradesmen send up chops and brussels sprouts in?'

'The service lift,' said Pat. 'Oh yes, but it's only a sort of wire-basket thing. Oh wait—I know. What about the coal lift?'

'Now that,' said Donovan, 'is an idea.'

Mildred made a discouraging suggestion. 'It'll be bolted,' she said. 'In Pat's kitchen, I mean, on the inside.'

But the idea was instantly negatived.

'Don't you believe it,' said Donovan.

'Not in *Pat's* kitchen,' said Jimmy. 'Pat never locks and bolts things.'

'I don't think it's bolted,' said Pat. 'I took the dustbin off this morning, and I'm sure I never bolted it afterwards, and I don't think I've been near it since.'

'Well,' said Donovan, 'that fact's going to be very useful to us tonight, but, all the same, young Pat, let me point out to you that these slack habits are leaving you at the mercy of burglars—non-feline—every night.'

Pat disregarded these admonitions.

'Come on,' she cried, and began racing down the four flights of stairs. The others followed her. Pat led them through a dark recess, apparently full to overflowing of perambulators, and through another door into the well of the flats, and guided them to the right lift. There was, at the moment, a dustbin on it. Donovan lifted it off and stepped gingerly on to the platform in its place. He wrinkled up his nose.

'A little noisome,' he remarked. 'But what of that? Do I go alone on this venture or is anyone coming with me?'

'I'll come, too,' said Jimmy.

He stepped on by Donovan's side.

'I suppose the lift will bear me,' he added doubtfully.

'You can't weigh much more than a ton of coal,' said Pat, who had never been particularly strong on her weights-and-measures table.

'And, anyway, we shall soon find out,' said Donovan cheerfully, as he hauled on the rope.

With a grinding noise they disappeared from sight.

'This thing makes an awful noise,' remarked Jimmy, as they passed up through blackness. 'What will the people in the other flats think?'

'Ghosts or burglars, I expect,' said Donovan. 'Hauling this rope is quite heavy work. The porter of Friars Mansions does more work than I ever suspected. I say, Jimmy, old son, are you counting the floors?'

'Oh, Lord! No. I forgot about it.'

'Well, I have, which is just as well. That's the third we're passing now. The next is ours.'

'And now, I suppose,' grumbled Jimmy, 'we shall find that Pat did bolt the door after all.'

But these fears were unfounded. The wooden door swung back at a touch, and Donovan and Jimmy stepped out into the inky blacknesss of Pat's kitchen.

'We ought to have a torch for this wild night work,' explained Donovan. 'If I know Pat, everything's on the floor, and we shall smash endless crockery before I can

204

get to the light switch. Don't move about, Jimmy, till I get the light on.'

He felt his way cautiously over the floor, uttering one fervent 'Damn!' as a corner of the kitchen table took him unawares in the ribs. He reached the switch, and in another moment another 'Damn!' floated out of the darkness.

'What's the matter?' asked Jimmy.

'Light won't come on. Dud bulb, I suppose. Wait a minute. I'll turn the sitting-room light on.'

The sitting-room was the door immediately across the passage. Jimmy heard Donovan go out of the door, and presently fresh muffled curses reached him. He himself edged his way cautiously across the kitchen.

'What's the matter?'

'I don't know. Rooms get bewitched at night, I believe. Everything seems to be in a different place. Chairs and tables where you least expected them. Oh, hell! Here's another!'

But at this moment Jimmy fortunately connected with the electric-light switch and pressed it down. In another minute two young men were looking at each other in silent horror.

This room was not Pat's sitting-room. They were in the wrong flat.

To begin with, the room was about ten times more crowded than Pat's, which explained Donovan's pathetic bewilderment at repeatedly cannoning into chairs and tables. There was a large round table in the centre of the room covered with a baize cloth, and there was an aspidistra in the window. It was, in fact, the kind of room whose owner,

205

the young men felt sure, would be difficult to explain to. With silent horror they gazed down at the table, on which lay a little pile of letters.

'Mrs Ernestine Grant,' breathed Donovan, picking them up and reading the name. 'Oh, help! Do you think she's heard us?'

'It's a miracle she hasn't heard you,' said Jimmy. 'What with your language and the way you've been crashing into the furniture. Come on, for the Lord's sake, let's get out of here quickly.'

They hastily switched off the light and retraced their steps on tiptoe to the lift. Jimmy breathed a sigh of relief as they regained the fastness of its depths without further incident.

'I do like a woman to be a good, sound sleeper,' he said approvingly. 'Mrs Ernestine Grant has her points.'

'I see it now,' said Donovan; 'why we made the mistake in the floor, I mean. Out in that well we started up from the basement.'

He heaved on the rope, and the lift shot up. 'We're right this time.'

'I devoutly trust we are,' said Jimmy as he stepped out into another inky void. 'My nerves won't stand many more shocks of this kind.'

But no further nerve strain was imposed. The first click of the light showed them Pat's kitchen, and in another minute they were opening the front door and admitting the two girls who were waiting outside.

'You have been a long time,' grumbled Pat. 'Mildred and I have been waiting here ages.'

'We've had an adventure,' said Donovan. 'We might have been hauled off to the police-station as dangerous malefactors.'

Pat had passed on into the sitting-room, where she switched on the light and dropped her wrap on the sofa. She listened with lively interest to Donovan's account of his adventures.

'I'm glad she didn't catch you,' she commented. 'I'm sure she's an old curmudgeon. I got a note from her this morning—wanted to see me some time—something she had to complain about—my piano, I suppose. People who don't like pianos over their heads shouldn't come and live in flats. I say, Donovan, you've hurt your hand. It's all over blood. Go and wash it under the tap.'

Donovan looked down at his hand in surprise. He went out of the room obediently and presently his voice called to Jimmy.

'Hullo,' said the other, 'what's up? You haven't hurt yourself badly, have you?'

'I haven't hurt myself at all.'

There was something so queer in Donovan's voice that Jimmy stared at him in surprise. Donovan held out his washed hand and Jimmy saw that there was no mark or cut of any kind on it.

'That's odd,' he said, frowning. 'There was quite a lot of blood. Where did it come from?' And then suddenly he realized what his quicker-witted friend had already seen.

'By Jove,' he said. 'It must have come from that flat.' He stopped, thinking over the possibilities his words implied. 'You're sure it was—er—blood?' he said. 'Not paint?'

Donovan shook his head. 'It was blood, all right,' he said, and shivered.

They looked at each other. The same thought was clearly in each of their minds. It was Jimmy who voiced it first.

'I say,' he said awkwardly. 'Do you think we ought to—well—go down again—and have—a—look around? See it's all right, you know?'

'What about the girls?'

'We won't say anything to them. Pat's going to put on an apron and make us an omelette. We'll be back by the time they wonder where we are.'

'Oh, well, come on,' said Donovan. 'I suppose we've got to go through with it. I dare say there isn't anything really wrong.'

But his tone lacked conviction. They got into the lift and descended to the floor below. They found their way across the kitchen without much difficulty and once more switched on the sitting-room light.

'It must have been in here,' said Donovan, 'that—that I got the stuff on me. I never touched anything in the kitchen.'

He looked round him. Jimmy did the same, and they both frowned. Everything looked neat and commonplace and miles removed from any suggestion of violence or gore.

Suddenly Jimmy started violently and caught his companion's arm.

'Look!'

Donovan followed the pointing finger, and in his turn uttered an exclamation. From beneath the heavy red curtains there protruded a foot—a woman's foot in a gaping patent leather shoe.

Jimmy went to the curtains and drew them sharply apart. In the recess of the window a woman's huddled body lay on the floor, a sticky dark pool beside it. She was dead, there was no doubt of that. Jimmy was attempting to raise her up when Donovan stopped him.

'You'd better not do that. She oughtn't to be touched till the police come.'

'The police. Oh, of course. I say, Donovan, what a ghastly business. Who do you think she is? Mrs Ernestine Grant?'

'Looks like it. At any rate, if there's anyone else in the flat they're keeping jolly quiet.'

'What do we do next?' asked Jimmy. 'Run out and get a policeman or ring up from Pat's flat?'

'I should think ringing up would be best. Come on, we might as well go out the front door. We can't spend the whole night going up and down in that evil-smelling lift.'

Jimmy agreed. Just as they were passing through the door he hesitated. 'Look here; do you think one of us ought to stay—just to keep an eye on things—till the police come?'

'Yes, I think you're right. If you'll stay I'll run up and telephone.'

He ran quickly up the stairs and rang the bell of the flat above. Pat came to open it, a very pretty Pat with a flushed face and a cooking apron on. Her eyes widened in surprise.

'You? But how—Donovan, what is it? Is anything the matter?'

He took both her hands in his. 'It's all right, Pat—only we've made a rather unpleasant discovery in the flat below. A woman—dead.'

'Oh!' She gave a little gasp. 'How horrible. Has she had a fit or something?'

'No. It looks—well—it looks rather as though she had been murdered.'

'Oh, Donovan!'

'I know. It's pretty beastly.'

Her hands were still in his. She had left them there—was even clinging to him. Darling Pat—how he loved her. Did she care at all for him? Sometimes he thought she did. Sometimes he was afraid that Jimmy Faulkener—remembrances of Jimmy waiting patiently below made him start guiltily.

'Pat, dear, we must telephone to the police.'

'Monsieur is right,' said a voice behind him. 'And in the meantime, while we are waiting their arrival, perhaps I can be of some slight assistance.'

They had been standing in the doorway of the flat, and now they peered out on the landing. A figure was standing on the stairs a little way above them. It moved down and into their range of vision.

They stood staring at the little man with a very fierce moustache and an egg-shaped head. He wore a resplendent dressing-gown and embroidered slippers. He bowed gallantly to Patricia.

'Mademoiselle!' he said. 'I am, as perhaps you know, the tenant of the flat above. I like to be up high—the air—the view over London. I take the flat in the name of Mr O'Connor. But I am not an Irishman. I have another name. That is why I venture to put myself at your service. Permit me.' With a flourish he pulled out a card and handed it to Pat. She read it.

'M. Hercule Poirot. Oh!' She caught her breath.

'*The* M. Poirot! The great detective? And you will really help?'

'That is my intention, mademoiselle. I nearly offered my help earlier in the evening.'

Pat looked puzzled.

'I heard you discussing how to gain admission to your flat. Me, I am very clever at picking locks. I could, without doubt, have opened your door for you, but I hesitated to suggest it. You would have had the grave suspicions of me.'

Pat laughed.

'Now, monsieur,' said Poirot to Donovan. 'Go in, I pray of you, and telephone to the police. I will descend to the flat below.'

Pat came down the stairs with him. They found Jimmy on guard, and Pat explained Poirot's presence. Jimmy, in his turn, explained to Poirot his and Donovan's adventures. The detective listened attentively.

'The lift door was unbolted, you say? You emerged into the kitchen, but the light it would not turn on.'

He directed his footsteps to the kitchen as he spoke. His fingers pressed the switch.

'*Tiens*! *Voilà ce qui est curieux*!' he said as the light flashed on. 'It functions perfectly now. I wonder—' He held up a finger to ensure silence and listened. A faint sound broke the stillness—the sound of an unmistakable snore. 'Ah!' said Poirot. '*La chambre de domestique.*'

He tiptoed across the kitchen into a little pantry, out of which led a door. He opened the door and switched on the light. The room was the kind of dog kennel designed by the builders of flats to accommodate a human being. The floor space was almost entirely occupied by the bed. In the bed was a rosy-cheeked girl lying on her back with her mouth wide open, snoring placidly.

Poirot switched off the light and beat a retreat.

'She will not wake,' he said. 'We will let her sleep till the police come.'

He went back to the sitting-room. Donovan had joined them.

'The police will be here almost immediately, they say,' he said breathlessly. 'We are to touch nothing.'

Poirot nodded. 'We will not touch,' he said. 'We will look, that is all.'

He moved into the room. Mildred had come down with Donovan, and all four young people stood in the doorway and watched him with breathless interest.

'What I can't understand, sir, is this,' said Donovan. 'I never went near the window—how did the blood come on my hand?'

'My young friend, the answer to that stares you in the face. Of what colour is the tablecloth? Red, is it not? and doubtless you did put your hand on the table.'

'Yes, I did. Is that—? He stopped.

Poirot nodded. He was bending over the table. He indicated with his hand a dark patch on the red.

'It was here that the crime was committed,' he said solemnly. 'The body was moved afterwards.'

Then he stood upright and looked slowly round the room. He did not move, he handled nothing, but nevertheless the four watching felt as though every object in that rather frowsty place gave up its secret to his observant eye.

Hercule Poirot nodded his head as though satisfied. A little sigh escaped him. 'I see,' he said.

'You see what?' asked Donovan curiously.

'I see,' said Poirot, 'what you doubtless felt—that the room is overfull of furniture.'

Donovan smiled ruefully. 'I did go barging about a bit,' he confessed. 'Of course, everything was in a different place to Pat's room, and I couldn't make it out.'

'Not everything,' said Poirot.

Donovan looked at him inquiringly.

'I mean,' said Poirot apologetically, 'that certain things are always fixed. In a block of flats the door, the window, the fireplace—they are in the same place in the rooms which are below each other.'

'Isn't that rather splitting hairs?' asked Mildred. She was looking at Poirot with faint disapproval.

'One should always speak with absolute accuracy. That is a little—how do you say?—fad of mine.'

There was the noise of footsteps on the stairs, and three men came in. They were a police inspector, a constable,

213

and the divisional surgeon. The inspector recognized Poirot and greeted him in an almost reverential manner. Then he turned to the others.

'I shall want statements from everyone,' he began, 'but in the first place—'

Poirot interrupted. 'A little suggestion. We will go back to the flat upstairs and mademoiselle here shall do what she was planning to do—make us an omelette. Me, I have a passion for the omelettes. Then, *M. l'Inspecteur*, when you have finished here, you will mount to us and ask questions at your leisure.'

It was arranged accordingly, and Poirot went up with them.

'M. Poirot,' said Pat, 'I think you're a perfect dear. And you shall have a lovely omelette. I really make omelettes frightfully well.'

'That is good. Once, mademoiselle, I loved a beautiful young English girl, who resembled you greatly—but alas!— she could not cook. So perhaps everything was for the best.'

There was a faint sadness in his voice, and Jimmy Faulkener looked at him curiously.

Once in the flat, however, he exerted himself to please and amuse. The grim tragedy below was almost forgotten.

The omelette had been consumed and duly praised by the time that Inspector Rice's footsteps were heard. He came in accompanied by the doctor, having left the constable below.

'Well, Monsieur Poirot,' he said. 'It all seems clear and above-board—not much in your line, though we may find it hard to catch the man. I'd just like to hear how the discovery came to be made.'

Donovan and Jimmy between them recounted the happenings of the evening. The inspector turned reproachfully to Pat.

'You shouldn't leave your lift door unbolted, miss. You really shouldn't.'

'I shan't again,' said Pat, with a shiver. 'Somebody might come in and murder me like that poor woman below.'

'Ah, but they didn't come in that way, though,' said the inspector.

'You will recount to us what you have discovered, yes?' said Poirot.

'I don't know as I ought to—but seeing it's you, M. Poirot—'

'*Précisément*,' said Poirot. 'And these young people—they will be discreet.'

'The newspapers will get hold of it, anyway, soon enough,' said the inspector. 'There's no real secret about the matter. Well, the dead woman's Mrs Grant, all right. I had the porter up to identify her. Woman of about thirty-five. She was sitting at the table, and she was shot with an automatic pistol of small calibre, probably by someone sitting opposite her at table. She fell forward, and that's how the bloodstain came on the table.'

'But wouldn't someone have heard the shot?' asked Mildred.

'The pistol was fitted with a silencer. No, you wouldn't hear anything. By the way, did you hear the screech the maid let out when we told her her mistress was dead? No. Well, that just shows how unlikely it was that anyone would hear the other.'

'Has the maid no story to tell?' asked Poirot.

'It was her evening out. She's got her own key. She came in about ten o'clock. Everything was quiet. She thought her mistress had gone to bed.'

'She did not look in the sitting-room, then?'

'Yes, she took the letters in there which had come by the evening post, but she saw nothing unusual—any more than Mr Faulkener and Mr Bailey did. You see, the murderer had concealed the body rather neatly behind the curtains.'

'But it was a curious thing to do, don't you think?'

Poirot's voice was very gentle, yet it held something that made the inspector look up quickly.

'Didn't want the crime discovered till he'd had time to make his getaway.'

'Perhaps, perhaps—but continue with what you were saying.'

'The maid went out at five o'clock. The doctor here puts the time of death as—roughly—about four to five hours ago. That's right, isn't it?'

The doctor, who was a man of few words, contented himself with jerking his head affirmatively.

'It's a quarter to twelve now. The actual time can, I think, be narrowed down to a fairly definite hour.'

He took out a crumpled sheet of paper.

'We found this in the pocket of the dead woman's dress. You needn't be afraid of handling it. There are no finger-prints on it.'

Poirot smoothed out the sheet. Across it some words were printed in small, prim capitals.

I WILL COME TO SEE YOU THIS EVENING AT
HALF PAST SEVEN.
    J.F.

'A compromising document to leave behind,' commented
Poirot, as he handed it back.

'Well, he didn't know she'd got it in her pocket,' said the
inspector. 'He probably thought she'd destroyed it. We've
evidence that he was a careful man, though. The pistol she
was shot with we found under the body—and there again
no fingerprints. They'd been wiped off very carefully with
a silk handkerchief.'

'How do you know,' said Poirot, 'that it was a silk
handkerchief?'

'Because we found it,' said the inspector triumphantly.
'At the last, as he was drawing the curtains, he must have
let it fall unnoticed.'

He handed across a big white silk handkerchief—a good-
quality handkerchief. It did not need the inspector's finger to
draw Poirot's attention to the mark on it in the centre. It was
neatly marked and quite legible. Poirot read the name out.

'John Fraser.'

'That's it,' said the inspector. 'John Fraser—J.F. in the
note. We know the name of the man we have to look for,
and I dare say when we find out a little about the dead
woman, and her relations come forward, we shall soon get
a line on him.'

'I wonder,' said Poirot. 'No, *mon cher*, somehow I do
not think he will be easy to find, your John Fraser. He is a

Agatha Christie

strange man—careful, since he marks his handkerchiefs and wipes the pistol with which he has committed the crime—yet careless since he loses his handkerchief and does not search for a letter that might incriminate him.'

'Flurried, that's what he was,' said the inspector.

'It is possible,' said Poirot. 'Yes, it is possible. And he was not seen entering the building?'

'There are all sorts of people going in and out all the time. These are big blocks. I suppose none of you—' he addressed the four collectively—'saw anyone coming out of the flat?'

Pat shook her head. 'We went out earlier—about seven o'clock.'

'I see.' The inspector rose. Poirot accompanied him to the door.

'As a little favour, may I examine the flat below?'

'Why, certainly, M. Poirot. I know what they think of you at headquarters. I'll leave you a key. I've got two. It will be empty. The maid cleared out to some relatives, too scared to stay there alone.'

'I thank you,' said M. Poirot. He went back into the flat, thoughtful.

'You're not satisfied, M. Poirot?' said Jimmy.

'No,' said Poirot. 'I am not satisfied.'

Donovan looked at him curiously. 'What is it that—well, worries you?'

Poirot did not answer. He remained silent for a minute or two, frowning, as though in thought, then he made a sudden impatient movement of the shoulders.

218

'I will say good night to you, mademoiselle. You must be tired. You have had much cooking to do—eh?'

Pat laughed. 'Only the omelette. I didn't do dinner. Donovan and Jimmy came and called for us, and we went out to a little place in Soho.'

'And then without doubt, you went to a theatre?'

'Yes. *The Brown Eyes of Caroline*.'

'Ah!' said Poirot. 'It should have been blue eyes—the blue eyes of mademoiselle.'

He made a sentimental gesture, and then once more wished Pat good night, also Mildred, who was staying the night by special request, as Pat admitted frankly that she would get the horrors if left alone on this particular night.

The two young men accompanied Poirot. When the door was shut, and they were preparing to say goodbye to him on the landing, Poirot forestalled them.

'My young friends, you heard me say I was not satisfied? *Eh bien*, it is true—I am not. I go now to make some little investigations of my own. You would like to accompany me—yes?'

An eager assent greeted this proposal. Poirot led the way to the flat below and inserted the key the inspector had given him in the lock. On entering, he did not, as the others had expected, enter the sitting-room. Instead he went straight to the kitchen. In a little recess which served as a scullery a big iron bin was standing. Poirot uncovered this and, doubling himself up, began to rootle in it with the energy of a ferocious terrier.

Both Jimmy and Donovan stared at him in amazement.

Agatha Christie

Suddenly with a cry of triumph he emerged. In his hand he held aloft a small stoppered bottle.

'*Voilà!*' he said. 'I find what I seek.' He sniffed at it delicately. 'Alas! I am *enrhumé*—I have the cold in the head.'

Donovan took the bottle from him and sniffed in his turn, but could smell nothing. He took out the stopper and held the bottle to his nose before Poirot's warning cry could stop him.

Immediately he fell like a log. Poirot, by springing forward, partly broke his fall.

'Imbecile!' he cried. 'The idea. To remove the stopper in that foolhardy manner! Did he not observe how delicately I handled it? Monsieur—Faulkener—is it not? Will you be so good as to get me a little brandy? I observed a decanter in the sitting-room.'

Jimmy hurried off, but by the time he returned, Donovan was sitting up and declaring himself quite all right again. He had to listen to a short lecture from Poirot on the necessity of caution in sniffing at possibly poisonous substances.

'I think I'll be off home,' said Donovan, rising shakily to his feet. 'That is, if I can't be any more use here. I feel a bit wonky still.'

'Assuredly,' said Poirot. 'That is the best thing you can do. M. Faulkener, attend me here a little minute. I will return on the instant.'

He accompanied Donovan to the door and beyond. They remained outside on the landing talking for some minutes. When Poirot at last re-entered the flat he found Jimmy standing in the sitting-room gazing round him with puzzled eyes.

'Well, M. Poirot,' he said, 'what next?'

'There is nothing next. The case is finished.'

'What?'

'I know everything—now.'

Jimmy stared at him. 'That little bottle you found?'

'Exactly. That little bottle.'

Jimmy shook his head. 'I can't make head or tail of it. For some reason or other I can see you are dissatisfied with the evidence against this John Fraser, whoever he may be.'

'Whoever he may be,' repeated Poirot softly. 'If he is anyone at all—well, I shall be surprised.'

'I don't understand.'

'He is a name—that is all—a name carefully marked on a handkerchief!'

'And the letter?'

'Did you notice that it was printed? Now, why? I will tell you. Handwriting might be recognized, and a typewritten letter is more easily traced than you would imagine—but if a real John Fraser wrote that letter those two points would not have appealed to him! No, it was written on purpose, and put in the dead woman's pocket for us to find. There is no such person as John Fraser.'

Jimmy looked at him inquiringly.

'And so,' went on Poirot, 'I went back to the point that first struck me. You heard me say that certain things in a room were always in the same place under given circumstances. I gave three instances. I might have mentioned a fourth—the electric-light switch, my friend.'

Jimmy still stared uncomprehendingly. Poirot went on.

'Your friend Donovan did not go near the window—it was by resting his hand on this table that he got it covered in blood! But I asked myself at once—why did he rest it there? What was he doing groping about this room in darkness? For remember, my friend, the electric-light switch is always in the same place—by the door. Why, when he came to this room, did he not at once feel for the light and turn it on? That was the natural, the normal thing to do. According to him, he tried to turn on the light in the kitchen, but failed. Yet when I tried the switch it was in perfect working order. Did he, then, not wish the light to go on just then? If it had gone on you would both have seen at once that you were in the wrong flat. There would have been no reason to come into this room.'

'What are you driving at, M. Poirot? I don't understand. What do you mean?'

'I mean—this.'

Poirot held up a Yale door key.

'The key of this flat?'

'No, *mon ami*, the key of the flat above. Mademoiselle Patricia's key, which M. Donovan Bailey abstracted from her bag some time during the evening.'

'But why—why?'

'*Parbleu*! So that he could do what he wanted to do—gain admission to this flat in a perfectly unsuspicious manner. He made sure that the lift door was unbolted earlier in the evening.'

'Where did you get the key?'

Poirot's smile broadened. 'I found it just now—where I looked for it—in M. Donovan's pocket. See you, that little bottle I pretended to find was a ruse. M. Donovan is taken in. He does what I knew he would do—unstoppers it and sniffs. And in that little bottle is ethyl chloride, a very powerful instant anaesthetic. It gives me just the moment or two of unconsciousness I need. I take from his pocket the two things that I knew would be there. This key was one of them—the other—'

He stopped and then went on.

'I questioned at the time the reason the inspector gave for the body being concealed behind the curtain. To gain time? No, there was more than that. And so I thought of just one thing—the post, my friend. The evening post that comes at half past nine or thereabouts. Say the murderer does not find something he expects to find, but that something may be delivered by post later. Clearly, then, he must come back. But the crime must not be discovered by the maid when she comes in, or the police would take possession of the flat, so he hides the body behind the curtain. And the maid suspects nothing and lays the letters on the table as usual.'

'The letters?'

'Yes, the letters.' Poirot drew something from his pocket. 'This is the second article I took from M. Donovan when he was unconscious.' He showed the superscription—a type-written envelope addressed to Mrs Ernestine Grant. 'But I will ask you one thing first. M. Faulkener, before we look at the contents of this letter. Are you or are you not in love with Mademoiselle Patricia?'

'I care for Pat damnably—but I've never thought I had a chance.'

'You thought that she cared for M. Donovan? It may be that she had begun to care for him—but it was only a beginning, my friend. It is for you to make her forget—to stand by her in her trouble.'

'Trouble?' said Jimmy sharply.

'Yes, trouble. We will do all we can to keep her name out of it, but it will be impossible to do so entirely. She was, you see, the motive.'

He ripped open the envelope that he held. An enclosure fell out. The covering letter was brief, and was from a firm of solicitors.

Dear Madam,
    The document you enclose is quite in order, and the fact of the marriage having taken place in a foreign country does not invalidate it in any way.
    Yours truly, etc.

Poirot spread out the enclosure. It was a certificate of marriage between Donovan Bailey and Ernestine Grant, dated eight years ago.

'Oh, my God!' said Jimmy. 'Pat said she'd had a letter from the woman asking to see her, but she never dreamed it was anything important.'

Poirot nodded. 'Donovan knew—he went to see his wife this evening before going to the flat above—a strange irony, by the way, that led the unfortunate woman to come to this building where her rival lived—he murdered her in cold blood, and then went on to his evening's amusement. His wife must have told him that she had sent the marriage certificate to her solicitors and was expecting to hear from them. Doubtless he himself had tried to make her believe that there was a flaw in the marriage.'

'He seemed in quite good spirits, too, all the evening. M. Poirot, you haven't let him escape?' Jimmy shuddered.

'There is no escape for him,' said Poirot gravely. 'You need not fear.'

'It's Pat I'm thinking about mostly,' said Jimmy. 'You don't think—she really cared.'

'*Mon ami*, that is your part,' said Poirot gently. 'To make her turn to you and forget. I do not think you will find it very difficult!'

Double Sin

I had called in at my friend Poirot's rooms to find him sadly overworked. So much had he become the rage that every rich woman who had mislaid a bracelet or lost a pet kitten rushed to secure the services of the great Hercule Poirot. My little friend was a strange mixture of Flemish thrift and artistic fervour. He accepted many cases in which he had little interest owing to the first instinct being predominant.

He also undertook cases in which there was a little or no monetary reward sheerly because the problem involved interested him. The result was that, as I say, he was overworking himself. He admitted as much himself, and I found little difficulty in persuading him to accompany me for a week's holiday to that well-known South Coast resort, Ebermouth.

We had spent four very agreeable days when Poirot came to me, an open letter in his hand.

'*Mon ami*, you remember my friend Joseph Aarons, the theatrical agent?'

I assented after a moment's thought. Poirot's friends are so many and so varied, and range from dustmen to dukes.

'*Eh bien*, Hastings, Joseph Aarons finds himself at Charlock Bay. He is far from well, and there is a little affair that it seems is worrying him. He begs me to go over and see him. I think, *mon ami*, that I must accede to his request. He is a faithful friend, the good Joseph Aarons, and has done much to assist me in the past.'

'Certainly, if you think so,' I said. 'I believe Charlock Bay is a beautiful spot, and as it happens I've never been there.'

'Then we combine business with pleasure,' said Poirot. 'You will inquire the trains, yes?'

'It will probably mean a change or two,' I said with a grimace. 'You know what these cross-country lines are. To go from the South Devon Coast to the North Devon coast is sometimes a day's journey.'

However, on inquiry, I found that the journey could be accomplished by only one change at Exeter and that the trains were good. I was hastening back to Poirot with the information when I happened to pass the offices of the Speedy cars and saw written up:

> *Tomorrow. All-day excursion to Charlock Bay. Starting 8.30 through some of the most beautiful scenery in Devon.*

I inquired a few particulars and returned to the hotel full of enthusiasm. Unfortunately, I found it hard to make Poirot share my feelings.

'My friend, why this passion for the motor coach? The train, see you, it is sure? The tyres, they do not burst; the accidents, they do not happen. One is not incommoded by too much air. The windows can be shut and no draughts admitted.'

I hinted delicately that the advantage of fresh air was what attracted me most to the motor-coach scheme.

'And if it rains? Your English climate is so uncertain.'

'There's a hood and all that. Besides, if it rains badly, the excursion doesn't take place.'

'Ah!' said Poirot. 'Then let us hope that it rains.'

'Of course, if you feel like that and...'

'No, no, *mon ami*. I see that you have set your heart on the trip. Fortunately, I have my greatcoat with me and two mufflers.' He sighed. 'But shall we have sufficient time at Charlock Bay?'

'Well, I'm afraid it means staying the night there. You see, the tour goes round by Dartmoor. We have lunch at Monkhampton. We arrive at Charlock Bay about four o'clock, and the coach starts back at five, arriving here at ten o'clock.'

'So!' said Poirot. 'And there are people who do this for pleasure! We shall, of course, get a reduction of the fare since we do not make the return journey?'

'I hardly think that's likely.'

'You must insist.'

'Come now, Poirot, don't be mean. You know you're coining money.'

'My friend, it is not the meanness. It is the business sense. If I were a millionaire, I would pay only what was just and right.'

As I had foreseen, however, Poirot was doomed to fail in this respect. The gentleman who issued tickets at the Speedy office was calm and unimpassioned but adamant.

His point was that we ought to return. He even implied that we ought to pay extra for the privilege of leaving the coach at Charlock Bay.

Defeated, Poirot paid over the required sum and left the office.

'The English, they have no sense of money,' he grumbled. 'Did you observe a young man, Hastings, who paid over the full fare and yet mentioned his intention of leaving the coach at Monkhampton?'

'I don't think I did. As a matter of fact...'

'You were observing the pretty young lady who booked No. 5, the next seat to ours. Ah! Yes, my friend, I saw you. And that is why when I was on the point of taking seats No. 13 and 14—which are in the middle and as well sheltered as it is possible to be—you rudely pushed yourself forward and said that 3 and 4 would be better.'

'Really, Poirot,' I said, blushing.

'Auburn hair—always the auburn hair!'

'At any rate, she was more worth looking at than an odd young man.'

'That depends upon the point of view. To me, the young man was interesting.'

Something rather significant in Poirot's tone made me look at him quickly. 'Why? What do you mean?'

'Oh, do not excite yourself. Shall I say that he interested me because he was trying to grow a moustache and as yet the result is poor.' Poirot stroked his own magnificent moustache tenderly. 'It is an art,' he murmured, 'the growing of the moustache! I have sympathy for all who attempt it.'

It is always difficult with Poirot to know when he is serious and when he is merely amusing himself at one's expense. I judged it safest to say no more.

The following morning dawned bright and sunny. A really glorious day! Poirot, however, was taking no chances. He wore a woolly waistcoat, a mackintosh, a heavy overcoat, and two mufflers, in addition to wearing his thickest suit. He also swallowed two tablets of 'Anti-grippe' before starting and packed a further supply.

We took a couple of small suitcases with us. The pretty girl we had noticed the day before had a small suitcase, and so did the young man whom I gathered to have been the object of Poirot's sympathy. Otherwise, there was no luggage. The four pieces were stowed away by the driver, and we all took our places.

Poirot, rather maliciously, I thought, assigned me the outside place as 'I had the mania for the fresh air' and himself occupied the seat next to our fair neighbour. Presently, however, he made amends. The man in seat 6 was a noisy fellow, inclined to be facetious and boisterous, and Poirot asked the girl in a low voice if she would like to change seats with him. She agreed gratefully, and the change having been effected, she entered into conversation with us and we were soon all three chattering together merrily.

She was evidently quite young, not more than nineteen, and as ingenuous as a child. She soon confided to us the reason for her trip. She was going, it seemed, on business for her aunt who kept a most interesting antique shop in Ebermouth.

This aunt had been left in very reduced circumstances on the death of her father and had used her small capital and a houseful of beautiful things which her father had left her to start in business. She had been extremely successful and had made quite a name for herself in the trade. This girl, Mary Durrant, had come to be with her aunt and learn the business and was very excited about it—much preferring it to the other alternative—becoming a nursery governess or companion.

Poirot nodded interest and approval to all this.

'Mademoiselle will be successful, I am sure,' he said gallantly. 'But I will give her a little word of advice. Do not be too trusting, mademoiselle. Everywhere in the world there are rogues and vagabonds, even it may be on this very coach of ours. One should always be on the guard, suspicious!'

She stared at him open-mouthed, and he nodded sapiently.

'But yes, it is as I say. Who knows? Even I who speak to you may be a malefactor of the worst description.'

And he twinkled more than ever at her surprised face.

We stopped for lunch at Monkhampton, and, after a few words with the waiter, Poirot managed to secure us a small table for three close by the window. Outside, in a big courtyard, about twenty char-à-bancs were parked—char-à-bancs which had come from all over the country. The hotel dining-room was full, and the noise was rather considerable.

'One can have altogether too much of the holiday spirit,' I said with a grimace.

Mary Durrant agreed. 'Ebermouth is quite spoiled in the summers nowadays. My aunt says it used to be quite different. Now one can hardly get along the pavements for the crowd.'

'But it is good for business, mademoiselle.'

'Not for ours particularly. We sell only rare and valuable things. We do not go in for cheap bric-a-brac. My aunt has clients all over England. If they want a particular period table or chair, or a certain piece of china, they write to her, and, sooner or later, she gets it for them. That is what has happened in this case.'

We looked interested and she went on to explain. A certain American gentleman, Mr J. Baker Wood, was a connoisseur and collector of miniatures. A very valuable set of miniatures had recently come into the market, and Miss Elizabeth Penn—Mary's aunt—had purchased them. She had written to Mr Wood describing the miniatures and naming a price. He had replied at once, saying that he was prepared to purchase if the miniatures were as represented and asking that someone should be sent with them for him to see where he was staying at Charlock Bay. Miss Durrant had accordingly been despatched, acting as representative for the firm.

'They're lovely things, of course,' she said. 'But I can't imagine anyone paying all that money for them. Five hundred pounds! Just think of it! They're by Cosway. Is it Cosway I mean? I get so mixed up in these things.'

Poirot smiled. 'You are not yet experienced, eh, mademoiselle?'

'I've had no training,' said Mary ruefully. 'We weren't brought up to know about old things. It's a lot to learn.'

She sighed. Then suddenly, I saw her eyes widen in surprise. She was sitting facing the window, and her glance now was directed out of that window, into the courtyard. With a hurried word, she rose from her seat and almost ran out of the room. She returned in a few moments, breathless and apologetic.

'I'm so sorry rushing off like that. But I thought I saw a man taking my suitcase out of the coach. I went flying after him, and it turned out to be his own. It's one almost exactly like mine. I felt like such a fool. It looked as though I were accusing him of stealing it.'

She laughed at the idea.

Poirot, however, did not laugh. 'What man was it, mademoiselle? Describe him to me.'

'He had on a brown suit. A thin weedy young man with a very indeterminate moustache.'

'Aha,' said Poirot. 'Our friend of yesterday, Hastings. You know this young man, mademoiselle? You have seen him before?'

'No, never. Why?'

'Nothing. It is rather curious—that is all.'

He relapsed into silence and took no further part in the conversation until something Mary Durrant said caught his attention.

'Eh, mademoiselle, what is that you say?'

'I said that on my return journey I should have to be careful of "malefactors", as you call them. I believe Mr Wood always pays for things in cash. If I have five hundred pounds in notes on me, I shall be worth some malefactor's attention.'

She laughed but Poirot did not respond. Instead, he asked her what hotel she proposed to stay at in Charlock Bay.

'The Anchor Hotel. It is small and not expensive, but quite good.'

'So!' said Poirot. 'The Anchor Hotel. Precisely where Hastings here has made up his mind to stay. How odd!'

He twinkled at me.

'You are staying long in Charlock Bay?' asked Mary.

'One night only. I have business there. You could not guess, I am sure, what my profession is, mademoiselle?'

I saw Mary consider several possibilities and reject them— probably from a feeling of caution. At last, she hazarded the suggestion that Poirot was a conjurer. He was vastly entertained.

'Ah! But it is an idea that! You think I take the rabbits out of the hat? No, mademoiselle. Me, I am the opposite of a conjurer. The conjurer, he makes things disappear. Me, I make things that have disappeared, reappear.' He leaned forward dramatically so as to give the words full effect. 'It is a secret, mademoiselle, but I will tell you, I am a detective!'

He leaned back in his chair pleased with the effect he had created. Mary Durrant stared at him spellbound. But any further conversation was barred for the braying of various horns outside announced that the road monsters were ready to proceed.

As Poirot and I went out together I commented on the charm of our luncheon companion. Poirot agreed.

'Yes, she is charming. But, also rather silly?'

'Silly?'

'Do not be outraged. A girl may be beautiful and have auburn hair and yet be silly. It is the height of foolishness to take two strangers into her confidence as she has done.'

'Well, she could see we were all right.'

'That is imbecile, what you say, my friend. Anyone who knows his job—naturally he will appear "all right". That little one she talked of being careful when she would have five hundred pounds in money with her. But she has five hundred pounds with her now.'

'In miniatures.'

'Exactly. In miniatures. And between one and the other, there is no great difference, *mon ami*.'

'But no one knew about them except us.'

'And the waiter and the people at the next table. And, doubtless, several people in Ebermouth! Mademoiselle Durrant, she is charming, but, if I were Miss Elizabeth Penn, I would first of all instruct my new assistant in the common sense.' He paused and then said in a different voice: 'You know, my friend, it would be the easiest thing in the world to remove a suitcase from one of those char-à-bancs while we were all at luncheon.'

'Oh, come, Poirot, somebody will be sure to see.'

'And what would they see? Somebody removing his luggage. It would be done in an open and above-board manner, and it would be nobody's business to interfere.'

'Do you mean—Poirot, are you hinting—But that fellow in the brown suit—it was his own suitcase?'

Poirot frowned. 'So it seems. All the same, it is curious, Hastings, that he should have not removed his suitcase

235

before, when the car first arrived. He has not lunched here, you notice.'

'If Miss Durrant hadn't been sitting opposite the window, she wouldn't have seen him,' I said slowly.

'And since it was his own suitcase, that would not have mattered,' said Poirot. 'So let us dismiss it from our thoughts, *mon ami*.'

Nevertheless, when we had resumed our places and were speeding along once more, he took the opportunity of giving Mary Durrant a further lecture on the dangers of indiscretion which she received meekly enough but with the air of thinking it all rather a joke.

We arrived at Charlock Bay at four o'clock and were fortunate enough to be able to get rooms at the Anchor Hotel—a charming old-world inn in one of the side streets.

Poirot had just unpacked a few necessaries and was applying a little cosmetic to his moustache preparatory to going out to call upon Joseph Aarons when there came a frenzied knocking at the door. I called 'Come in,' and, to my utter amazement, Mary Durrant appeared, her face white and large tears standing in her eyes.

'I do beg your pardon—but—but the most awful thing has happened. And you did say you were a detective?' This to Poirot.

'What has happened, mademoiselle?'

'I opened my suitcase. The miniatures were in a crocodile despatch case—locked, of course. Now, look!'

She held out a small square crocodile-covered case. The lid hung loose. Poirot took it from her. The case had been forced; great strength must have been used. The marks were plain enough. Poirot examined it and nodded.

'The miniatures?' he asked, though we both knew the answer well enough.

'Gone. They've been stolen. Oh, what shall I do?'

'Don't worry,' I said. 'My friend is Hercule Poirot. You must have heard of him. He'll get them back for you if anyone can.'

'Monsieur Poirot. The great Monsieur Poirot.'

Poirot was vain enough to be pleased at the obvious reverence in her voice. 'Yes, my child,' he said. 'It is I, myself. And you can leave your little affair in my hands. I will do all that can be done. But I fear—I much fear—that it will be too late. Tell me, was the lock of your suitcase forced also?'

She shook her head.

'Let me see it, please.'

We went together to her room, and Poirot examined the suitcase closely. It had obviously been opened with a key.

'Which is simple enough. These suitcase locks are all much of the same pattern. *Eh bien*, we must ring up the police and we must also get in touch with Mr Baker Wood as soon as possible. I will attend to that myself.'

I went with him and asked what he meant by saying it might be too late. '*Mon cher*, I said today that I was the opposite of the conjurer—that I make the disappearing things reappear—but suppose someone has been before-hand with me. You do not understand? You will in a minute.'

He disappeared into the telephone box. He came out five minutes later looking very grave. 'It is as I feared. A lady called upon Mr Wood with the miniatures half an hour ago. She represented herself as coming from Miss Elizabeth Penn. He was delighted with the miniatures and paid for them forthwith.'

'Half an hour ago—before we arrived here.'

Poirot smiled rather enigmatically. 'The Speedy cars are quite speedy, but a fast motor from, say, Monkhampton would get here a good hour ahead of them at least.'

'And what do we do now?'

'The good Hastings—always practical. We inform the police, do all we can for Miss Durrant, and—yes, I think decidedly, we have an interview with Mr J. Baker Wood.'

We carried out this programme. Poor Mary Durrant was terribly upset, fearing her aunt would blame her.

'Which she probably will,' observed Poirot, as we set out for the Seaside Hotel where Mr Wood was staying. 'And with perfect justice. The idea of leaving five hundred pounds' worth of valuables in a suitcase and going to lunch! All the same, *mon ami*, there are one or two curious points about the case. That despatch box, for instance, why was it forced?'

'To get out the miniatures.'

'But was not that a foolishness? Say our thief is tampering with the luggage at lunch-time under the pretext of getting out his own. Surely it is much simpler to open the suitcase, transfer the despatch case unopened to his own suitcase, and get away, than to waste the time forcing the lock?'

'He had to make sure the miniatures were inside.'

Poirot did not look convinced, but, as we were just being shown into Mr Wood's suite, we had no time for more discussion.

I took an immediate dislike to Mr Baker Wood.

He was a large vulgar man, very much overdressed and wearing a diamond solitaire ring. He was blustering and noisy.

Of course, he'd not suspected anything amiss. Why should he? The woman said she had the miniatures all right. Very fine specimens, too! Had he the numbers of the notes? No, he hadn't. And who was Mr—er—Poirot, anyway, to come asking him all these questions?

'I will not ask you anything more, monsieur, except for one thing. A description of the woman who called upon you. Was she young and pretty?'

'No, sir, she was not. Most emphatically not. A tall woman, middle-aged, grey hair, blotchy complexion and a budding moustache. A siren? Not on your life.'

'Poirot,' I cried, as we took our departure. 'A moustache. Did you hear?'

'I have the use of my ears, thank you, Hastings!'

'But what a very unpleasant man.'

'He has not the charming manner, no.'

'Well, we ought to get the thief all right,' I remarked. 'We can identify him.'

'You are of such a naïve simplicity, Hastings. Do you not know that there is such a thing as an alibi?'

'You think he will have an alibi?'

Poirot replied unexpectedly: 'I sincerely hope so.'

'The trouble with you is,' I said, 'that you like a thing to be difficult.'

'Quite right, *mon ami*. I do not like—how do you say it—the bird who sits!'

Poirot's prophecy was fully justified. Our travelling companion in the brown suit turned out to be a Mr Norton Kane. He had gone straight to the George Hotel at Monkhampton and had been there during the afternoon. The only evidence against him was that of Miss Durrant who declared that she had seen him getting out his luggage from the car while we were at lunch.

'Which in itself is not a suspicious act,' said Poirot meditatively.

After that remark, he lapsed into silence and refused to discuss the matter any further, saying when I pressed him, that he was thinking of moustaches in general, and that I should be well advised to do the same.

I discovered, however, that he had asked Joseph Aarons—with whom he spent the evening—to give him every detail possible about Mr Baker Wood. As both men were staying at the same hotel, there was a chance of gleaning some stray crumbs of information. Whatever Poirot learned, he kept to himself, however.

Mary Durrant, after various interviews with the police, had returned to Ebermouth by an early morning train. We lunched with Joseph Aarons, and after lunch, Poirot announced to me that he had settled the theatrical agent's problem satisfactorily, and that we could return to Ebermouth as soon as we liked. 'But not by road, *mon ami*; we go by rail this time.'

'Are you afraid of having your pocket picked, or of meeting another damsel in distress?'

'Both those affairs, Hastings, might happen to me on the train. No, I am in haste to be back in Ebermouth, because I want to proceed with our case.'

'Our case?'

'But, yes, my friend. Mademoiselle Durrant appealed to me to help her. Because the matter is now in the hands of the police, it does not follow that I am free to wash my hands of it. I came here to oblige an old friend, but it shall never be said of Hercule Poirot that he deserted a stranger in need!' And he drew himself up grandiloquently.

'I think you were interested before that,' I said shrewdly. 'In the office of cars, when you first caught sight of that young man, though what drew your attention to him I don't know.'

'Don't you, Hastings? You should. Well, well, that must remain my little secret.'

We had a short conversation with the police inspector in charge of the case before leaving. He had interviewed Mr Norton Kane, and told Poirot in confidence that the young man's manner had not impressed him favourably. He had blustered, denied, and contradicted himself.

'But just how the trick was done, I don't know,' he confessed. 'He could have handed the stuff to a confederate who pushed off at once in a fast car. But that's just theory. We've got to find the car and the confederate and pin the thing down.'

Poirot nodded thoughtfully.

'Do you think that was how it was done?' I asked him, as we were seated in the train.

'No, my friend, that was not how it was done. It was cleverer than that.'

'Won't you tell me?'

'Not yet. You know—it is my weakness—I like to keep my little secrets till the end.'

'Is the end going to be soon?'

'Very soon now.'

We arrived in Ebermouth a little after six and Poirot drove at once to the shop which bore the name 'Elizabeth Penn'. The establishment was closed, but Poirot rang the bell, and presently Mary herself opened the door, and expressed surprise and delight at seeing us.

'Please come in and see my aunt,' she said.

She led us into a back room. An elderly lady came forward to meet us; she had white hair and looked rather like a miniature herself with her pink-and-white skin and her blue eyes. Round her rather bent shoulders she wore a cape of priceless old lace.

'Is this the great Monsieur Poirot?' she asked in a low charming voice. 'Mary has been telling me. I could hardly believe it. And you will really help us in our trouble. You will advise us?'

Poirot looked at her for a moment, then bowed.

'Mademoiselle Penn—the effect is charming. But you should really grow a moustache.'

Miss Penn gave a gasp and drew back.

'You were absent from business yesterday, were you not?'

'I was here in the morning. Later I had a bad headache and went directly home.'

'Not home, mademoiselle. For your headache you tried the change of air, did you not? The air of Charlock Bay is very bracing, I believe.'

He took me by the arm and drew me towards the door. He paused there and spoke over his shoulder.

'You comprehend, I know everything. This little—farce—it must cease.'

There was a menace in his tone. Miss Penn, her face ghastly white, nodded mutely. Poirot turned to the girl.

'Mademoiselle,' he said gently, 'you are young and charming. But participating in these little affairs will lead to that youth and charm being hidden behind prison walls—and I, Hercule Poirot, tell you that that will be a pity.'

Then he stepped out into the street and I followed him, bewildered.

'From the first, *mon ami*, I was interested. When that young man booked his place as far as Monkhampton only, I saw the girl's attention suddenly riveted on him. Now why? He was not of the type to make a woman look at him for himself alone. When we started on the coach, I had a feeling that something would happen. Who saw the young man tampering with the luggage? Mademoiselle and mademoiselle only, and remember she chose that seat—a seat facing the window—a most unfeminine choice.

'And then she comes to us with the tale of robbery—the despatch box forced which makes not the common sense, as I told you at the time.

'And what is the result of it all? Mr Baker Wood has paid over good money for stolen goods. The miniatures

243

will be returned to Miss Penn. She will sell them and will have made a thousand pounds instead of five hundred. I make the discreet inquiries and learn that her business is in a bad state—touch and go. I say to myself—the aunt and niece are in this together.'

'Then you never suspected Norton Kane?'

'*Mon ami*! With that moustache? A criminal is either clean shaven or he has a proper moustache that can be removed at will. But what an opportunity for the clever Miss Penn—a shrinking elderly lady with a pink-and-white complexion as we saw her. But if she holds herself erect, wears large boots, alters her complexion with a few unseemly blotches and—crowning touch—adds a few sparse hairs to her upper lip. What then? A masculine woman, says Mr Wood and "a man in disguise" say we at once.'

'She really went to Charlock yesterday?'

'Assuredly. The train, as you may remember telling me, left here at eleven and got to Charlock Bay at two o'clock. Then the return train is even quicker—the one we came by. It leaves Charlock at four-five and gets here at six-fifteen. Naturally, the miniatures were never in the despatch case at all. That was artistically forced before being packed. Mademoiselle Mary has only to find a couple of mugs who will be sympathetic to her charm and champion beauty in distress. But one of the mugs was no mug—he was Hercule Poirot!'

I hardly liked the inference. I said hurriedly: 'Then when you said you were helping a stranger, you were wilfully deceiving me. That's exactly what you were doing.'

'Never do I deceive you, Hastings. I only permit you to deceive yourself. I was referring to Mr Baker Wood—a stranger to these shores.' His face darkened. 'Ah! When I think of that imposition, that iniquitous over-charge, the same fare single to Charlock as return, my blood boils to protect the visitor! Not a pleasant man, Mr Baker Wood, not, as you would say, sympathetic. But a visitor! And we visitors, Hastings, must stand together. Me, I am all for the visitors!'

The Market Basing Mystery

'After all, there's nothing like the country, is there?' said Inspector Japp, breathing in heavily through his nose and out through his mouth in the most approved fashion.

Poirot and I applauded the sentiment heartily. It had been the Scotland Yard inspector's idea that we should all go for the weekend to the little country town of Market Basing. When off duty, Japp was an ardent botanist, and discoursed upon minute flowers possessed of unbelievably lengthy Latin names (somewhat strangely pronounced) with an enthusiasm even greater than that he gave to his cases.

'Nobody knows us, and we know nobody,' explained Japp. 'That's the idea.'

This was not to prove quite the case, however, for the local constable happened to have been transferred from a village fifteen miles away where a case of arsenical poisoning had brought him into contact with the Scotland Yard man. However, his delighted recognition of the great man only enhanced Japp's sense of well-being, and as we sat down to breakfast on Sunday morning in the parlour of the village inn, with the sun shining, and tendrils of honeysuckle thrusting themselves in at the window, we were all in the best of spirits. The bacon and eggs were excellent, the coffee not so good, but passable and boiling hot.

'This is the life,' said Japp. 'When I retire, I shall have a little place in the country. Far from crime, like this!'

'*Le crime, il est partout,*' remarked Poirot, helping himself to a neat square of bread, and frowning at a sparrow which had balanced itself impertinently on the windowsill.

I quoted lightly:

> *'That rabbit has a pleasant face,*
> *His private life is a disgrace*
> *I really could not tell to you*
> *The awful things that rabbits do.'*

'Lord,' said Japp, stretching himself backward, 'I believe I could manage another egg, and perhaps a rasher or two of bacon. What do you say, Captain?'

'I'm with you,' I returned heartily. 'What about you, Poirot?'

Poirot shook his head.

'One must not so replenish the stomach that the brain refuses to function,' he remarked.

'I'll risk replenishing the stomach a bit more,' laughed Japp. 'I take a large size in stomachs; and by the way, you're getting stout yourself, M. Poirot. Here, miss, eggs and bacon twice.'

At that moment, however, an imposing form blocked the doorway. It was Constable Pollard.

'I hope you'll excuse me troubling the inspector, gentlemen, but I'd be glad of his advice.'

'I'm on holiday,' said Japp hastily. 'No work for me. What is the case?'

'Gentleman up at Leigh House—shot himself—through the head.'

'Well, they will do it,' said Japp prosaically. 'Debt, or a woman, I suppose. Sorry I can't help you, Pollard.'

'The point is,' said the constable, 'that he can't have shot himself. Leastways, that's what Dr Giles says.'

Japp put down his cup.

'*Can't* have shot himself? What do you mean?'

'That's what Dr Giles says,' repeated Pollard. 'He says it's plumb impossible. He's puzzled to death, the door being locked on the inside and the windows bolted; but he sticks to it that the man couldn't have committed suicide.'

That settled it. The further supply of bacon and eggs was waved aside, and a few minutes later we were all walking as fast as we could in the direction of Leigh House, Japp eagerly questioning the constable.

The name of the deceased was Walter Protheroe; he was a man of middle age and something of a recluse. He had come to Market Basing eight years ago and rented Leigh House, a rambling, dilapidated old mansion fast falling into ruin. He lived in a corner of it, his wants attended to by a housekeeper whom he had brought with him. Miss Clegg was her name, and she was a very superior woman and highly thought of in the village. Just lately Mr Protheroe had had visitors staying with him, a Mr and Mrs Parker from London. This morning, unable to get a reply when she went to call her master, and finding the door locked, Miss Clegg became alarmed, and telephoned for the police and the doctor. Constable Pollard and Dr Giles had arrived at the same moment. Their united efforts had succeeded in breaking down the oak door of his bedroom.

Mr Protheroe was lying on the floor, shot through the head, and the pistol was clasped in his right hand. It looked a clear case of suicide.

After examining the body, however, Dr Giles became clearly perplexed, and finally he drew the constable aside, and communicated his perplexities to him; whereupon Pollard had at once thought of Japp. Leaving the doctor in charge, he had hurried down to the inn.

By the time the constable's recital was over, we had arrived at Leigh House, a big, desolate house surrounded by an unkempt, weed-ridden garden. The front door was open, and we passed at once into the hall and from there into a small morning-room whence proceeded the sound of voices. Four people were in the room: a somewhat flashily dressed man with a shifty, unpleasant face to whom I took an immediate dislike; a woman of much the same type, though handsome in a coarse fashion; another woman dressed in neat black who stood apart from the rest, and whom I took to be the housekeeper; and a tall man dressed in sporting tweeds, with a clever, capable face, and who was clearly in command of the situation.

'Dr Giles,' said the constable, 'this is Detective-Inspector Japp of Scotland Yard, and his two friends.'

The doctor greeted us and made us known to Mr and Mrs Parker. Then we accompanied them upstairs. Pollard, in obedience to a sign from Japp, remained below, as it were on guard over the household. The doctor led us upstairs and along a passage. A door was open at the end; splinters hung from the hinges, and the door itself had crashed to the floor inside the room.

We went in. The body was still lying on the floor. Mr Protheroe had been a man of middle age, bearded, with hair grey at the temples. Japp went and knelt by the body.

'Why couldn't you leave it as you found it?' he grumbled.

The doctor shrugged his shoulders.

'We thought it a clear case of suicide.'

'H'm!' said Japp. 'Bullet entered the head behind the left ear.'

'Exactly,' said the doctor. 'Clearly impossible for him to have fired it himself. He'd have had to twist his hand right round his head. It couldn't have been done.'

'Yet you found the pistol clasped in his hand? Where is it, by the way?'

The doctor nodded to the table.

'But it wasn't clasped in his hand,' he said. 'It was inside the hand, but the fingers weren't closed over it.'

'Put there afterwards,' said Japp; 'that's clear enough.' He was examining the weapon. 'One cartridge fired. We'll test it for fingerprints, but I doubt if we'll find any but yours, Dr Giles. How long has he been dead?'

'Some time last night. I can't give the time to an hour or so, as those wonderful doctors in detective stories do. Roughly, he's been dead about twelve hours.'

So far, Poirot had not made a move of any kind. He had remained by my side, watching Japp at work and listening to his questions. Only, from time to time, he had sniffed the air very delicately, and as if puzzled. I too had sniffed, but could detect nothing to arouse interest. The air seemed perfectly fresh and devoid of odour. And yet, from time to time, Poirot continued to sniff it dubiously, as though his keener nose detected something I had missed.

Now, as Japp moved away from the body, Poirot knelt down by it. He took no interest in the wound. I thought at first that he was examining the fingers of the hand that had held the pistol, but in a minute I saw that it was a handkerchief carried in the coat-sleeve that interested him. Mr Protheroe was dressed in a dark grey lounge-suit. Finally Poirot got up from his knees, but his eyes still strayed back to the handkerchief as though puzzled.

Japp called to him to come and help to lift the door. Seizing my opportunity, I too knelt down, and taking the handkerchief from the sleeve, scrutinized it minutely. It was a perfectly plain handkerchief of white cambric; there was no mark or stain on it of any kind. I replaced it, shaking my head and confessing myself baffled.

The others had raised the door. I realized that they were hunting for the key. They looked in vain.

'That settles it,' said Japp. 'The window's shut and bolted. The murderer left by the door, locking it and taking the key with him. He thought it would be accepted that Protheroe had locked himself in and shot himself, and that the absence of the key would not be noticed. You agree, M. Poirot?'

'I agree, yes; but it would have been simpler and better to slip the key back inside the room under the door. Then it would look as though it had fallen from the lock.'

'Ah, well, you can't expect everybody to have the bright ideas that you have. You'd have been a holy terror if you'd taken to crime. Any remarks to make, M. Poirot?'

Poirot, it seemed to me, was somewhat at a loss. He looked round the room and remarked mildly and almost apologetically: 'He smoked a lot, this monsieur.'

True enough, the grate was filled with cigarette-stubs, as was an ashtray that stood on a small table near the big armchair.

'He must have got through about twenty cigarettes last night,' remarked Japp. Stooping down, he examined the contents of the grate carefully, then transferred his attention to the ashtray. 'They're all the same kind,' he announced, 'and smoked by the same man. There's nothing there, M. Poirot.'

'I did not suggest that there was,' murmured my friend.

'Ha,' cried Japp, 'what's this?' He pounced on something bright and glittering that lay on the floor near the dead man. 'A broken cuff-link. I wonder who this belongs to. Dr Giles, I'd be obliged if you'd go down and send up the housekeeper.'

'What about the Parkers? He's very anxious to leave the house—says he's got urgent business in London.'

'I dare say. It'll have to get on without him. By the way things are going, it's likely that there'll be some urgent business down here for him to attend to! Send up the housekeeper, and don't let either of the Parkers give you and Pollard the slip. Did any of the household come in here this morning?'

The doctor reflected.

'No, they stood outside in the corridor while Pollard and I came in.'

'Sure of that?'

'Absolutely certain.'

The doctor departed on his mission.

'Good man, that,' said Japp approvingly. 'Some of these sporting doctors are first-class fellows. Well, I wonder who shot this chap. It looks like one of the three in the house. I hardly suspect the housekeeper. She's had eight years to shoot him in if she wanted to. I wonder who these Parkers are? They're not a prepossessing-looking couple.'

Miss Clegg appeared at this juncture. She was a thin, gaunt woman with neat grey hair parted in the middle, very staid and calm in manner. Nevertheless there was an air of efficiency about her which commanded respect. In answer to Japp's questions, she explained that she had been with the dead man for fourteen years. He had been a generous and considerate master. She had never seen Mr and Mrs Parker until three days ago, when they arrived unexpectedly to stay. She was of the opinion that they had asked themselves—the master had certainly not seemed pleased to see them. The cuff-links which Japp showed her had not belonged to Mr Protheroe—she was sure of that. Questioned about the pistol, she said that she believed her master had a weapon of that kind. He kept it locked up. She had seen it once some years ago, but could not say whether this was the same one. She had heard no shot last night, but that was not surprising, as it was a big, rambling house, and her rooms and those prepared for the Parkers were at the other end of the building. She did not know what time Mr Protheroe had gone to bed—he was still up when she retired at half past nine. It was not his habit to go at once to bed when he went to his room. Usually he would sit up half the night, reading and smoking. He was a great smoker.

Then Poirot interposed a question:

'Did your master sleep with his window open or shut, as a rule?'

Miss Clegg considered.

'It was usually open, at any rate at the top.'

'Yet now it is closed. Can you explain that?'

'No, unless he felt a draught and shut it.'

Japp asked her a few more questions and then dismissed her. Next he interviewed the Parkers separately. Mrs Parker was inclined to be hysterical and tearful; Mr Parker was full of bluster and abuse. He denied that the cuff-link was his, but as his wife had previously recognized it, this hardly improved matters for him; and as he had also denied ever having been in Protheroe's room, Japp considered that he had sufficient evidence to apply for a warrant.

Leaving Pollard in charge, Japp bustled back to the village and got into telephonic communication with headquarters. Poirot and I strolled back to the inn.

'You're unusually quiet,' I said. 'Doesn't the case interest you?'

'*Au contraire*, it interests me enormously. But it puzzles me also.'

'The motive is obscure,' I said thoughtfully, 'but I'm certain that Parker's a bad lot. The case against him seems pretty clear but for the lack of motive, and that may come out later.'

'Nothing struck you as being especially significant, although overlooked by Japp?'

I looked at him curiously.

'What have you got up your sleeve, Poirot?'

'What did the dead man have up his sleeve?'

'Oh, that handkerchief!'

'Exactly, that handkerchief.'

'A sailor carries his handkerchief in his sleeve,' I said thoughtfully.

'An excellent point, Hastings, though not the one I had in mind.'

'Anything else?'

'Yes, over and over again I go back to the smell of cigarette-smoke.'

'I didn't smell any,' I cried wonderingly.

'No more did I, *cher ami*.'

I looked earnestly at him. It is so difficult to know when Poirot is pulling one's leg, but he seemed thoroughly in earnest and was frowning to himself.

The inquest took place two days later. In the meantime other evidence had come to light. A tramp had admitted that he had climbed over the wall into the Leigh House garden, where he often slept in a shed that was left unlocked. He declared that at twelve o'clock he had heard two men quarrelling loudly in a room on the first floor. One was demanding a sum of money; the other was angrily refusing. Concealed behind a bush, he had seen the two men as they passed and repassed the lighted window. One he knew well as being Mr Protheroe, the owner of the house; the other he identified positively as Mr Parker.

It was clear now that the Parkers had come to Leigh House to blackmail Protheroe, and when later it was discovered that the dead man's real name was Wendover, and that he had been a lieutenant in the Navy and had been concerned in the blowing up of the first-class cruiser *Merrythought*, in 1910, the case seemed to be rapidly clearing. It was supposed that Parker, cognizant of the part Wendover had played, had tracked him down and demanded hush-money which the other refused to pay. In the course of the quarrel, Wendover drew his revolver, and Parker snatched it from him and shot him, subsequently endeavouring to give it the appearance of suicide.

Parker was committed for trial, reserving his defence. We had attended the police-court proceedings. As we left, Poirot nodded his head.

'It must be so,' he murmured to himself. 'Yes, it must be so. I will delay no longer.'

He went into the post office, and wrote off a note which he despatched by special messenger. I did not see to whom it was addressed. Then we returned to the inn where we had stayed on that memorable weekend.

Poirot was restless, going to and from the window.

'I await a visitor,' he explained. 'It cannot be—surely it cannot be that I am mistaken? No, here she is.'

To my utter astonishment, in another minute Miss Clegg walked into the room. She was less calm than usual, and was breathing hard as though she had been running. I saw the fear in her eyes as she looked at Poirot.

'Sit down, mademoiselle,' he said kindly. 'I guessed rightly, did I not?'

For answer she burst into tears.

'Why did you do it?' asked Poirot gently. 'Why?'

'I loved him so,' she answered. 'I was nursemaid to him when he was a little boy. Oh, be merciful to me!'

'I will do all I can. But you understand that I cannot permit an innocent man to hang—even though he is an unpleasing scoundrel.'

She sat up and said in a low voice: 'Perhaps in the end I could not have, either. Do whatever must be done.'

Then, rising, she hurried from the room.

'Did she shoot him?' I asked utterly bewildered.

Poirot smiled and shook his head.

'He shot himself. Do you remember that he carried his handkerchief in his *right* sleeve? That showed me that he was left-handed. Fearing exposure, after his stormy interview with Mr Parker, he shot himself. In the morning Miss Clegg came to call him as usual and found him lying dead. As she has just told us, she had known him from a little boy upward, and was filled with fury against the Parkers, who had driven him to this shameful death. She regarded them as murderers, and then suddenly she saw a chance of making them suffer for the deed they had inspired. She alone knew that he was left-handed. She changed the pistol to his right hand, closed and bolted the window, dropped the bit of cuff-link she had picked up in one of the downstairs rooms, and went out, locking the door and removing the key.'

'Poirot,' I said, in a burst of enthusiasm, 'you are magnificent. All that from the one little clue of the handkerchief.'

'And the cigarette-smoke. If the window had been closed, and all those cigarettes smoked, the room ought to have been full of stale tobacco. Instead, it was perfectly fresh, so I deduced at once that the window must have been open all night, and only closed in the morning, and that gave me a very interesting line of speculation. I could conceive of no circumstances under which a murderer could want to shut the window. It would be to his advantage to leave it open, and pretend that the murderer had escaped that way, if the theory of suicide did not go down. Of course, the tramp's evidence, when I heard it, confirmed my suspicions. He could never have overheard that conversation unless the window had been open.'

'Splendid!' I said heartily. 'Now, what about some tea?'

'Spoken like a true Englishman,' said Poirot with a sigh. 'I suppose it is not likely that I could obtain here a glass of *sirop*?'

Wasps' Nest

Out of the house came John Harrison and stood a moment on the terrace looking out over the garden. He was a big man with a lean, cadaverous face. His aspect was usually somewhat grim but when, as now, the rugged features softened into a smile, there was something very attractive about him.

John Harrison loved his garden, and it had never looked better than it did on this August evening, summery and languorous. The rambler roses were still beautiful; sweet peas scented the air.

A well-known creaking sound made Harrison turn his head sharply. Who was coming in through the garden gate? In another minute, an expression of utter astonishment came over his face, for the dandified figure coming up the path was the last he expected to see in this part of the world.

'By all that's wonderful,' cried Harrison. 'Monsieur Poirot!'

It was, indeed, the famous Hercule Poirot whose renown as a detective had spread over the whole world.

'Yes,' he said, 'it is. You said to me once: "If you are ever in this part of the world, come and see me." I take you at your word. I arrive.'

'And I'm delighted,' said Harrison heartily. 'Sit down and have a drink.'

With a hospitable hand, he indicated a table on the veranda bearing assorted bottles.

'I thank you,' said Poirot, sinking down into a basket chair. 'You have, I suppose, no *sirop*? No, no. I thought not. A little plain soda water then—no whisky.' And he added in a feeling voice as the other placed the glass beside him: 'Alas, my moustaches are limp. It is this heat!'

'And what brings you into this quiet spot?' asked Harrison as he dropped into another chair. 'Pleasure?'

'No, *mon ami*, business.'

'Business? In this out-of-the-way place?'

Poirot nodded gravely. 'But yes, my friend, all crimes are not committed in crowds, you know?'

The other laughed. 'I suppose that was rather an idiotic remark of mine. But what particular crime are you investigating down here, or is that a thing I mustn't ask?'

'You may ask,' said the detective. 'Indeed, I would prefer that you asked.'

Harrison looked at him curiously. He sensed something a little unusual in the other's manner. 'You are investigating a crime, you say?' he advanced rather hesitatingly. 'A serious crime?'

'A crime of the most serious there is.'

'You mean...'

'Murder.'

So gravely did Hercule Poirot say that word that Harrison was quite taken aback. The detective was looking straight at him and again there was something so unusual in his glance that Harrison hardly knew how to proceed. At last, he said: 'But I have heard of no murder.'

'No,' said Poirot, 'you would not have heard of it.'

'Who has been murdered?'

'As yet,' said Hercule Poirot, 'nobody.'

'What?'

'That is why I said you would not have heard of it. I am investigating a crime that has not yet taken place.'

'But look here, that is nonsense.'

'Not at all. If one can investigate a murder before it has happened, surely that is very much better than afterwards. One might even—a little idea—prevent it.'

Harrison stared at him. 'You are not serious, Monsieur Poirot.'

'But yes, I am serious.'

'You really believe that a murder is going to be committed? Oh, it's absurd!'

Hercule Poirot finished the first part of the sentence without taking any notice of the exclamation.

'Unless we can manage to prevent it. Yes, *mon ami*, that is what I mean.'

'We?'

'I said we. I shall need your co-operation.'

'Is that why you came down here?'

Again Poirot looked at him, and again an indefinable something made Harrison uneasy.

'I came here, Monsieur Harrison because I—well—like you.'

And then he added in an entirely different voice: 'I see, Monsieur Harrison, that you have a wasps' nest there. You should destroy it.'

The change of subject made Harrison frown in a puzzled way. He followed Poirot's glance and said in a bewildered voice: 'As a matter of fact, I'm going to. Or rather, young Langton is. You remember Claude Langton? He was at that same dinner where I met you. He's coming over this evening to take the nest. Rather fancies himself at the job.'

'Ah,' said Poirot. 'And how is he going to do it?'

'Petrol and the garden syringe. He's bringing his own syringe over; it's a more convenient size than mine.'

'There is another way, is there not?' asked Poirot. 'With cyanide of potassium?'

Harrison looked a little surprised. 'Yes, but that's rather dangerous stuff. Always a risk having it about the place.'

Poirot nodded gravely. 'Yes, it is deadly poison.' He waited a minute and then repeated in a grave voice, 'Deadly poison.'

'Useful if you want to do away with your mother-in-law, eh?' said Harrison with a laugh.

But Hercule Poirot remained grave. 'And you are quite sure, Monsieur Harrison, that it is with petrol that Monsieur Langton is going to destroy your wasps' nest?'

'Quite sure. Why?'

'I wondered. I was at the chemist's in Barchester this afternoon. For one of my purchases I had to sign the poison book. I saw the last entry. It was for cyanide of potassium and it was signed by Claude Langton.'

Harrison stared. 'That's odd,' he said. 'Langton told me the other day that he'd never dream of using the stuff; in fact, he said it oughtn't to be sold for the purpose.'

Poirot looked out over the roses. His voice was very quiet as he asked a question. 'Do you like Langton?'

The other started. The question somehow seemed to find him quite unprepared. 'I—I—well, I mean—of course, I like him. Why shouldn't I?'

'I only wondered,' said Poirot placidly, 'whether you did.'

And as the other did not answer, he went on. 'I also wondered if he liked you?'

'What are you getting at, Monsieur Poirot? There's something in your mind I can't fathom.'

'I am going to be very frank. You are engaged to be married, Monsieur Harrison. I know Miss Molly Deane. She is a very charming, a very beautiful girl. Before she was engaged to you, she was engaged to Claude Langton. She threw him over for you.'

Harrison nodded.

'I do not ask what her reasons were: she may have been justified. But I tell you this, it is not too much to suppose that Langton has not forgotten or forgiven.'

'You're wrong, Monsieur Poirot. I swear you're wrong. Langton's been a sportsman; he's taken things like a man. He's been amazingly decent to me—gone out of his way to be friendly.'

'And that does not strike you as unusual? You use the word "amazingly", but you do not seem to be amazed.'

'What do you mean, M. Poirot?'

Agatha Christie

'I mean,' said Poirot, and his voice had a new note in it, 'that a man may conceal his hate till the proper time comes.'

'Hate?' Harrison shook his head and laughed.

'The English are very stupid,' said Poirot. 'They think that they can deceive anyone but that no one can deceive them. The sportsman—the good fellow—never will they believe evil of him. And because they are brave, but stupid, sometimes they die when they need not die.'

'You are warning me,' said Harrison in a low voice. 'I see it now—what has puzzled me all along. You are warning me against Claude Langton. You came here today to warn me...'

Poirot nodded. Harrison sprang up suddenly. 'But *you* are mad, Monsieur Poirot. This is England. Things don't happen like that here. Disappointed suitors don't go about stabbing people in the back and poisoning them. And you're wrong about Langton. That chap wouldn't hurt a fly.'

'The lives of flies are not my concern,' said Poirot placidly. 'And although you say Monsieur Langton would not take the life of one, yet you forget that he is even now preparing to take the lives of several thousand wasps.'

Harrison did not at once reply. The little detective in his turn sprang to his feet. He advanced to his friend and laid a hand on his shoulder. So agitated was he that he almost shook the big man, and, as he did so, he hissed into his ear: 'Rouse yourself, my friend, rouse yourself. And look— look where I am pointing. There on the bank, close by that tree root. See you, the wasps returning home, placid at the end of the day? In a little hour, there will be destruction, and they know it not. There is no one to tell them. They

264

have not, it seems, a Hercule Poirot. I tell you, Monsieur Harrison, I am down here on business. Murder is my business. And it is my business before it has happened as well as afterwards. At what time does Monsieur Langton come to take this wasps' nest?'

'Langton would never...'

'At what time?'

'At nine o'clock. But I tell you, you're all wrong. Langton would never...'

'These English!' cried Poirot in a passion. He caught up his hat and stick and moved down the path, pausing to speak over his shoulder. 'I do not stay to argue with you. I should only enrage myself. But you understand, I return at nine o'clock?'

Harrison opened his mouth to speak, but Poirot did not give him the chance. 'I know what you would say: "Langton would never", et cetera. Ah, Langton would never! But all the same I return at nine o'clock. But, yes, it will amuse me—put it like that—it will amuse me to see the taking of a wasps' nest. Another of your English sports!'

He waited for no reply but passed rapidly down the path and out through the door that creaked. Once outside on the road, his pace slackened. His vivacity died down, his face became grave and troubled. Once he drew his watch from his pocket and consulted it. The hands pointed to ten minutes past eight. 'Over three quarters of an hour,' he murmured. 'I wonder if I should have waited.'

His footsteps slackened; he almost seemed on the point of returning. Some vague foreboding seemed to assail him.

He shook it off resolutely, however, and continued to walk in the direction of the village. But his face was still troubled, and once or twice he shook his head like a man only partly satisfied.

It was still some minutes off nine when he once more approached the garden door. It was a clear, still evening; hardly a breeze stirred the leaves. There was, perhaps, something a little sinister in the stillness, like the lull before a storm.

Poirot's footsteps quickened ever so slightly. He was suddenly alarmed—and uncertain. He feared he knew not what.

And at that moment the garden door opened and Claude Langton stepped quickly out into the road. He started when he saw Poirot.

'Oh—er—good evening.'

'Good evening, Monsieur Langton. You are early.'

Langton stared at him. 'I don't know what you mean.'

'You have taken the wasps' nest?'

'As a matter of fact, I didn't.'

'Oh,' said Poirot softly. 'So you did not take the wasps' nest. What did you do then?'

'Oh, just sat and yarned a bit with old Harrison. I really must hurry along now, Monsieur Poirot. I'd no idea you were remaining in this part of the world.'

'I had business here, you see.'

'Oh! Well, you'll find Harrison on the terrace. Sorry I can't stop.'

He hurried away. Poirot looked after him. A nervous young fellow, good-looking with a weak mouth!

'So I shall find Harrison on the terrace,' murmured Poirot. 'I wonder.' He went in through the garden door and up the path. Harrison was sitting in a chair by the table. He sat motionless and did not even turn his head as Poirot came up to him.

'Ah! *Mon ami*,' said Poirot. 'You are all right, eh?'

There was a long pause and then Harrison said in a queer, dazed voice, 'What did you say?'

'I said—are you all right?'

'All right? Yes, I'm all right. Why not?'

'You feel no ill effects? That is good.'

'Ill effects? From what?'

'Washing soda.'

Harrison roused himself suddenly. 'Washing soda? What do you mean?'

Poirot made an apologetic gesture. 'I infinitely regret the necessity, but I put some in your pocket.'

'You put some in my pocket? What on earth for?'

Harrison stared at him. Poirot spoke quietly and impersonally like a lecturer coming down to the level of a small child.

'You see, one of the advantages, or disadvantages, of being a detective is that it brings you into contact with the criminal classes. And the criminal classes, they can teach you some very interesting and curious things. There was a pickpocket once—I interested myself in him because for once in a way he had not done what they say he has done—and so I get him off. And because he is grateful he pays me in the only way he can think of—which is to show me the tricks of his trade.

'And so it happens that I can pick a man's pocket if I choose without his ever suspecting the fact. I lay one hand on his shoulder, I excite myself, and he feels nothing. But all the same I have managed to transfer what is in his pocket to my pocket and leave washing soda in its place.

'You see,' continued Poirot dreamily, 'if a man wants to get at some poison quickly to put in a glass, unobserved, he positively must keep it in his right-hand coat pocket; there is nowhere else. I knew it would be there.'

He dropped his hand into his pocket and brought out a few white, lumpy crystals. 'Exceedingly dangerous,' he murmured, 'to carry it like that—loose.'

Calmly and without hurrying himself, he took from another pocket a wide-mouthed bottle. He slipped in the crystals, stepped to the table and filled up the bottle with plain water. Then carefully corking it, he shook it until all the crystals were dissolved. Harrison watched him as though fascinated.

Satisfied with his solution, Poirot stepped across to the nest. He uncorked the bottle, turned his head aside, and poured the solution into the wasps' nest, then stood back a pace or two watching.

Some wasps that were returning alighted, quivered a little and then lay still. Other wasps crawled out of the hole only to die. Poirot watched for a minute or two and then nodded his head and came back to the veranda.

'A quick death,' he said. 'A very quick death.'

Harrison found his voice. 'How much do you know?'

Poirot looked straight ahead. 'As I told you, I saw Claude Langton's name in the book. What I did not tell you was that almost immediately afterwards, I happened to meet him. He told me he had been buying cyanide of potassium at your request—to take a wasps' nest. That struck me as a little odd, my friend, because I remember that at that dinner of which you spoke, you held forth on the superior merits of petrol and denounced the buying of cyanide as dangerous and unnecessary.'

'Go on.'

'I knew something else. I had seen Claude Langton and Molly Deane together when they thought no one saw them. I do not know what lovers' quarrel it was that originally parted them and drove her into your arms, but I realized that misunderstandings were over and that Miss Deane was drifting back to her love.'

'Go on.'

'I knew something more, my friend. I was in Harley Street the other day, and I saw you come out of a certain doctor's house. I know the doctor and for what disease one consults him, and I read the expression on your face. I have seen it only once or twice in my lifetime, but it is not easily mistaken. It was the face of a man under sentence of death. I am right, am I not?'

'Quite right. He gave me two months.'

'You did not see me, my friend, for you had other things to think about. I saw something else on your face—the thing that I told you this afternoon men try to conceal. I saw hate there, my friend. You did not trouble to conceal it, because you thought there were none to observe.'

'Go on,' said Harrison.

'There is not much more to say. I came down here, saw Langton's name by accident in the poison book as I tell you, met him, and came here to you. I laid traps for you. You denied having asked Langton to get cyanide, or rather you expressed surprise at his having done so. You were taken aback at first at my appearance, but presently you saw how well it would fit in and you encouraged my suspicions. I knew from Langton himself that he was coming at half past eight. You told me nine o'clock, thinking I should come and find everything over. And so I knew everything.'

'Why did you come?' cried Harrison. 'If only you hadn't come!'

Poirot drew himself up. 'I told you,' he said, 'murder is my business.'

'Murder? Suicide, you mean.'

'No.' Poirot's voice rang out sharply and clearly. 'I mean murder. Your death was to be quick and easy, but the death you planned for Langton was the worst death any man can die. He bought the poison; he comes to see you, and he is alone with you. You die suddenly, and the cyanide is found in your glass, and Claude Langton hangs. That was your plan.'

Again Harrison moaned.

'Why did you come? Why did you come?'

'I have told you, but there is another reason. I liked you. Listen, *mon ami*, you are a dying man; you have lost the girl you loved, but there is one thing that you are not; you are not a murderer. Tell me now: are you glad or sorry that I came?'

There was a moment's pause and Harrison drew himself up. There was a new dignity in his face—the look of a man who has conquered his own baser self. He stretched out his hand across the table.

'Thank goodness you came,' he cried. 'Oh, thank goodness you came.'

The Veiled Lady

I had noticed that for some time Poirot had been growing increasingly dissatisfied and restless. We had had no interesting cases of late, nothing on which my little friend could exercise his keen wits and remarkable powers of deduction. This morning he flung down the newspaper with an impatient '*Tchah!*'—a favourite exclamation of his which sounded exactly like a cat sneezing.

'They fear me, Hastings; the criminals of your England they fear me! When the cat is there, the little mice, they come no more to the cheese!'

'I don't suppose the greater part of them even know of your existence,' I said, laughing.

Poirot looked at me reproachfully. He always imagines that the whole world is thinking and talking of Hercule Poirot. He had certainly made a name for himself in London, but I could hardly believe that his existence struck terror into the criminal world.

'What about that daylight robbery of jewels in Bond Street the other day?' I asked.

'A neat *coup*,' said Poirot approvingly, 'though not in my line. *Pas de finesse, seulement de l'audace*! A man with a loaded cane smashes the plate-glass window of a jeweller's shop and grabs a number of precious stones. Worthy citizens immediately seize him; a policeman arrives. He is caught red-handed with the jewels on him. He is marched off to the police, and then it is discovered that the stones are paste. He has passed the real ones to a confederate—one of the aforementioned worthy citizens. He will go to prison—true; but when he comes out, there will be a nice little fortune awaiting him. Yes, not badly imagined. But I could do better than that. Sometimes, Hastings, I regret that I am of such a moral disposition. To work against the law, it would be pleasing, for a change.'

'Cheer up, Poirot; you know you are unique in your own line.'

'But what is there on hand in my own line?'

I picked up the paper.

'Here's an Englishman mysteriously done to death in Holland,' I said.

'They always say that—and later they find that he ate the tinned fish and that his death is perfectly natural.'

'Well, if you're determined to grouse!'

'*Tiens*!' said Poirot, who had strolled across to the window. 'Here in the street is what they call in novels a "heavily veiled lady". She mounts the steps; she rings the bell—she comes to consult us. Here is a possibility of something interesting. When one is as young and pretty as that one, one does not veil the face except for a big affair.'

A minute later our visitor was ushered in. As Poirot had said, she was indeed heavily veiled. It was impossible to

273

distinguish her features until she raised her veil of black Spanish lace. Then I saw that Poirot's intuition had been right; the lady was extremely pretty, with fair hair and blue eyes. From the costly simplicity of her attire, I deduced at once that she belonged to the upper strata of society.

'Monsieur Poirot,' said the lady in a soft, musical voice, 'I am in great trouble. I can hardly believe that you can help me, but I have heard such wonderful things of you that I come literally as the last hope to beg you to do the impossible.'

'The impossible, it pleases me always,' said Poirot. 'Continue, I beg of you, mademoiselle.'

Our fair guest hesitated.

'But you must be frank,' added Poirot. 'You must not leave me in the dark on any point.'

'I will trust you,' said the girl suddenly. 'You have heard of Lady Millicent Castle Vaughan?'

I looked up with keen interest. The announcement of Lady Millicent's engagement to the young Duke of Southshire had appeared a few days previously. She was, I knew, the fifth daughter of an impecunious Irish peer, and the Duke of Southshire was one of the best matches in England.

'I am Lady Millicent,' continued the girl. 'You may have read of my engagement. I should be one of the happiest girls alive; but oh, M. Poirot, I am in terrible trouble! There is a man, a horrible man—his name is Lavington; and he—I hardly know how to tell you. There was a letter I wrote—I was only sixteen at the time; and he—he—'

'A letter that you wrote to this Mr Lavington?'

'Oh *no*—not to him! To a young soldier—I was very fond of him—he was killed in the war.'

I understand,' said Poirot kindly.

'It was a foolish letter, an indiscreet letter, but indeed, M. Poirot, nothing more. But there are phrases in it which—which might bear a different interpretation.'

'I see,' said Poirot. 'And this letter has come into the possession of Mr Lavington?'

'Yes, and he threatens, unless I pay him an enormous sum of money, a sum that is quite impossible for me to raise, to send it to the Duke.'

'The dirty swine!' I ejaculated. 'I beg your pardon, Lady Millicent.'

'Would it not be wiser to confess all to your future husband?'

'I dare not, M. Poirot. The Duke is a rather peculiar character, jealous and suspicious and prone to believe the worst. I might as well break off my engagement at once.'

'Dear, dear,' said Poirot with an expressive grimace. 'And what do you want me to do, milady?'

'I thought perhaps that I might ask Mr Lavington to call upon you. I would tell him that you were empowered by me to discuss the matter. Perhaps you could reduce his demands.'

'What sum does he mention?'

'Twenty thousand pounds—an impossibility. I doubt if I could raise a thousand, even.'

'You might perhaps borrow the money on the prospect of your approaching marriage—but I doubt if you could get hold of half that sum. Besides—*eh bien*, it is repugnant to me that you should pay! No, the ingenuity of Hercule Poirot

shall defeat your enemies! Send me this Mr Lavington. Is
he likely to bring the letter with him?'

The girl shook her head.

'I do not think so. He is very cautious.'

'I suppose there is no doubt that he really has it?'

'He showed it to me when I went to his house.'

'You went to his house? That was very imprudent, milady.'

'Was it? I was so desperate. I hoped my entreaties might
move him.'

'*Oh, là là*! The Lavingtons of this world are not moved
by entreaties! He would welcome them as showing how
much importance you attached to the document. Where
does he live, this fine gentleman?'

'At Buona Vista, Wimbledon. I went there after dark—'
Poirot groaned. 'I declared that I would inform the police in
the end, but he only laughed in a horrid, sneering manner.
"By all means, my dear Lady Millicent, do so if you wish,"
he said.'

'Yes, it is hardly an affair for the police,' murmured Poirot.

'"But I think you will be wiser than that," he continued.
"See, here is your letter—in this little Chinese puzzle box!"
He held it so that I could see. I tried to snatch at it, but he
was too quick for me. With a horrid smile he folded it up
and replaced it in the little wooden box. "It will be quite
safe here, I assure you," he said, "and the box itself lives in
such a clever place that you would never find it." My eyes
turned to the small wall-safe, and he shook his head and
laughed. "I have a better safe than that," he said. Oh, he
was odious! M. Poirot, do you think that you can help me?'

'Have faith in Papa Poirot. I will find a way.'

These reassurances were all very well, I thought, as Poirot gallantly ushered his fair client down the stairs, but it seemed to me that we had a tough nut to crack. I said as much to Poirot when he returned. He nodded ruefully.

'Yes—the solution does not leap to the eye. He has the whip hand, this M. Lavington. For the moment I do not see how we are to circumvent him.'

Mr Lavington duly called upon us that afternoon. Lady Millicent had spoken truly when she described him as an odious man. I felt a positive tingling in the end of my boot, so keen was I to kick him down the stairs. He was blustering and overbearing in manner, laughed Poirot's gentle suggestions to scorn, and generally showed himself as master of the situation. I could not help feeling that Poirot was hardly appearing at his best. He looked discouraged and crestfallen.

'Well, gentlemen,' said Lavington, as he took up his hat, 'we don't seem to be getting much further. The case stands like this: I'll let the Lady Millicent off cheap, as she is such a charming young lady.' He leered odiously. 'We'll say eighteen thousand. I'm off to Paris today—a little piece of business to attend to over there. I shall be back on Tuesday. Unless the money is paid by Tuesday evening, the letter goes to the Duke. Don't tell me Lady Millicent can't raise the money. Some of her gentlemen friends would be only too willing to oblige such a pretty woman with a loan—if she goes the right way about it.'

My face flushed, and I took a step forward, but Lavington had wheeled out of the room as he finished his sentence.

'My God!' I cried. 'Something has got to be done. You seem to be taking this lying down, Poirot.'

'You have an excellent heart, my friend—but your grey cells are in a deplorable condition. I have no wish to impress Mr Lavington with my capabilities. The more pusillanimous he thinks me, the better.'

'Why?'

'It is curious,' murmured Poirot reminiscently, 'that I should have uttered a wish to work against the law just before Lady Millicent arrived!'

'You are going to burgle his house while he is away?' I gasped.

'Sometimes, Hastings, your mental processes are amazingly quick.'

'Suppose he takes the letter with him?'

Poirot shook his head.

'That is very unlikely. He has evidently a hiding-place in his house that he fancies to be pretty impregnable.'

'When do we—er—do the deed?'

'Tomorrow night. We will start from here about eleven o'clock.'

At the time appointed I was ready to set off. I had donned a dark suit, and a soft dark hat. Poirot beamed kindly on me.

'You have dressed the part, I see,' he observed. 'Come let us take the underground to Wimbledon.'

'Aren't we going to take anything with us? Tools to break in with?'

'My dear Hastings, Hercule Poirot does not adopt such crude methods.'

I retired, snubbed, but my curiosity was alert.

It was just on midnight that we entered the small suburban garden of Buona Vista. The house was dark and silent. Poirot went straight to a window at the back of the house, raised the sash noiselessly and bade me enter.

'How did you know this window would be open?' I whispered, for really it seemed uncanny.

'Because I sawed through the catch this morning.'

'What?'

'But yes, it was most simple. I called, presented a fictitious card and one of Inspector Japp's official ones. I said I had been sent, recommended by Scotland Yard, to attend to some burglar-proof fastenings that Mr Lavington wanted fixed while he was away. The housekeeper welcomed me with enthusiasm. It seems they have had two attempted burglaries here lately—evidently our little idea has occurred to other clients of Mr Lavington's—with nothing of value taken. I examined all the windows, made my little arrangement, forbade the servants to touch the windows until tomorrow, as they were electrically connected up, and withdrew gracefully.'

'Really, Poirot, you are wonderful.'

'*Mon ami*, it was of the simplest. Now, to work! The servants sleep at the top of the house, so we will run little risk of disturbing them.'

'I presume the safe is built into the wall somewhere?'

'Safe? Fiddlesticks! There is no safe. Mr Lavington is an intelligent man. You will see, he will have devised a hiding-place much more intelligent than a safe. A safe is the first thing everyone looks for.'

Whereupon we began a systematic search of the entire place. But after several hours' ransacking of the house, our search had been unavailing. I saw symptoms of anger gathering on Poirot's face.

'*Ah, sapristi*, is Hercule Poirot to be beaten? Never! Let us be calm. Let us reflect. Let us reason. Let us—*enfin*!—employ our little grey cells!'

He paused for some moments, bending his brows in concentration; then the green light I knew so well stole into his eyes.

'I have been an imbecile! The kitchen!'

'The kitchen,' I cried. 'But that's impossible. The servants!'

'Exactly. Just what ninety-nine people out of a hundred would say! And for that very reason the kitchen is the ideal place to choose. It is full of various homely objects. *En avant*, to the kitchen!'

I followed him, completely sceptical, and watched whilst he dived into bread-bins, tapped saucepans, and put his head into the gas-oven. In the end, tired of watching him, I strolled back to the study. I was convinced that there, and there only, would we find the *cache*. I made a further minute search, noted that it was now a quarter past four and that therefore it would soon be growing light, and then went back to the kitchen regions.

To my utter amazement, Poirot was now standing right inside the coal-bin, to the utter ruin of his neat light suit. He made a grimace.

'But yes, my friend, it is against all my instincts so to ruin my appearance, but what will you?'

'But Lavington can't have buried it under the coal?'

'If you would use your eyes, you would see that it is not the coal that I examine.'

I then saw on a shelf behind the coal-bunker some logs of wood were piled. Poirot was dexterously taking them down one by one. Suddenly he uttered a low exclamation.

'Your knife, Hastings!'

I handed it to him. He appeared to insert it in the wood, and suddenly the log split in two. It had been neatly sawn in half and a cavity hollowed out in the centre. From this cavity Poirot took a little wooden box of Chinese make.

'Well done!' I cried, carried out of myself.

'Gently, Hastings! Do not raise your voice too much. Come, let us be off, before the daylight is upon us.'

Slipping the box into his pocket, he leaped lightly out of the coal-bunker, brushed himself down as well as he could, and leaving the house by the same way as we had come, we walked rapidly in the direction of London.

'But what an extraordinary place!' I expostulated. 'Anyone might have used the log.'

'In July, Hastings? And it was at the bottom of the pile—a very ingenious hiding-place. Ah, here is a taxi! Now for home, a wash, and a refreshing sleep.'

After the excitement of the night, I slept late. When I finally strolled into our sitting-room just before one o'clock, I was surprised to see Poirot, leaning back in an armchair, the Chinese box open beside him, calmly reading the letter he had taken from it.

He smiled at me affectionately, and tapped the sheet he held.

'She was right, the Lady Millicent; never would the Duke have pardoned this letter! It contains some of the most extravagant terms of affection I have ever come across.'

'Really, Poirot,' I said, rather disgustedly, 'I don't think you should have read the letter. 'That's the sort of thing that isn't done.'

'It is done by Hercule Poirot,' replied my friend imperturbably.

'And another thing,' I said. 'I don't think using Japp's official card yesterday was quite playing the game.'

'But I was not playing a game, Hastings. I was conducting a case.'

I shrugged my shoulders. One can't argue with a point of view.

'A step on the stairs,' said Poirot. 'That will be Lady Millicent.'

Our fair client came in with an anxious expression on her face which changed to one of delight on seeing the letter and box which Poirot held up.

'Oh, M. Poirot. How wonderful of you! How did you do it?'

'By rather reprehensible methods, milady. But Mr Lavington will not prosecute. This is your letter, is it not?'

She glanced through it.

'Yes. Oh, how can I ever thank you! You are a wonderful, wonderful man. Where was it hidden?'

Poirot told her.

'How very clever of you!' She took up the small box from the table. 'I shall keep this as a souvenir.'

'I had hoped, milady, that you would permit me to keep it—also as a souvenir.'

'I hope to send you a better souvenir than that—on my wedding-day. You shall not find me ungrateful, M. Poirot.'

'The pleasure of doing you a service will be more to me than a cheque—so you permit that I retain the box.'

'Oh no, M. Poirot, I simply must have that,' she cried laughingly.

She stretched out her hand, but Poirot was before her. His hand closed over it.

'I think not.' His voice had changed.

'What do you mean?' Her voice seemed to have grown sharper.

'At any rate, permit me to abstract its further contents. You observed that the original cavity has been reduced by half. In the top half, the compromising letter; in the bottom—'

He made a nimble gesture, then held out his hand. On the palm were four large glittering stones, and two big milky white pearls.

'The jewels stolen in Bond Street the other day, I rather fancy,' murmured Poirot. 'Japp will tell us.'

To my utter amazement, Japp himself stepped out from Poirot's bedroom.

283

'An old friend of yours, I believe,' said Poirot politely to Lady Millicent.

'Nabbed, by the Lord!' said Lady Millicent, with a complete change of manner. 'You nippy old devil!' She looked at Poirot with almost affectionate awe.

'Well, Gertie, my dear,' said Japp, 'the game's up this time, I fancy. Fancy seeing you again so soon! We've got your pal, too, the gentleman who called here the other day calling himself Lavington. As for Lavington himself, alias Croker, alias Reed, I wonder which of the gang it was who stuck a knife into him the other day in Holland? Thought he'd got the goods with him, didn't you? And he hadn't. He double-crossed you properly—hid 'em in his own house. You had two fellows looking for them, and then you tackled M. Poirot here, and by a piece of amazing luck he found them.'

'You do like talking, don't you?' said the late Lady Millicent. 'Easy there, now. I'll go quietly. You can't say that I'm not the perfect lady. Ta-ta, all!'

'The shoes were wrong,' said Poirot dreamily, while I was still too stupefied to speak. 'I have made my little observations of your English nation, and a lady, a born lady, is always particular about her shoes. She may have shabby clothes, but she will be well shod. Now, this Lady Millicent had smart, expensive clothes, and cheap shoes. It was not likely that either you or I should have seen the real Lady Millicent; she has been very little in London, and this girl had a certain superficial resemblance which would pass well enough. As I say, the shoes first awakened my suspicions, and then her story—and her veil—were a little

Poirot's Early Cases

melodramatic, eh? The Chinese box with a bogus compromising letter in the top must have been known to all the gang, but the log of wood was the late Mr Lavington's idea. *Eh, par exemple*, Hastings, I hope you will not again wound my feelings as you did yesterday by saying that I am unknown to the criminal classes. *Ma foi*, they even employ me when they themselves fail!'

285

Problem at Sea

'Colonel Clapperton!' said General Forbes.

He said it with an effect midway between a snort and a sniff.

Miss Ellie Henderson leaned forward, a strand of her soft grey hair blowing across her face. Her eyes, dark and snapping, gleamed with a wicked pleasure.

'Such a *soldierly*-looking man!' she said with malicious intent, and smoothed back the lock of hair to await the result.

'Soldierly!' exploded General Forbes. He tugged at his military moustache and his face became bright red.

'In the Guards, wasn't he?' murmured Miss Henderson, completing her work.

'Guards? Guards? Pack of nonsense. Fellow was on the music hall stage! Fact! Joined up and was out in France counting tins of plum and apple. Huns dropped a stray bomb and he went home with a flesh wound in the arm. Somehow or other got into Lady Carrington's hospital.'

'So that's how they met.'

'Fact! Fellow played the wounded hero. Lady Carrington had no sense and oceans of money. Old Carrington had

286

been in munitions. She'd been a widow only six months. This fellow snaps her up in no time. She wangled him a job at the War Office. *Colonel* Clapperton! Pah!' he snorted.

'And before the war he was on the music hall stage,' mused Miss Henderson, trying to reconcile the distinguished grey-haired Colonel Clapperton with a red-nosed comedian singing mirth-provoking songs.

'Fact!' said General Forbes. 'Heard it from old Bassington-ffrench. And he heard it from old Badger Cotterill who'd got it from Snooks Parker.'

Miss Henderson nodded brightly. 'That does seem to settle it!' she said.

A fleeting smile showed for a minute on the face of a small man sitting near them. Miss Henderson noticed the smile. She was observant. It had shown appreciation of the irony underlying her last remark—irony which the General never for a moment suspected.

The General himself did not notice the smile. He glanced at his watch, rose and remarked: 'Exercise. Got to keep oneself fit on a boat,' and passed out through the open door on to the deck.

Miss Henderson glanced at the man who had smiled. It was a well-bred glance indicating that she was ready to enter into conversation with a fellow traveller.

'He is energetic—yes?' said the little man.

'He goes round the deck forty-eight times exactly,' said Miss Henderson. 'What an old gossip! And they say *we* are the scandal-loving sex.'

'What an impoliteness!'

'Frenchmen are always polite,' said Miss Henderson—there was the nuance of a question in her voice.

The little man responded promptly. 'Belgian, mademoiselle.'

'Oh! Belgian.'

'Hercule Poirot. At your service.'

The name aroused some memory. Surely she had heard it before—? 'Are you enjoying this trip, M. Poirot?'

'Frankly, no. It was an imbecility to allow myself to be persuaded to come. I detest *la mer*. Never does it remain tranquil—no, not for a little minute.'

'Well, you admit it's quite calm now.'

M. Poirot admitted this grudgingly. '*A ce moment*, yes. That is why I revive. I once more interest myself in what passes around me—your very adept handling of the General Forbes, for instance.'

'You mean—' Miss Henderson paused.

Hercule Poirot bowed. 'Your methods of extracting the scandalous matter. Admirable!'

Miss Henderson laughed in an unashamed manner. 'That touch about the Guards? I knew that would bring the old boy up spluttering and gasping.' She leaned forward confidentially. 'I admit I *like* scandal—the more ill-natured, the better!'

Poirot looked thoughtfully at her—her slim well-preserved figure, her keen dark eyes, her grey hair; a woman of forty-five who was content to look her age.

Ellie said abruptly: 'I have it! Aren't you the great detective?'

Poirot bowed. 'You are too amiable, mademoiselle.' But he made no disclaimer.

'How thrilling,' said Miss Henderson. 'Are you "hot on the trail" as they say in books? Have we a criminal secretly in our midst? Or am I being indiscreet?'

'Not at all. Not at all. It pains me to disappoint your expectations, but I am simply here, like everyone else, to amuse myself.'

He said it in such a gloomy voice that Miss Henderson laughed.

'Oh! Well, you will be able to get ashore tomorrow at Alexandria. You have been to Egypt before?'

'Never, mademoiselle.'

Miss Henderson rose somewhat abruptly.

'I think I shall join the General on his constitutional,' she announced.

Poirot sprang politely to his feet.

She gave him a little nod and passed on to the deck.

A faint puzzled look showed for a moment in Poirot's eyes, then, a little smile creasing his lips, he rose, put his head through the door and glanced down the deck. Miss Henderson was leaning against the rail talking to a tall, soldierly-looking man.

Poirot's smile deepened. He drew himself back into the smoking-room with the same exaggerated care with which a tortoise withdraws itself into its shell. For the moment he had the smoking-room to himself, though he rightly conjectured that that would not last long.

It did not. Mrs Clapperton, her carefully waved platinum head protected with a net, her massaged and dieted form dressed in a smart sports suit, came through the door from the bar with the purposeful air of a woman who has always been able to pay top price for anything she needed.

She said: 'John—? Oh! Good morning, M. Poirot—have you seen John?'

'He's on the starboard deck, madame. Shall I—?'

She arrested him with a gesture. 'I'll sit here a minute.' She sat down in a regal fashion in the chair opposite him. From the distance she had looked a possible twenty-eight. Now, in spite of her exquisitely made-up face, her delicately plucked eyebrows, she looked not her actual forty-nine years, but a possible fifty-five. Her eyes were a hard pale blue with tiny pupils.

'I was sorry not to have seen you at dinner last night,' she said. 'It was just a shade choppy, of course—'

'*Précisément*,' said Poirot with feeling.

'Luckily, I am an excellent sailor,' said Mrs Clapperton. 'I say luckily, because, with my weak heart, seasickness would probably be the death of me.'

'You have the weak heart, madame?'

'Yes, I have to be *most* careful. I must *not* overtire myself! *All* the specialists say so!' Mrs Clapperton had embarked on the—to her—ever-fascinating topic of her health. 'John, poor darling, wears himself out trying to prevent me from doing too much. I live so intensely, if you know what I mean, M. Poirot?'

'Yes, yes.'

'He always says to me: "Try to be more of a vegetable, Adeline." But I can't. Life was meant to be *lived*, I feel. As a matter of fact I wore myself out as a girl in the war.

My hospital—you've heard of my hospital? Of course I had nurses and matrons and all that—but *I* actually ran it.' She sighed.

'Your vitality is marvellous, dear lady,' said Poirot, with the slightly mechanical air of one responding to his cue.

Mrs Clapperton gave a girlish laugh.

'Everyone tells me how young I am! It's absurd. I never try to pretend I'm a day less than forty-three,' she continued with slightly mendacious candour, 'but a lot of people find it hard to believe. "You're so *alive*, Adeline," they say to me. But really, M. Poirot, what would one *be* if one wasn't alive?'

'Dead,' said Poirot.

Mrs Clapperton frowned. The reply was not to her liking. The man, she decided, was trying to be funny. She got up and said coldly: 'I must find John.'

As she stepped through the door she dropped her handbag. It opened and the contents flew far and wide. Poirot rushed gallantly to the rescue. It was some few minutes before the lipsticks, vanity boxes, cigarette case and lighter and other odds and ends were collected. Mrs Clapperton thanked him politely, then she swept down the deck and said, 'John—'

Colonel Clapperton was still deep in conversation with Miss Henderson. He swung round and came quickly to meet his wife. He bent over her protectively. Her deck chair—was it in the right place? Wouldn't it be better—? His manner was courteous—full of gentle consideration. Clearly an adored wife spoilt by an adoring husband.

Miss Ellie Henderson looked out at the horizon as though something about it rather disgusted her.

Standing in the smoking-room door, Poirot looked on.

A hoarse quavering voice behind him said: 'I'd take a hatchet to that woman if I were her husband.' The old gentleman known disrespectfully among the younger set on board as the Grandfather of All the Tea Planters, had just shuffled in. 'Boy!' he called. 'Get me a whisky peg.'

Poirot stooped to retrieve a torn scrap of notepaper, an overlooked item from the contents of Mrs Clapperton's bag. Part of a prescription, he noted, containing digitalin. He put it in his pocket, meaning to restore it to Mrs Clapperton later.

'Yes,' went on the aged passenger. 'Poisonous woman. I remember a woman like that in Poona. In '87 that was.'

'Did anyone take a hatchet to her?' inquired Poirot.

The old gentleman shook his head sadly.

'Worried her husband into his grave within the year. Clapperton ought to assert himself. Gives his wife her head too much.'

'She holds the purse strings,' said Poirot gravely.

'Ha, ha!' chuckled the old gentleman. 'You've put the matter in a nutshell. Holds the purse strings. Ha, ha!'

Two girls burst into the smoking-room. One had a round face with freckles and dark hair streaming out in a windswept confusion, the other had freckles and curly chestnut hair.

'A rescue—a rescue!' cried Kitty Mooney. 'Pam and I are going to rescue Colonel Clapperton.'

'From his wife,' gasped Pamela Cregan.

'We think he's a *pet*...'

'And she's just awful—she won't let him do *anything*,' the two girls exclaimed.

'And if he isn't with her, he's usually grabbed by the Henderson woman...'

'Who's quite nice. But terribly *old*...'

They ran out, gasping in between giggles. 'A rescue—a rescue...'

That the rescue of Colonel Clapperton was no isolated sally, but a fixed project was made clear that same evening when the eighteen-year-old Pam Cregan came up to Hercule Poirot, and murmured: 'Watch us, M. Poirot. He's going to be cut out from under her nose and taken to walk in the moonlight on the boat deck.'

It was just at that moment that Colonel Clapperton was saying: 'I grant you the price of a Rolls-Royce. But it's practically good for a lifetime. Now my car—'

'*My* car, I think, John.' Mrs Clapperton's voice was shrill and penetrating.

He showed no annoyance at her ungraciousness. Either he was used to it by this time, or else—

'Or else?' thought Poirot and let himself speculate.

'Certainly, my dear, *your* car,' Clapperton bowed to his wife and finished what he had been saying, perfectly unruffled.

'*Voilà ce qu'on appelle le pukka sahib*,' thought Poirot. 'But the General Forbes says that Clapperton is no gentleman at all. I wonder now.'

There was a suggestion of bridge. Mrs Clapperton, General Forbes and a hawk-eyed couple sat down to it. Miss Henderson had excused herself and gone out on deck.

'What about your husband?' asked General Forbes, hesitating.

'John won't play,' said Mrs Clapperton. 'Most tiresome of him.'

The four bridge players began shuffling the cards.

Pam and Kitty advanced on Colonel Clapperton. Each one took an arm.

'You're coming with us!' said Pam. 'To the boat deck. There's a moon.'

'Don't be foolish, John,' said Mrs Clapperton. 'You'll catch a chill.'

'Not with us, he won't,' said Kitty. 'We're hot stuff!'

He went with them, laughing.

Poirot noticed that Mrs Clapperton said No Bid to her initial bid of Two Clubs.

He strolled out on to the promenade deck. Miss Henderson was standing by the rail. She looked round expectantly as he came to stand beside her and he saw the drop in her expression.

They chatted for a while. Then presently as he fell silent she asked: 'What are you thinking about?'

Poirot replied: 'I am wondering about my knowledge of English. Mrs Clapperton said: "John won't play bridge." Is not "can't play" the usual term?'

'She takes it as a personal insult that he doesn't, I suppose,' said Ellie drily. 'The man was a fool ever to have married her.'

In the darkness Poirot smiled. 'You don't think it's just possible that the marriage may be a success?' he asked diffidently.

'With a woman like that?'

Poirot shrugged his shoulders. 'Many odious women have devoted husbands. An enigma of nature. You will admit that nothing she says or does appears to gall him.' Miss Henderson was considering her reply when Mrs Clapperton's voice floated out through the smoking-room window.

'No—I don't think I will play another rubber. So stuffy. I think I'll go up and get some air on the boat deck.'

'Good night,' said Miss Henderson. 'I'm going to bed.' She disappeared abruptly.

Poirot strolled forward to the lounge—deserted save for Colonel Clapperton and the two girls. He was doing card tricks for them and noting the dexterity of his shuffling and handling of the cards, Poirot remembered the General's story of a career on the music hall stage.

'I see you enjoy the cards even though you do not play bridge,' he remarked.

'I've my reasons for not playing bridge,' said Clapperton, his charming smile breaking out. 'I'll show you. We'll play one hand.'

He dealt the cards rapidly. 'Pick up your hands. Well, what about it?' He laughed at the bewildered expression on Kitty's face. He laid down his hand and the others followed suit. Kitty held the entire club suit, M. Poirot the hearts, Pam the diamonds and Colonel Clapperton the spades.

'You see?' he said. 'A man who can deal his partner and his adversaries any hand he pleases had better stand aloof from a friendly game! If the luck goes too much his way, ill-natured things might be said.'

'Oh!' gasped Kitty. 'How *could* you do that? It all looked perfect ordinary.'

'The quickness of the hand deceives the eye,' said Poirot sententiously—and caught the sudden change in the Colonel's expression.

It was as though he realized that he had been off his guard for a moment or two.

Poirot smiled. The conjuror had shown himself through the mask of the pukka sahib.

The ship reached Alexandria at dawn the following morning.

As Poirot came up from breakfast he found the two girls all ready to go on shore. They were talking to Colonel Clapperton.

'We ought to get off now,' urged Kitty. 'The passport people will be going off the ship presently. You'll come with us won't you? You wouldn't let us go ashore all by ourselves? Awful things might happen to us.'

'I certainly don't think you ought to go by yourselves,' said Clapperton, smiling. 'But I'm not sure my wife feels up to it.'

'That's too bad,' said Pam. 'But she can have a nice long rest.'

Colonel Clapperton looked a little irresolute. Evidently the desire to play truant was strong upon him. He noticed Poirot.

'Hullo, M. Poirot—you going ashore?'

'No, I think not,' M. Poirot replied.

'I'll—I'll—just have a word with Adeline,' decided Colonel Clapperton.

'We'll come with you,' said Pam. She flashed a wink at Poirot. 'Perhaps we can persuade her to come too,' she added gravely.

Colonel Clapperton seemed to welcome this suggestion. He looked decidedly relieved.

'Come along then, the pair of you,' he said lightly. They all three went along the passage of B deck together.

Poirot, whose cabin was just opposite the Clappertons', followed them out of curiosity.

Colonel Clapperton rapped a little nervously at the cabin door.

'Adeline, my dear, are you up?'

The sleepy voice of Mrs Clapperton from within replied: 'Oh, bother—what is it?'

'It's John. What about going ashore?'

'Certainly not.' The voice was shrill and decisive. 'I've had a very bad night. I shall stay in bed most of the day.'

Pam nipped in quickly. 'Oh, Mrs Clapperton, I'm so sorry. We did so want you to come with us. Are you sure you're not up to it?'

'I'm quite certain.' Mrs Clapperton's voice sounded even shriller.

The Colonel was turning the door-handle without result.

'What is it, John? The door's locked. I don't want to be disturbed by the stewards.'

Agatha Christie

'Sorry, my dear, sorry. Just wanted my Baedeker.'

'Well, you can't have it,' snapped Mrs Clapperton. 'I'm not going to get out of bed. Do go away, John, and let me have a little peace.'

'Certainly, certainly, my dear.' The Colonel backed away from the door. Pam and Kitty closed in on him.

'Let's start at once. Thank goodness your hat's on your head. Oh, gracious—your passport isn't in the cabin, is it?'

'As a matter of fact it's in my pocket—' began the Colonel.

Kitty squeezed his arm. 'Glory be!' she exclaimed. 'Now, come on.'

Leaning over the rail, Poirot watched the three of them leave the ship. He heard a faint intake of breath beside him and turned to see Miss Henderson. Her eyes were fastened on the three retreating figures.

'So they've gone ashore,' she said flatly.

'Yes. Are you going?'

She had a shade hat, he noticed, and a smart bag and shoes. There was a shore-going appearance about her. Nevertheless, after the most infinitesimal of pauses, she shook her head.

'No,' she said. 'I think I'll stay on board. I have a lot of letters to write.'

She turned and left him.

Puffing after his morning tour of forty-eight rounds of the deck, General Forbes took her place. 'Aha!' he exclaimed as his eyes noted the retreating figures of the Colonel and the two girls. 'So *that's* the game! Where's the Madam?'

Poirot explained that Mrs Clapperton was having a quiet day in bed.

298

'Don't you believe it!' the old warrior closed one knowing eye. 'She'll be up for tiffin—and if the poor devil's found to be absent without leave, there'll be ructions.'

But the General's prognostications were not fulfilled. Mrs Clapperton did not appear at lunch and by the time the Colonel and his attendant damsels returned to the ship at four o'clock, she had not shown herself.

Poirot was in his cabin and heard the husband's slightly guilty knock on his cabin door. Heard the knock repeated, the cabin door tried, and finally heard the Colonel's call to a steward.

'Look here, I can't get an answer. Have you a key?'

Poirot rose quickly from his bunk and came out into the passage.

The news went like wildfire round the ship. With horrified incredulity people heard that Mrs Clapperton had been found dead in her bunk—a native dagger driven through her heart. A string of amber beads was found on the floor of her cabin.

Rumour succeeded rumour. All bead sellers who had been allowed on board that day were being rounded up and questioned! A large sum in cash had disappeared from a drawer in the cabin! The notes had been traced! They had not been traced! Jewellery worth a fortune had been taken! No jewellery had been taken at all! A steward had been arrested and had confessed to the murder!

'What is the truth of it all?' demanded Miss Ellie Henderson waylaying Poirot. Her face was pale and troubled.

'My dear lady, how should I know?'

'Of course you know,' said Miss Henderson.

It was late in the evening. Most people had retired to their cabins. Miss Henderson led Poirot to a couple of deck chairs on the sheltered side of the ship. 'Now tell me,' she commanded.

Poirot surveyed her thoughtfully. 'It's an interesting case,' he said.

'Is it true that she had some very valuable jewellery stolen?'

Poirot shook his head. 'No. No jewellery was taken. A small amount of loose cash that was in a drawer has disappeared, though.'

'I'll never feel safe on a ship again,' said Miss Henderson with a shiver. 'Any clue as to which of those brutes did it?'

'No,' said Hercule Poirot. 'The whole thing is rather— strange.'

'What do you mean?' asked Ellie sharply.

Poirot spread out his hands. '*Eh bien*—take the facts. Mrs Clapperton had been dead at least five hours when she was found. Some money had disappeared. A string of beads was on the floor by her bed. The door was locked and the key was missing. The window—*window*, not port-hole—gives on the deck and was open.'

'Well?' asked the woman impatiently.

'Do you not think it is curious for a murder to be committed under those particular circumstances? Remember that the postcard sellers, money changers and bead sellers who are allowed on board are all well known to the police.'

'The stewards usually lock your cabin, all the same,' Ellie pointed out.

'Yes, to prevent any chance of petty pilfering. But this— was murder.'

'What exactly are you thinking of, M. Poirot?' Her voice sounded a little breathless.

'I am thinking of the *locked door*.'

Miss Henderson considered this. 'I don't see anything in that. The man left by the door, locked it and took the key with him so as to avoid having the murder discovered too soon. Quite intelligent of him, for it wasn't discovered until four o'clock in the afternoon.'

'No, no, mademoiselle, you don't appreciate the point I'm trying to make. I'm not worried as to how he got *out*, but as to how he got *in*.'

'The window of course.'

'*C'est possible*. But it would be a very narrow fit—and there were people passing up and down the deck all the time, remember.'

'Then through the door,' said Miss Henderson impatiently.

'But you forget, mademoiselle. *Mrs Clapperton had locked the door on the inside*. She had done so before Colonel Clapperton left the boat this morning. He actually tried it—so we *know* that is so.'

'Nonsense. It probably stuck—or he didn't turn the handle properly.'

'But it does not rest on his word. We actually heard *Mrs Clapperton herself say so*.'

'We?'

'Miss Mooney, Miss Cregan, Colonel Clapperton and myself.'

Ellie Henderson tapped a neatly shod foot. She did not speak for a moment or two. Then she said in a slightly irritable tone: 'Well—what exactly do you deduce from that? If Mrs Clapperton could lock the door she could unlock it too, I suppose.'

'Precisely, precisely.' Poirot turned a beaming face upon her. 'And you see where that leaves us. *Mrs Clapperton unlocked the door and let the murderer in.* Now would she be likely to do that for a bead seller?'

Ellie objected: 'She might not have known who it was. He may have knocked—she got up and opened the door—and he forced his way in and killed her.'

Poirot shook his head. '*Au contraire*. She was lying peacefully in bed when she was stabbed.'

Miss Henderson stared at him. 'What's your idea?' she asked abruptly.

Poirot smiled. 'Well, it looks, does it not, as though she *knew* the person she admitted...'

'You mean,' said Miss Henderson and her voice sounded a little harsh, '*that the murderer is a passenger on the ship?*'

Poirot nodded. 'It seems indicated.'

'And the string of beads left on the floor was a blind?'

'Precisely.'

'The theft of the money also?'

'Exactly.'

There was a pause, then Miss Henderson said slowly: 'I thought Mrs Clapperton a very unpleasant woman and

I don't think anyone on board really liked her—but there wasn't anyone who had any reason to kill her.'

'Except her husband, perhaps,' said Poirot.

'You don't really think—' She stopped.

'It is the opinion of every person on this ship that Colonel Clapperton would have been quite justified in "taking a hatchet to her". That was, I think, the expression used.'

Ellie Henderson looked at him—waiting.

'But I am bound to say,' went on Poirot, 'that I myself have not noted any signs of exasperation on the good Colonel's part. Also what is more important, he had an alibi. He was with those two girls all day and did not return to the ship till four o'clock. By then, Mrs Clapperton had been dead many hours.'

There was another minute of silence. Ellie Henderson said softly: 'But you still think—a passenger on the ship?'

Poirot bowed his head.

Ellie Henderson laughed suddenly—a reckless defiant laugh. 'Your theory may be difficult to prove, M. Poirot. There are a good many passengers on this ship.'

Poirot bowed to her. 'I will use a phrase from one of your detective stories. "I have my methods, Watson."'

The following evening, at dinner, every passenger found a typewritten slip by his plate requesting him to be in the main lounge at 8.30. When the company were assembled, the Captain stepped on to the raised platform where the orchestra usually played and addressed them.

'Ladies and gentlemen, you all know of the tragedy which took place yesterday. I am sure you all wish to co-operate in bringing the perpetrator of that foul crime to justice.' He paused and cleared his throat. 'We have on board with us M. Hercule Poirot who is probably known to you all as a man who has had wide experience in—er—such matters. I hope you will listen carefully to what he has to say.'

It was at this moment that Colonel Clapperton, who had not been at dinner, came in and sat down next to General Forbes. He looked like a man bewildered by sorrow—not at all like a man conscious of great relief. Either he was a very good actor or else he had been genuinely fond of his disagreeable wife.

'M. Hercule Poirot,' said the Captain and stepped down. Poirot took his place. He looked comically self-important as he beamed on his audience.

'*Messieurs, mesdames*,' he began. 'It is most kind of you to be so indulgent as to listen to me. *M. le Capitaine* has told you that I have had a certain experience in these matters. I have, it is true, a little idea of my own about how to get to the bottom of this particular case.' He made a sign and a steward pushed forward and passed on to him a bulky, shapeless object wrapped in a sheet.

'What I am about to do may surprise you a little,' Poirot warned them. 'It may occur to you that I am eccentric, perhaps mad. Nevertheless I assure you that behind my madness there is—as you English say—a method.'

His eyes met those of Miss Henderson for just a minute. He began unwrapping the bulky object.

'I have here, *messieurs* and *mesdames*, an important witness to the truth of who killed Mrs Clapperton.' With a deft hand he whisked away the last enveloping cloth, and the object it concealed was revealed—an almost life-sized wooden doll, dressed in a velvet suit and lace collar.

'Now, Arthur,' said Poirot and his voice changed subtly— it was no longer foreign—it had instead a confident English, a slightly Cockney inflection. 'Can you tell me—I repeat— can you tell me—anything at all about the death of Mrs Clapperton?'

The doll's neck oscillated a little, its wooden lower jaw dropped and wavered and a shrill high-pitched woman's voice spoke:

'*What is it, John? The door's locked. I don't want to be disturbed by the stewards...*'

There was a cry—an overturned chair—a man stood swaying, his hand to his throat—trying to speak—trying... Then suddenly, his figure seemed to crumple up. He pitched headlong.

It was Colonel Clapperton.

Poirot and the ship's doctor rose from their knees by the prostrate figure.

'All over, I'm afraid. Heart,' said the doctor briefly.

Poirot nodded. 'The shock of having his trick seen through,' he said.

He turned to General Forbes. 'It was you, General, who gave me a valuable hint with your mention of the music hall stage. I puzzle—I think—and then it comes to me. Supposing that before the war Clapperton was a *ventriloquist*. In that case, it would be perfectly possible for three people to hear Mrs Clapperton speak from inside her cabin *when she was already dead...*'

Ellie Henderson was beside him. Her eyes were dark and full of pain. 'Did you know his heart was weak?' she asked.

'I guessed it... Mrs Clapperton talked of her own heart being affected, but she struck me as the type of woman who likes to be thought ill. Then I picked up a torn prescription with a very strong dose of digitalin in it. Digitalin is a heart medicine but it couldn't be Mrs Clapperton's because digitalin dilates the pupils of the eyes. I have never noticed such a phenomenon with her—but when I looked at his eyes I saw the signs at once.'

Ellie murmured: 'So you thought—it might end—this way?'

'The best way, don't you think, mademoiselle?' he said gently.

He saw the tears rise in her eyes. She said: 'You've known. You've known all along... That I cared... But he didn't do it for *me*... It was those girls—youth—it made him feel his slavery. He wanted to be free before it was too late... Yes, I'm sure that's how it was... When did you guess—that it was he?'

'His self-control was too perfect,' said Poirot simply. 'No matter how galling his wife's conduct, it never seemed to touch him. That meant either that he was so used to it that it no longer stung him, or else—*eh bien*—I decided on the latter alternative... And I was right...'

'And then there was his insistence on his conjuring ability—the evening before the crime he pretended to give himself away. But a man like Clapperton doesn't give himself away. There must be a reason. So long as people thought he had been a *conjuror* they weren't likely to think of his having been a *ventriloquist*.'

'And the voice we heard—Mrs Clapperton's voice?'

'One of the stewardesses had a voice not unlike hers. I induced her to hide behind the stage and taught her the words to say.'

'It was a trick—a cruel trick,' cried out Ellie.

'I do not approve of murder,' said Hercule Poirot.

How Does Your Garden Grow?

Hercule Poirot arranged his letters in a neat pile in front of him. He picked up the topmost letter, studied the address for a moment, then neatly slit the back of the envelope with a little paper-knife that he kept on the breakfast table for that express purpose and extracted the contents. Inside was yet another envelope, carefully sealed with purple wax and marked 'Private and Confidential'.

Hercule Poirot's eyebrows rose a little on his egg-shaped head. He murmured, '*Patience! Nous allons arriver!*' and once more brought the little paper-knife into play. This time the envelope yielded a letter—written in a rather shaky and spiky handwriting. Several words were heavily underlined.

Hercule Poirot unfolded it and read. The letter was headed once again 'Private and Confidential'. On the right-hand side was the address—Rosebank, Charman's Green, Bucks—and the date—March twenty-first.

> *Dear M. Poirot,*
>   *I have been recommended to you by an old and valued friend of mine who knows the* worry *and* distress *I have been in lately. Not that this friend knows the actual*

circumstances—*those I have kept* entirely *to myself—the matter being strictly private. My friend assures me that you are* discretion *itself—and that there will be no fear of my being involved in a* police *matter which, if my suspicions should prove correct, I should* very much dislike. *But it is of course possible that I am* entirely *mistaken. I do not feel myself clear-headed enough nowadays—suffering as I do from insomnia and the result of a severe illness last winter— to investigate things for myself. I have neither the* means nor *the* ability. *On the other hand, I must reiterate once more that this is a very delicate family matter and that for many reasons I may want the* whole thing hushed up. *If I am once assured of the* facts, *I can deal with the matter myself and should prefer to do so. I hope that I have made myself clear on this point. If you will undertake this investigation perhaps you will let me know to the above address?*

    Yours very truly,
    Amelia Barrowby

Poirot read the letter through twice. Again his eyebrows rose slightly. Then he placed it on one side and proceeded to the next envelope in the pile.

At ten o'clock precisely he entered the room where Miss Lemon, his confidential secretary, sat awaiting her instructions for the day. Miss Lemon was forty-eight and of unprepossessing appearance. Her general effect was that of a lot of bones flung together at random. She had a passion for order almost equalling that of Poirot himself; and though capable of thinking, she never thought unless told to do so.

Poirot handed her the morning correspondence. 'Have the goodness, mademoiselle, to write refusals couched in correct terms to all of these.'

Miss Lemon ran an eye over the various letters, scribbling in turn a hieroglyphic on each of them. These marks were legible to her alone and were in a code of her own: 'Soft soap'; 'slap in the face'; 'purr purr'; 'curt'; and so on. Having done this, she nodded and looked up for further instructions.

Poirot handed her Amelia Barrowby's letter. She extracted it from its double envelope, read it through and looked up inquiringly.

'Yes, M. Poirot?' Her pencil hovered—ready—over her shorthand pad.

'What is your opinion of that letter, Miss Lemon?'

With a slight frown Miss Lemon put down the pencil and read through the letter again.

The contents of a letter meant nothing to Miss Lemon except from the point of view of composing an adequate reply. Very occasionally her employer appealed to her human, as opposed to her official, capacities. It slightly annoyed Miss Lemon when he did so—she was very nearly the perfect machine, completely and gloriously uninterested in all human affairs. Her real passion in life was the perfection of a filing system beside which all other filing systems should sink into oblivion. She dreamed of such a system at night. Nevertheless, Miss Lemon was perfectly capable of intelligence on purely human matters, as Hercule Poirot well knew.

'Well?' he demanded.

'Old lady,' said Miss Lemon. 'Got the wind up pretty badly.'

'Ah! The wind rises in her, you think?'

Miss Lemon, who considered that Poirot had been long enough in Great Britain to understand its slang terms, did not reply. She took a brief look at the double envelope.

'Very hush-hush,' she said. 'And tells you nothing at all.'

'Yes,' said Hercule Poirot. 'I observed that.'

Miss Lemon's hand hung once more hopefully over the shorthand pad. This time Hercule Poirot responded.

'Tell her I will do myself the honour to call upon her at any time she suggests, unless she prefers to consult me here. Do not type the letter—write it by hand.'

'Yes, M. Poirot.'

Poirot produced more correspondence. 'These are bills.'

Miss Lemon's efficient hands sorted them quickly. 'I'll pay all but these two.'

'Why those two? There is no error in them.'

'They are firms you've only just begun to deal with. It looks bad to pay too promptly when you've just opened an account—looks as though you were working up to get some credit later on.'

'Ah!' murmured Poirot. 'I bow to your superior knowledge of the British tradesman.'

'There's nothing much I don't know about them,' said Miss Lemon grimly.

The letter to Miss Amelia Barrowby was duly written and sent, but no reply was forthcoming. Perhaps, thought Hercule Poirot, the old lady had unravelled her mystery herself. Yet he felt a shade of surprise that in that case she should not have written a courteous word to say that his services were no longer required.

It was five days later when Miss Lemon, after receiving her morning's instructions, said, 'That Miss Barrowby we wrote to—no wonder there's been no answer. She's dead.'

Hercule Poirot said very softly, 'Ah—dead.' It sounded not so much like a question as an answer.

Opening her handbag, Miss Lemon produced a newspaper cutting. 'I saw it in the tube and tore it out.'

Just registering in his mind approval of the fact that, though Miss Lemon used the word 'tore', she had neatly cut the entry out with scissors, Poirot read the announcement taken from the Births, Deaths and Marriages in the *Morning Post*: 'On March 26th—suddenly—at Rosebank, Charman's Green, Amelia Jane Barrowby, in her seventy-third year. No flowers, by request.'

Poirot read it over. He murmured under his breath, 'Suddenly.' Then he said briskly, 'If you will be so obliging as to take a letter, Miss Lemon?'

The pencil hovered. Miss Lemon, her mind dwelling on the intricacies of the filing system, took down in rapid and correct shorthand:

Dear Miss Barrowby,

I have received no reply from you, but as I shall be in the neighbourhood of Charman's Green on Friday, I will call upon you on that day and discuss more fully the matter mentioned to me in your letter.

Yours, etc.

'Type this letter, please; and if it is posted at once, it should get to Charman's Green tonight.'

On the following morning a letter in a black-edged envelope arrived by the second post:

Dear Sir,

In reply to your letter my aunt, Miss Barrowby, passed away on the twenty-sixth, so the matter you speak of is no longer of importance.

Yours truly,

Mary Delafontaine

Poirot smiled to himself. 'No longer of importance... Ah—that is what we shall see. *En avant*—to Charman's Green.'

Rosebank was a house that seemed likely to live up to its name, which is more than can be said for most houses of its class and character.

Hercule Poirot paused as he walked up the path to the front door and looked approvingly at the neatly planned beds on either side of him. Rose trees that promised a good harvest later in the year, and at present daffodils, early tulips, blue hyacinths—the last bed was partly edged with shells.

Poirot murmured to himself, 'How does it go, the English rhyme the children sing?

'Mistress Mary, quite contrary,
How does your garden grow?
With cockle-shells, and silver bells.
And pretty maids all in a row.

313

'Not a row, perhaps,' he considered, 'but here is at least one pretty maid to make the little rhyme come right.'

The front door had opened and a neat little maid in cap and apron was looking somewhat dubiously at the spectacle of a heavily moustached foreign gentleman talking aloud to himself in the front garden. She was, as Poirot had noted, a very pretty little maid, with round blue eyes and rosy cheeks.

Poirot raised his hat with courtesy and addressed her: 'Pardon, but does a Miss Amelia Barrowby live here?'

The little maid gasped and her eyes grew rounder. 'Oh, sir, didn't you know? She's dead. Ever so sudden it was. Tuesday night.'

She hesitated, divided between two strong instincts: the first, distrust of a foreigner; the second, the pleasurable enjoyment of her class in dwelling on the subject of illness and death.

'You amaze me,' said Hercule Poirot, not very truthfully. 'I had an appointment with the lady for today. However, I can perhaps see the other lady who lives here.'

The little maid seemed slightly doubtful. 'The mistress? Well, you could see her, perhaps, but I don't know whether she'll be seeing anyone or not.'

'She will see me,' said Poirot, and handed her a card.

The authority of his tone had its effect. The rosy-cheeked maid fell back and ushered Poirot into a sitting-room on the right of the hall. Then, card in hand, she departed to summon her mistress.

Hercule Poirot looked round him. The room was a perfectly conventional drawing-room—oatmeal-coloured paper with a frieze round the top, indeterminate cretonnes, rose-coloured cushions and curtains, a good many china knick-knacks and ornaments. There was nothing in the room that stood out, that announced a definite personality.

Suddenly Poirot, who was very sensitive, felt eyes watching him. He wheeled round. A girl was standing in the entrance of the french window—a small, sallow girl, with very black hair and suspicious eyes.

She came in, and as Poirot made a little bow she burst out abruptly, 'Why have you come?'

Poirot did not reply. He merely raised his eyebrows.

'You are not a lawyer—no?' Her English was good, but not for a minute would anyone have taken her to be English.

'Why should I be a lawyer, mademoiselle?'

The girl stared at him sullenly. 'I thought you might be. I thought you had come perhaps to say that she did not know what she was doing. I have heard of such things—the not due influence; that is what they call it, no? But that is not right. She wanted me to have the money, and I shall have it. If it is needful I shall have a lawyer of my own. The money is mine. She wrote it down so, and so it shall be.' She looked ugly, her chin thrust out, her eyes gleaming.

The door opened and a tall woman entered and said, 'Katrina.'

The girl shrank, flushed, muttered something and went out through the window.

Poirot turned to face the newcomer who had so effectually dealt with the situation by uttering a single word. There had been authority in her voice, and contempt and a shade of well-bred irony. He realized at once that this was the owner of the house, Mary Delafontaine.

'M. Poirot? I wrote to you. You cannot have received my letter.'

'Alas, I have been away from London.'

'Oh, I see; that explains it. I must introduce myself. My name is Delafontaine. This is my husband. Miss Barrowby was my aunt.'

Mr Delafontaine had entered so quietly that his arrival had passed unnoticed. He was a tall man with grizzled hair and an indeterminate manner. He had a nervous way of fingering his chin. He looked often towards his wife, and it was plain that he expected her to take the lead in any conversation.

'I much regret that I intrude in the midst of your bereavement,' said Hercule Poirot.

'I quite realize that it is not your fault,' said Mrs Delafontaine. 'My aunt died on Tuesday evening. It was quite unexpected.'

'Most unexpected,' said Mr Delafontaine. 'Great blow.' His eyes watched the window where the foreign girl had disappeared.

'I apologize,' said Hercule Poirot. 'And I withdraw.' He moved a step towards the door.

'Half a sec,' said Mr Delafontaine. 'You—er—had an appointment with Aunt Amelia, you say?'

'*Parfaitement.*'

'Perhaps you will tell us about it,' said his wife. 'If there is anything we can do—'

316

'It was of a private nature,' said Poirot. 'I am a detective,' he added simply.

Mr Delafontaine knocked over a little china figure he was handling. His wife looked puzzled.

'A detective? And you had an appointment with Auntie? But how extraordinary!' She stared at him. 'Can't you tell us a little more, M. Poirot? It—it seems quite fantastic.'

Poirot was silent for a moment. He chose his words with care.

'It is difficult for me, madame, to know what to do.'

'Look here,' said Mr Delafontaine. 'She didn't mention Russians, did she?'

'Russians?'

'Yes, you know—Bolshies, Reds, all that sort of thing.'

'Don't be absurd, Henry,' said his wife.

Mr Delafontaine collapsed. 'Sorry—sorry—I just wondered.'

Mary Delafontaine looked frankly at Poirot. Her eyes were very blue—the colour of forget-me-nots. 'If you can tell us anything, M. Poirot, I should be glad if you would do so. I can assure you that I have a—a reason for asking.'

Mr Delafontaine looked alarmed. 'Be careful, old girl—you know there may be nothing in it.'

Again his wife quelled him with a glance. 'Well, M. Poirot?'

Slowly, gravely, Hercule Poirot shook his head. He shook it with visible regret, but he shook it. 'At present, madame,' he said, 'I fear I must say nothing.'

He bowed, picked up his hat and moved to the door. Mary Delafontaine came with him into the hall. On the doorstep he paused and looked at her.

'You are fond of your garden, I think, madame?'

'I? Yes, I spend a lot of time gardening.'

'Je vous fait mes compliments.'

He bowed once more and strode down to the gate. As he passed out of it and turned to the right he glanced back and registered two impressions—a sallow face watching him from the first-floor window, and a man of erect and soldierly carriage pacing up and down on the opposite side of the street.

Hercule Poirot nodded to himself. *'Definitivement,'* he said. 'There is a mouse in this hole! What move must the cat make now?'

His decision took him to the nearest post office. Here he put through a couple of telephone calls. The result seemed to be satisfactory. He bent his steps to Charman's Green police station, where he inquired for Inspector Sims.

Inspector Sims was a big, burly man with a hearty manner. 'M. Poirot?' he inquired. 'I thought so. I've just this minute had a telephone call through from the chief constable about you. He said you'd be dropping in. Come into my office.'

The door shut, the inspector waved Poirot to one chair, settled himself in another, and turned a gaze of acute inquiry upon his visitor.

'You're very quick on to the mark, M. Poirot. Come to see us about this Rosebank case almost before we know it is a case. What put you on to it?'

Poirot drew out the letter he had received and handed it to the inspector. The latter read it with some interest.

'Interesting,' he said. 'The trouble is, it might mean so many things. Pity she couldn't have been a little more explicit. It would have helped us now.'

'Or there might have been no need for help.'

'You mean?'

'She might have been alive.'

'You go as far as that, do you? H'm—I'm not sure you're wrong.'

'I pray of you, Inspector, recount to me the facts. I know nothing at all.'

'That's easily done. Old lady was taken bad after dinner on Tuesday night. Very alarming. Convulsions—spasms—whatnot. They sent for the doctor. By the time he arrived she was dead. Idea was she'd died of a fit. Well, he didn't much like the look of things. He hemmed and hawed and put it with a bit of soft sawder, but he made it clear that he couldn't give a death certificate. And as far as the family go, that's where the matter stands. They're awaiting the result of the post-mortem. We've got a bit further. The doctor gave us the tip right away—he and the police surgeon did the autopsy together—and the result is in no doubt whatever. The old lady died of a large dose of strychnine.'

'Aha!'

'That's right. Very nasty bit of work. Point is, who gave it to her? It must have been administered very shortly before death. First idea was it was given to her in her food at dinner—but, frankly, that seems to be a washout. They had artichoke soup, served from a tureen, fish pie and apple tart.

'Miss Barrowby, Mr Delafontaine and Mrs Delafontaine. Miss Barrowby had a kind of nurse-attendant—a half-Russian girl—but she didn't eat with the family. She had the remains as they came out from the dining-room. There's a maid, but it was her night out. She left the soup on the stove and the fish pie in the oven, and the apple tart was cold. All three of them ate the same thing—and, apart from that, I don't think you could get strychnine down anyone's throat that way. Stuff's as bitter as gall. The doctor told me you could taste it in a solution of one in a thousand, or something like that.'

'Coffee?'

'Coffee's more like it, but the old lady never took coffee.'

'I see your point. Yes, it seems an insuperable difficulty. What did she drink at the meal?'

'Water.'

'Worse and worse.'

'Bit of a teaser, isn't it?'

'She had money, the old lady?'

'Very well to do, I imagine. Of course, we haven't got exact details yet. The Delafontaines are pretty badly off, from what I can make out. The old lady helped with the upkeep of the house.'

Poirot smiled a little. He said, 'So you suspect the Delafontaines. Which of them?'

'I don't exactly say I suspect either of them in particular. But there it is; they're her only near relations, and her death brings them a tidy sum of money, I've no doubt. We all know what human nature is!'

'Sometimes inhuman—yes, that is very true. And there was nothing else the old lady ate or drank?'

'Well, as a matter of fact—'

'Ah, *voilà*! I felt that you had something, as you say, up your sleeve—the soup, the fish pie, the apple tart—a *bêtise*! Now we come to the hub of the affair.'

'I don't know about that. But as a matter of fact, the old girl took a cachet before meals. You know, not a pill or a tablet; one of those rice-paper things with a powder inside. Some perfectly harmless thing for the digestion.'

'Admirable. Nothing is easier than to fill a cachet with strychnine and substitute it for one of the others. It slips down the throat with a drink of water and is not tasted.'

'That's all right. The trouble is, the girl gave it to her.'

'The Russian girl?'

'Yes. Katrina Rieger. She was a kind of lady-help, nurse-companion to Miss Barrowby. Fairly ordered about by her, too, I gather. Fetch this, fetch that, fetch the other, rub my back, pour out my medicine, run round to the chemist—all that sort of business. You know how it is with these old women—they mean to be kind, but what they need is a sort of slave!'

Poirot smiled.

'And there you are, you see,' continued Inspector Sims. 'It doesn't fit in what you might call nicely. Why should the girl poison her? Miss Barrowby dies and now the girl will be out of a job, and jobs aren't easy to find—she's not trained or anything.'

'Still,' suggested Poirot, 'if the box of cachets was left about, anyone in the house might have the opportunity.'

'Naturally we're on to that, M. Poirot. I don't mind telling you we're making our inquiries—quiet like, if you understand me. When the prescription was last made up, where it was usually kept; patience and a lot of spade work—that's what will do the trick in the end. And then there's Miss Barrowby's solicitor. I'm having an interview with him tomorrow. And the bank manager. There's a lot to be done still.'

Poirot rose. 'A little favour, Inspector Sims; you will send me a little word how the affair marches. I would esteem it a great favour. Here is my telephone number.'

'Why, certainly, M. Poirot. Two heads are better than one; and besides, you ought to be in on this, having had that letter and all.'

'You are too amiable, Inspector.' Politely, Poirot shook hands and took his leave.

He was called to the telephone on the following afternoon. 'Is that M. Poirot? Inspector Sims here. Things are beginning to sit up and look pretty in the little matter you and I know of.'

'In verity? Tell me, I pray of you.'

'Well, here's item No. 1—and a pretty big item. Miss B. left a small legacy to her niece and everything else to K. In consideration of her great kindness and attention—that's the way it was put. That alters the complexion of things.'

A picture rose swiftly in Poirot's mind. A sullen face and a passionate voice saying, 'The money is mine. She wrote it down and so it shall be.' The legacy would not come as a surprise to Katrina—she knew about it beforehand.

'Item No. 2,' continued the voice of Inspector Sims. 'Nobody but K. handled that cachet.'

'You can be sure of that?'

'The girl herself doesn't deny it. What do you think of that?'

'Extremely interesting.'

'We only want one thing more—evidence of how the strychnine came into her possession. That oughtn't to be difficult.'

'But so far you haven't been successful?'

'I've barely started. The inquest was only this morning.'

'What happened at it?'

'Adjourned for a week.'

'And the young lady—K.?'

'I'm detaining her on suspicion. Don't want to run any risks. She might have some funny friends in the country who'd try to get her out of it.'

'No,' said Poirot. 'I do not think she has any friends.'

'Really? What makes you say that, M. Poirot?'

'It is just an idea of mine. There were no other "items", as you call them?'

'Nothing that's strictly relevant. Miss B. seems to have been monkeying about a bit with her shares lately—must have dropped quite a tidy sum. It's rather a funny business, one way and another, but I don't see how it affects the main issue—not at present, that is.'

'No, perhaps you are right. Well, my best thanks to you. It was most amiable of you to ring me up.'

'Not at all. I'm a man of my word. I could see you were interested. Who knows, you may be able to give me a helping hand before the end.'

'That would give me great pleasure. It might help you, for instance, if I could lay my hand on a friend of the girl Katrina.'

'I thought you said she hadn't got any friends?' said Inspector Sims, surprised.

'I was wrong,' said Hercule Poirot. 'She has one.'

Before the inspector could ask a further question, Poirot had rung off.

With a serious face he wandered into the room where Miss Lemon sat at her typewriter. She raised her hands from the keys at her employer's approach and looked at him inquiringly.

'I want you,' said Poirot, 'to figure to yourself a little history.'

Miss Lemon dropped her hands into her lap in a resigned manner. She enjoyed typing, paying bills, filing papers and entering up engagements. To be asked to imagine herself in hypothetical situations bored her very much, but she accepted it as a disagreeable part of a duty.

'You are a Russian girl,' began Poirot.

'Yes,' said Miss Lemon, looking intensely British.

'You are alone and friendless in this country. You have reasons for not wishing to return to Russia. You are employed as a kind of drudge, nurse-attendant and companion to an old lady. You are meek and uncomplaining.'

'Yes,' said Miss Lemon obediently, but entirely failing to see herself being meek to any old lady under the sun.

'The old lady takes a fancy to you. She decides to leave her money to you. She tells you so.' Poirot paused.

Miss Lemon said 'Yes' again.

'And then the old lady finds out something; perhaps it is a matter of money—she may find that you have not been honest with her. Or it might be more grave still—a medicine that tasted different, some food that disagreed. Anyway, she begins to suspect you of something and she writes to a very famous detective—*enfin*, to the most famous detective—me! I am to call upon her shortly. And then, as you say, the dripping will be in the fire. The great thing is to act quickly. And so—before the great detective arrives—the old lady is dead. And the money comes to you... Tell me, does that seem to you reasonable?'

'Quite reasonable,' said Miss Lemon. 'Quite reasonable for a Russian, that is. Personally, I should never take a post as a companion. I like my duties clearly defined. And of course I should not dream of murdering anyone.'

Poirot sighed. 'How I miss my friend Hastings. He had such imagination. Such a romantic mind! It is true that he always imagined wrong—but that in itself was a guide.'

Miss Lemon was silent. She had heard about Captain Hastings before and was not interested. She looked longingly at the typewritten sheet in front of her.

'So it seems to you reasonable,' mused Poirot.

'Doesn't it to you?'

'I am almost afraid it does,' sighed Poirot.

The telephone rang and Miss Lemon went out of the room to answer it. She came back to say 'It's Inspector Sims again.' Poirot hurried to the instrument. ''Allo, 'allo. What is that you say?'

Sims repeated his statement. 'We've found a packet of strychnine in the girl's bedroom—tucked underneath the mattress. The sergeant's just come in with the news. That about clinches it, I think.'

'Yes,' said Poirot, 'I think that clinches it.' His voice had changed. It rang with sudden confidence.

When he had rung off, he sat down at his writing table and arranged the objects on it in a mechanical manner. He murmured to himself, 'There was something wrong. I felt it—no, not felt. It must have been something I saw. *En avant*, the little grey cells. Ponder—reflect. Was everything logical and in order? The girl—her anxiety about the money: Mme Delafontaine; her husband—his suggestion of Russians—imbecile, but he is an imbecile; the room; the garden—ah! Yes, the garden.'

He sat up very stiff. The green light shone in his eyes. He sprang up and went into the adjoining room.

'Miss Lemon, will you have the kindness to leave what you are doing and make an investigation for me?'

'An investigation, M. Poirot? I'm afraid I'm not very good—'

Poirot interrupted her. 'You said one day that you knew all about tradesmen.'

'Certainly I do,' said Miss Lemon with confidence.

'Then the matter is simple. You are to go to Charman's Green and you are to discover a fishmonger.'

'A fishmonger?' asked Miss Lemon, surprised.

'Precisely. The fishmonger who supplied Rosebank with fish. When you have found him you will ask him a certain question.'

He handed her a slip of paper. Miss Lemon took it, noted its contents without interest, then nodded and slipped the lid on her typewriter.

'We will go to Charman's Green together,' said Poirot. 'You go to the fishmonger and I to the police station. It will take us but half an hour from Baker Street.'

On arrival at his destination, he was greeted by the surprised Inspector Sims. 'Well, this is quick work, M. Poirot. I was talking to you on the phone only an hour ago.'

'I have a request to make to you; that you allow me to see this girl Katrina—what is her name?'

'Katrina Rieger. Well, I don't suppose there's any objection to that.'

The girl Katrina looked even more sallow and sullen than ever.

Poirot spoke to her very gently. 'Mademoiselle, I want you to believe that I am not your enemy. I want you to tell me the truth.'

Her eyes snapped defiantly. 'I have told the truth. To everyone I have told the truth! If the old lady was poisoned, it was not I who poisoned her. It is all a mistake. You wish to prevent me having the money.' Her voice was rasping. She looked, he thought, like a miserable little cornered rat.

'Did no one handle it but you?'

'I have said so, have I not? They were made up at the chemist's that afternoon. I brought them back with me in my bag—that was just before supper. I opened the box and gave Miss Barrowby one with a glass of water.'

'No one touched them but you?'

'No.' A cornered rat—with courage!

'And Miss Barrowby had for supper only what we have been told. The soup, the fish pie, the tart?'

'Yes.' A hopeless 'yes'—dark, smouldering eyes that saw no light anywhere.

Poirot patted her shoulder. 'Be of good courage, mademoiselle. There may yet be freedom—yes, and money—a life of ease.'

She looked at him suspiciously.

As she went out Sims said to him, 'I didn't quite get what you said through the telephone—something about the girl having a friend.'

'She has one. Me!' said Hercule Poirot, and had left the police station before the inspector could pull his wits together.

At the Green Cat tearooms, Miss Lemon did not keep her employer waiting. She went straight to the point.

'The man's name is Rudge, in the High Street, and you were quite right. A dozen and a half exactly. I've made a note of what he said.' She handed it to him.

'Arrr.' It was a deep, rich sound like a purr of a cat.

Hercule Poirot betook himself to Rosebank. As he stood in the front garden, the sun setting behind him, Mary Delafontaine came out to him.

'M. Poirot?' Her voice sounded surprised. 'You have come back?'

'Yes, I have come back.' He paused and then said, 'When I first came here, madame, the children's nursery rhyme came into my head:

> *'Mistress Mary, quite contrary,*
> *How does your garden grow?*
> *With cockle-shells, and silver bells,*
> *And pretty maids all in a row.*

'Only they are not *cockle* shells, are they, madame? They are *oyster* shells.' His hand pointed.

He heard her catch her breath and then stay very still. Her eyes asked a question.

He nodded. '*Mais, oui*, I know! The maid left the dinner ready—she will swear and Katrina will swear that that is all you had. Only you and your husband know that you brought back a dozen and a half oysters—a little treat *pour la bonne tante*. So easy to put the strychnine in an oyster. It is swallowed—*comme ça*! But there remain the shells—they must not go in the bucket. The maid would see them. And so you thought of making an edging of them to a bed. But there were not enough—the edging is not complete. The effect is bad—it spoils the symmetry of the otherwise charming garden. Those few oyster shells struck an alien note—they displeased my eye on my first visit.'

Mary Delafontaine said, 'I suppose you guessed from the letter. I knew she had written—but I didn't know how much she'd said.'

Poirot answered evasively, 'I knew at least that it was a family matter. If it had been a question of Katrina there would have been no point in hushing things up. I understand that you or your husband handled Miss Barrowby's securities to your own profit, and that she found out—'

Mary Delafontaine nodded. 'We've done it for years—a little here and there. I never realized she was sharp enough to find out. And then I learned she had sent for a detective; and I found out, too, that she was leaving her money to Katrina—that miserable little creature!'

'And so the strychnine was put in Katrina's bedroom? I comprehend. You save yourself and your husband from what I may discover, and you saddle an innocent child with murder. Had you no pity, madame?'

Mary Delafontaine shrugged her shoulders—her blue forget-me-not eyes looked into Poirot's. He remembered the perfection of her acting the first day he had come and the bungling attempts of her husband. A woman above the average—but inhuman.

She said, 'Pity? For that miserable intriguing little rat?' Her contempt rang out.

Hercule Poirot said slowly, 'I think, madame, that you have cared in your life for two things only. One is your husband.'

He saw her lips tremble.

'And the other—is your garden.'

He looked round him. His glance seemed to apologize to the flowers for that which he had done and was about to do.

330